# BUNTER DOES HIS BEST!

A LATIN DICTIONARY WHIZZED ACROSS THE STUDY AND IMPINGED UPON THE FATTEST CHIN AT GREYFRIARS SCHOOL

(*Page* 20)

# BUNTER DOES HIS BEST!

*By*
*FRANK RICHARDS*

*Illustrated by*
R. J. MACDONALD

HAWK
BOOKS

First published 1954 by Charles Skilton Ltd.

This edition published 1991 by:
HAWK BOOKS LTD
Suite 309
Canalot Studios
222 Kensal Road
London W10 5BN



ISBN 0-948248-87-4



*Printed in England by Redwood Press Ltd.*

# CONTENTS

## CHAPTER 1

# TRIBULATIONS OF A FOOTBALL CAPTAIN

"Ass!" said Harry Wharton.

"Thanks!"

"Silly ass, if you like that better."

Bob Cherry grinned.

"Pile it on, old chap, if it does you any good!" he said. "Let off all the steam you like, and don't mind me."

Three fellows in No. 1 Study grinned.

Harry Wharton did not grin. He frowned.

"You had to get in the way of Bolsover's hoof!" he grunted.

"Not Bob's fault, old bean," said Frank Nugent, mildly. "Bob didn't ask that clumsy ass to hack him in practice this afternoon."

"Br-r-r-r-r!" was Harry Wharton's reply to that.

It was an expressive, but not very intelligible, reply: so none of the fellows in No. 1 Study in the Remove made any rejoinder.

There were five fellows in the study: the "Famous Five" of the Greyfriars Remove. Harry Wharton sat at the table, a football list before him, a pencil in his hand, and a frown on his brow.

His look indicated that matters were serious: as, indeed, they were! The captain of the Remove had a problem on his mind: not an easy one. And Bob Cherry had certainly added to its difficulty of solution, by stopping a clumsy kick from Bolsover major with his knee.

Bob sat in the study armchair, with a leg extended over

another chair. He had rolled up a trouser-leg, revealing a bruised knee. He was rubbing that knee tenderly, and a sweet scent of Elliman's filled the study.

Frank Nugent, Johnny Bull, and Hurree Jamset Ram Singh were sympathetic. They knew what a fellow felt like with a crocked knee: especially a couple of days before a football fixture in which that fellow was booked to play.

Harry Wharton, no doubt, would have sympathised too: but for the circumstance that he was football captain, and that Bob's disaster deprived him of his best half-back. At the moment he was thinking of Soccer, not of sympathy. His brows were knitted as he lifted the pencil to cross out the name of R. Cherry in the list. He paused and glanced across at Bob in the armchair.

"Sure it won't mend by Wednesday?"

Bob made a rueful grimace.

"Look at it!" he said. "My dear chap, I shouldn't be able to play marbles on Wednesday, let alone Soccer."

"Br-r-r-r!"

"All right for the Rookwood match later on," said Bob. "Right as rain when we go over to Rookwood——."

"Fathead! We're playing Courtfield on Wednesday—never mind Rookwood now." Harry Wharton drew the pencil through "R. Cherry". "That's the limit! The team's all at sixes and sevens already: Browney laid up with a cold, Linley gone home for the week—that's two of the halves gone: and now you have to shove your silly knee just where the clumsiest ass in the Remove was planting his hoof—it's rotten."

"The rottenfulness is terrific," remarked Hurree Jamset Ram Singh, "but what cannot be cured is a stitch in time that must go longest to the well, as the English proverb remarks."

"Br-r-r-r!" repeated the captain of the Remove; apparently deriving no consolation from that spot of proverbial wisdom.

"Can't be helped!" remarked Johnny Bull, philosophically.

"Oh, rot!" The captain of the Remove seemed to have no more use for Johnny's philosophy, than for Hurree Singh's proverbial wisdom. "Looks like Trumper's gang walking over us on Wednesday. Perhaps you like the idea of Greyfriars being wiped off the map by a village team!" he added, sarcastically.

"Courtfield aren't a village team," said Johnny, stolidly. "They're jolly good men at Soccer—they beat us last time."

"All the more reason why we should put a good team into the field to play them this time! For goodness sake don't argue!"

"I'm not arguing! But——."

"Well, don't! Three duds all in a row, in the half-way line, and a weak spot in the front line too, as Penfold's away, and I've had to put Nugent in his place——."

"Awful!" said Frank Nugent, solemnly.

"Oh, don't be an ass, Franky. You know I'm jolly glad to play you, but you're not going to say you're a patch on Pen at inside-right, are you?" hooted Wharton.

"Not at all, old chap!" said Frank, soothingly. "Don't get shirty."

"Who's getting shirty?"

Nobody in No. 1 Study answered that question. Four fellows had an impression that Harry Wharton was in a frame of mind perilously near "shirtiness". But they forbore to say so.

There was silence in the study, while the captain of the Remove frowned over his unsatisfactory football list. It was broken by Bob Cherry uttering a sudden exclamation, or rather a howl.

"Ow! wow! wow!" Bob had inadvertently given his damaged knee an extra hard rub, and was rewarded with a devastating pang.

Wharton stared at him across the table.

"Eh! what's up?" he asked.

"Wow! My knee——!" gasped Bob. "Oh, crikey!"

"Oh!" It seemed to dawn on the captain of the Remove, at last, that his chum was in a painful state, and his expression changed. "Sorry, old chap! Does it feel very bad?"

"Wow!" mumbled Bob: a reply which seemed to indicate that it did! He resumed rubbing, with a more cautious rub.

"Tough on you, old fellow." Sympathy had the upper hand of Soccer now. "That clumsy ass Bolsover ought to be booted. You'll have to go easy."

"I shall be dotting and carrying-one for the rest of the week!" groaned Bob. "It would happen, just before a fixture! Wow!"

"Oh, we'll pull out of it all right!" said Harry, more cheerfully. "Don't you worry, old son. We shall be weak in the halves, but we've got good backs, and Johnny in goal. And the front line's strong—Frank's jolly nearly as good as Pen at inside-right—what are you grinning at, Frank?"

"Oh! Nothing! Carry on."

"Well, Smithy at outside-right is worth his weight in gold," said Harry, glancing at the list again. "Thank goodness Smithy's at the top of his form, and that he kept out of the way of Bolsover's hoofs this afternoon. Smith, Nugent, little me, Ogilvy, and Inky—that's a good forward line. We shall have to attack all the time, and keep them busy, that's all."

"And I'll stand on one leg like a stork and watch you getting the goals!" said Bob.

Harry Wharton laughed.

"We'll get the goals all right!" he said. "We simply can't let a team of townies beat us a second time. Don't you worry, old chap! Now, I've got to find a man to shove in, in your place, Bob——."

"I say, you fellows." A fat squeak interrupted.

A fat face, and a big pair of spectacles, blinked in at the half open door of the study. Five fellows glanced round, not with welcoming looks. Billy Bunter was often superfluous: and more superfluous than ever when troublesome football problems had to be solved.

"Hook it, Bunter," said Harry, briefly.

"Oh, really, Wharton——."

"Buzz off, you fat ass!"

"I heard what you were saying, old chap," said Bunter, blinking at the captain of the Remove through his big spectacles. "You're in a jam for a man on Wednesday. If you want a good man, I can tell you where to find him."

"Oh, do!" said Harry Wharton, sarcastically. "Always willing to learn! Who's that good man?"

"Me!" said Bunter.

"You fat ass!" roared the captain of the Remove, while the other fellows in the study chuckled.

"Well, why not?" demanded Bunter, warmly. "I'm a better forward than half, I know—but I can play half, I suppose——."

"Something wrong with your supposer, then! Travel!"

"Look here, you cheeky beast——."

Harry Wharton picked up a cushion.

"Where will you have it?" he asked.

"Beast!"

Bunter, apparently, did not want it anywhere. The study door closed with a bang, and the fat Owl of the Remove disappeared.

Harry Wharton threw down the cushion, and picked up the football list again. Billy Bunter's happy suggestion was not, evidently, regarded as a present help in time of need: and at that moment, the captain of the Remove little dreamed of what was destined to happen on the eventful Wednesday when the Courtfield men came over to Greyfriars. He wrinkled his brow over the list.

"After all, we've got good men in the Remove," he said. "There's nobody like your form to take your place, Bob, but Morgan and Russell are good—and there's Redwing—Redwing's a good man, and jolly keen. Smithy would like his pal in the team, too, and this is a chance for him. Now—let's see—." He was interrupted by a tap, and the turning of the door-handle. "Oh, my hat! Is that that fat ass again?"

He stared round, exasperated, as the door opened.

"You howling fathead, what are you barging in for?" he hooted. "Do you want your silly head banged on the table? Oh!" Harry Wharton broke off quite suddenly. "Is that you, Smithy?"

It was not Bunter this time. It was Herbert Vernon-Smith who looked in at the door. He stared at Wharton.

"Are you always as polite as that to callers?" he asked.

"I thought it was that fat chump Bunter! Trot in, Smithy—you're just the man I want to see."

"Trot in, Smithy," said the four other fellows, in chorus.

And the Bounder of Greyfriars "trotted" in.

## CHAPTER 2

# LET DOWN!

HERBERT VERNON-SMITH stood with his hands in his trousers pockets, without speaking for the moment. Evidently he had come to No. 1 Study with something to say: but he did not seem in a hurry to begin. There was a faint trace of embarrassment in his somewhat hard-featured face.

It was not like the cool, self-assured Bounder to feel disconcerted at any time. But he was not at his ease now. Four fellows in the study noted it at once. Harry Wharton, completely absorbed in Soccer, did not. His manner to Smithy could not have been more cordial.

Smithy was not always *persona grata* in that study. His ways were not the ways of Harry Wharton and Co. Breaking bounds after lights out, smoking surreptitious cigarettes, "cheeking" prefects, ragging "beaks", were not amusements in which the Famous Five indulged: and they had their own opinion about such things, which they did not by any means keep a secret. But Soccer was the order of the day now: and there was no doubt that in Soccer Herbert Vernon-Smith was a tower of strength to his side. His unruly manners and customs were his own affair: as a footballer, at least, he was a man whom the captain of his form delighted to honour—especially at the present moment, with four good men out of the team, and a hard match ahead.

"Squat down, old chap," said Harry. Probably Wharton did not address Smithy as "old chap" once in a term: but at the moment the scapegrace of Greyfriars was, so to speak, a man and a brother!

The Bounder did not "squat" down.

"I've only looked in to speak to you about the footer," he said, and just the faintest flush came into his cheeks.

"Just what we're chinning about," said Bob Cherry. "Wharton's been ragging me for contacting Bolsover's hoof this afternoon: he's feeling better now he's got it off his chest."

"Crocked?" asked Vernon-Smith, glancing at the bared knee, and sniffing the scent of embrocation.

"K.O. for Wednesday," said Bob, with a grimace. "If I could stand on this leg, I'd jolly well boot Bolsover with the other. Ow!"

"Rotten luck," said Smithy.

"Rotten enough," said Harry Wharton. "We'd already lost Browney, and Linley, and Penfold—now Bob's out of it. I was just thinking of Redwing to take Bob's place on Wednesday. What do you think, Smithy?"

He expected an immediate and very cheerful affirmative. If there was one fellow at Greyfriars about whom the Bounder cared, it was his chum Tom Redwing. Smithy was very keen on pushing his chum's claims in football matters: sometimes too keen for Tom's own comfort. But he hesitated now.

"Reddy's a better forward than half," he said, after a pause.

"Perhaps: but he can play half, and it's a half we want now," said Harry. "Not in the same street with Bob, I know——."

"I don't see that!" interrupted the Bounder, sharply.

Harry Wharton smiled.

"Well, never mind that," he said. "Reddy's a good

man, at any rate, and we want a half. The front line's filled."

The Bounder's colour deepened a little: and Nugent, Johnny Bull, Bob, and Hurree Singh all regarded him curiously. They could see that something was coming, though they did not as yet guess what. Wharton, still unobservant, picked up the pencil to put the name of T. Redwing under the crossed-out R. Cherry.

"Hold on a minute," said Smithy, hastily.

Wharton looked up.

"My dear chap, surely you're glad for Reddy to be in the team," he exclaimed. "Why, you've told me a dozen times——."

"Well, yes! But——."

"But what?" asked Harry, puzzled.

"You'll want a forward——."

"That's all right: I've put Nugent into Pen's place in the front line——."

"I don't mean that! I mean—well, look here, I came in to tell you that I shan't be able to play on Wednesday!" Smithy had got it out at last.

Harry Wharton dropped the pencil, and stared at him.

"Not play on Wednesday!" he ejaculated.

"No! You—you see——!" For once, the Bounder was stammering.

"Great pip! Mean to say you've gone and got yourself crocked, like Bob?" exclaimed the captain of the Remove, blankly.

"No! But——."

"Then what do you mean?" demanded Wharton, hotly. "Have you come here to tell me that you're going to let us down, for no reason at all?"

"I've got a reason, of course——."

"Well, what is it?"

"I—I just can't play on Wednesday, that's all!" said Vernon-Smith. "There's something else that I can't put off——."

"And you can't tell me what it is?"

"No need, that I can see," answered the Bounder. "I'm giving you plenty of time to find another man. There's Redwing——."

"Cut that out! Why are you going to cut on Wednesday?"

"That's my business," muttered Smith, sullenly. "Look here, it's not one of our big fixtures. If it were a St. Jim's match, or Rookwood, or Carcroft, or Felgate, it would be different. But a lot of townies——."

"That lot of townies beat us on their own ground," said Johnny Bull.

"Well, I can't play."

"You mean that you won't?" asked Harry Wharton, very quietly.

"Put it like that, if you like!" said Vernon-Smith: and he turned to leave the study.

"Hold on a minute, Smithy!" said Harry, still very quietly. "That's not all." The cordiality was quite gone from his manner now. His eyes were like steel, as he looked across the study at the sullen Bounder.

Smithy turned back.

"It's no good talking," he said. "It's settled——."

"I'll talk, all the same. You needn't tell me what you've got on for Wednesday that's more important than a Soccer match—I can guess that!" said Wharton, scornfully. "Some stunt out of gates, with Pon and his crew from High-cliffe, I've no doubt—something you'd be sacked for, if Quelch or the Head knew."

"I didn't come here for a sermon, thanks."

"You know how we stand," went on Wharton, unheeding, "four men out of the team, already. Now you propose to leave the team in the lurch, to carry on with your blackguardly stunts. Well, you can't do it! You'll be playing Soccer for the Remove on Wednesday afternoon, Vernon-Smith."

The Bounder's jaw squared.

"I shall be miles from Greyfriars on Wednesday afternoon!" he answered, deliberately. "That's that! You can put that pencil through my name in the list."

"Look here, Smithy——!" began Bob Cherry.

"That's all!" said Smithy.

"Worm!" said Johnny Bull.

"The wormfulness is terrific, my esteemed and execrable Smithy!" said Hurree Jamset Ram Singh, with a shake of his dusky head.

The Bounder, without replying, stepped to the door. But he stopped again, as Harry Wharton spoke. Wharton picked up the pencil.

"One word more, Smithy," he said. "If you've made up your mind to let the Remove down, I can't stop you——."

"Has that just dawned on you?" asked the Bounder, sarcastically.

"Am I to cross your name out?"

"I've said so."

"I'll cross it out if you like. But put this in your pipe and smoke it—if I take your name out of the football now, it stays out. You won't play Soccer for the Remove again this season. If that's what you want, you can have it. If you stand out of the Courtfield match on Wednesday, you stand out of St. Jim's, and Rookwood, and Carcroft, and

Felgate, and every other match we play. You can't play fast and loose with footer, as you seem to think you can. If we can't trust you to play when you're wanted, we can't trust you at all. If your name goes out of this list, it will never go into another—or into this again, if you change your mind. So think it over for a minute before I put the pencil through it."

The Bounder's eyes glinted.

"Do you think I'm a fellow to be threatened?" he sneered.

"It's not a threat—only a warning. And I mean every word of it."

"For goodness sake, Smithy, don't be such an ass!" urged Bob Cherry. "Let Pon and his crew go and eat coke, and play up for your school."

"The playfulness of the game is the proper caper, my esteemed Smithy!" urged Hurree Jamset Ram Singh.

"Smithy, old chap——!" said Nugent.

"Well?" asked Harry Wharton, as the Bounder did not speak. He stood with the pencil poised in his hand.

The Bounder gave him a black look.

"I'm goin' out of gates on Wednesday," he said. "If you fancy you can boot me out of the footer afterwards, you'll find that you have another guess coming. That's the lot!"

With that, Herbert Vernon-Smith walked out of the study, and closed the door after him with a bang.

Harry Wharton drew a deep breath.

"That's that!" he said.

And he drew the pencil through the name of H. Vernon-Smith in the football list.

## CHAPTER 3

# SIX FOR SMITHY

"I SAY, you fellows——."

"Get out!" The Bounder almost yelled.

Half-an-hour ago, Billy Bunter had seemed superfluous in No. 1 Study. Now he seemed still more superfluous in No. 4.

Indeed the look that Herbert Vernon-Smith gave him was almost deadly, as he blinked in at the doorway through his big spectacles.

"Tantrums" were not uncommon in that study. When Smithy's temper was bad, as not infrequently it was, he was accustomed to letting it rip. Remove fellows often wondered how so quiet and good-tempered a fellow as Tom Redwing could tolerate a study-mate like Smithy. Yet different as they were, they were fast friends: though Tom's almost inexhaustible patience was often tried to the very limit.

At the present moment, Smithy was in the worst temper ever. His conscience, which did not often trouble him very much, troubled him a little now. He was quite determined to carry out his own plans for the half-holiday on Wednesday, and go on his own reckless way regardless of others. But it gave him an unpleasant twinge to let down his football captain: and he had left No. 1 Study angry with Wharton, angry with himself, dissatisfied and disgruntled generally. In his own study he found no comfort when he joined Tom Redwing there for tea. Quite a hot argument was going on, across the table, when the door opened and

Billy Bunter blinked in. Tom Redwing was expressing his opinion in unusually plain language.

"You can't do it, Smithy," he was saying. "I tell you——."

"Oh, shut up!"

"I tell you it's rotten—you can't let a man down like that—you ought to be jolly well ashamed of yourself——."

Redwing broke off as the door opened. He did not want other ears to hear him "slanging" his chum. Vernon-Smith, who was scowling at him across the table, transferred his scowl to Billy Bunter at the door. It was one of Billy Bunter's happy ways to butt into a study at tea-time: and had he found the Bounder in a good temper, he might have been permitted to share in the good things in that well-provided study. But he had found Smithy in an extremely bad temper: on the verge of a quarrel with his best chum, and certainly not in a mood to be patient with the fat and fatuous Owl of the Remove.

"But I say——!" babbled Bunter, as Vernon-Smith glared at him rather like the fabled basilisk. "I say——."

"Shut that door, you fat fool!"

"Oh! Yes! But I say. I—I haven't come to tea, if that's what you think, Smithy—I came here to say—Yarooooooh!"

Bunter broke off, with a frantic yell, as a Latin dictionary whizzed across the study, and impinged upon the fattest chin at Greyfriars School.

The fat Owl went backwards into the passage, and sat down there, with a heavy bump! His yell woke the echoes in most of the studies along the passage.

"Yarooh! wow! Oh, ow! Beast! Wow!"

Vernon-Smith rose from the table, and kicked the door shut after him, with a bang louder than Bunter's yell. He came back scowling to his chair; his scowl deepening as he read contemptuous disapproval on Tom Redwing's face.

"Did you want that fat guzzler to tea here?" he snapped.

"No! But you needn't have let your rotten temper rip on the fat ass. He may have come with a message or something, too."

"Oh, rot!"

"Look here, Smithy——."

"If the fat ass butts in where he's not wanted, he can take what comes to him!" snarled Smithy. "Don't jaw me about Bunter."

Tom Redwing breathed hard.

"Well, never mind Bunter," he said. "Look here, Smithy, you simply can't let the team down on Wednesday. You——."

Redwing was interrupted by a howl through the keyhole.

"Yah! Beast! Rotter! I jolly well won't tell you now that Quelch wants your lines, Smithy, you cad, so yah!"

And with that valediction, the Owl of the Remove rolled away down the passage.

"So that was it," said Redwing. "A message from Quelch—and you tipped him over with that dick——."

"Oh, rats!"

"If you haven't done those lines for Quelch——."

"I haven't! I've had other things to think about! Blow Quelch and his lines," snapped the Bounder. "I'm fed up with Quelch—and jolly nearly fed up with you, if you want to know. Hasn't a fellow ever cut a football match before?"

"Not like this, if he was a decent fellow," answered Redwing.

"So I'm not a decent fellow?"

"You're not acting like one. Wharton's skipper, and he's short of three men already, and I hear that Cherry was crocked this afternoon, too—that makes four. Now he's losing his best winger, because you've got some disreputable stunt on with those cads at Highcliffe—and I expect Wharton knows that as well as I do——."

"I don't care two hoots for his opinion, or for yours either."

"You ought to, Smithy," said Tom Redwing, quietly. "I can tell you that every man in the Remove will be down on you for this."

The Bounder shrugged his shoulders.

"Let them!" he answered.

"It's rotten," said Tom. "Even Skinner wouldn't do this, or Snoop—you can't do it, Smithy. It's rotten."

"So I'm a rotter too?" sneered the Bounder. "So glad to know what you really think of me. But you'd better shut up at that, Tom Redwing. I'd have punched any other fellow's head for half as much."

"I hope you'll think better of it before Wednesday, Smithy! Look here, old fellow, why not go back to Wharton and say——."

"Rats!"

Vernon-Smith groped in the table-drawer, selected a cigarette from a box therein, and struck a match. He gave his chum a stare of scornful defiance as he lighted the cigarette. The Bounder seldom or never put on his smokes when Redwing was in the study: but he was in an angry and hostile mood now. Redwing gave him an expressive glance, as he blew out a cloud of smoke.

"For goodness sake, chuck that silly rot!" he snapped.

"If you don't like it, you can get out."

"I'll get out, then."

Redwing rose from the table. The Bounder, with a derisive sneer, blew a stream of smoke towards him as he did so. At the same moment, there was a sharp tap at the door, and it opened.

"Oh!" ejaculated Redwing, as a tall angular figure appeared in the doorway, and he stared in dismay at Mr. Quelch, the master of the Remove.

Quelch frowned into the study.

"Vernon-Smith! I sent Bunter to tell you—why—what is this?" The Remove master stared blankly at the scapegrace of his form. "Vernon-Smith! Upon my word! How dare you, Vernon-Smith?"

The Bounder whipped the cigarette from his mouth. But it was too late—seconds too late. There was the cigarette, still glowing, with a curl of smoke, under the gimlet-eyes of his form-master. He dropped it to the floor and put his foot on it, and stood up, with a crimson face.

"Vernon-Smith! On Saturday I gave you a hundred lines for smoking. Now I find you smoking in your study. It is useless to be lenient with you. I shall cane you for this, Vernon-Smith."

The Bounder stood sullenly silent. Mr. Quelch had his cane under his arm. Possibly it had been intended for use if Smithy's lines were not forthcoming. At all events it was intended for use now. He pointed with it to the chair from which Vernon-Smith had risen.

"Bend over that chair, Vernon-Smith."

With a black brow, the Bounder obeyed. Tom Redwing looked on with a clouded face, as the cane swished. He could scarcely blame Quelch for taking severe measures with that reckless and rebellious member of his form: but it was painful to him to see his chum going through it.

And Smithy was going through it hard. Six times the cane rose and fell, and every swipe rang through the study. Lines had had no effect on the scapegrace of his form: no doubt Quelch hoped that "six of the best" would prove more effective. And they were six of the very best.

The Bounder uttered no sound: but he had to shut his teeth hard to keep back a yell. His face was almost pale as he rose after the infliction.

"That, I trust, will be a warning to you, Vernon-Smith, to respect the rules laid down by your head-master," said Mr. Quelch: and he tucked the cane under his arm, and still frowning portentously, rustled out of the study, closing the door after him with a snap.

The Bounder stood breathing hard, with fury in his face.

"Sorry, old chap," said Redwing, in a low voice.

"I'll get level with him for it!" muttered the Bounder. "Six—for putting on a fag! By gad, I'll get level with Quelch for this——."

"Quiet!" breathed Redwing, hurriedly, as the study door reopened. Mr. Quelch looked in again.

With all his nerve, the Bounder felt a tremor. He knew that Quelch must have heard his words, as he opened the door. And the look that the Remove master gave him showed only too plainly that he had heard.

But Quelch was not the man to take official note of words not intended for his ears. His look was expressive: but he made no reference to what he had heard.

"Vernon-Smith! I sent Bunter to tell you to bring your lines to me in my study at once. Have you written them?"

"No!" muttered Smithy.

The gimlet-eyes glinted.

"What did you say, Vernon-Smith?"

"I—I—No, sir!" breathed the Bounder.

"Very well! The lines are doubled," said Mr. Quelch. "Unless they are delivered to me before preparation this evening, I shall send you to Dr. Locke. That is all!"

The door snapped shut again, and Mr. Quelch departed: this time for good. The Bounder stood with clenched hands. There was a grim silence in the study. Redwing broke it at last.

"I'll help you with the lines, Smithy."

"Don't be a fool! Think Quelch wouldn't spot it, and jump at the chance to send me up to the Head? I don't want your help, either."

"But——!"

"Oh, don't jaw!"

Tom Redwing gave him a look, and quietly left the study. Smithy was in a mood to quarrel with friend or foe: and he did not want a "row" with his disgruntled chum. Left alone, the Bounder moved about the study, restlessly, rather like a tiger in a cage. He had two hundred lines to write: and with all his reckless disregard of authority, he knew that he had to deliver those lines on time: he did not want an interview with his head-master. But he had to wait till the first effects of the "six" had worn off, before he settled down to lines. He was still roaming about the study like a caged animal when the door opened, and Skinner of the Remove looked in.

"I say, Smithy——."

"Oh, get out!"

"But I say, Wharton's posted the list in the Rag, and your name's out of it," said Skinner. "What——."

"Leave me alone, will you?"

"Well, you needn't jump down a fellow's throat," said

Skinner, staring at him. "If Wharton's turned you out, it's not my fault, is it?"

The Bounder clutched up the Latin dictionary which Billy Bunter had already found so discomforting on his fat chin.

"If you don't want this at your head, get out!" he snarled.

Skinner got out promptly, slamming the door after him.

With a black brow, Smithy settled down, at last, to his lines: comforted only by a resentful determination to "get level" with Quelch somehow, at a later date.

## CHAPTER 4

# BILLY BUNTER'S BOOBY-TRAP

"HALLO, hallo, hallo! What's that game?"

"Oh!" gasped Billy Bunter, startled.

The fat Owl blinked round through his big spectacles with a startled blink, at Bob Cherry's sudden genial roar.

Bunter had fancied himself alone in the Remove passage. So he was, till Bob came out of No. 13. Bunter wanted to be alone just then: he had work on hand which he did not desire other eyes to behold.

And really he had chosen his time well. Prep was not yet due: and fellows were not yet coming up to the studies. There was a spot of excitement in the Rag, in connection with the football list recently posted up by the captain of the Remove. Everybody there was talking Soccer, which was likely to keep them interested till the bell rang for prep. Bunter was not interested in Soccer: he was interested in quite other things.

Bob had been in his study, giving his damaged knee an extra rub with Elliman's. He was surprised, when he came out, to see the fat Owl of the Remove standing outside the door of No. 4 Study, with a large paper bag of flour in his fat hand, blinking at the half-open door with a meditative and calculating blink.

Bunter, evidently, was up to something with that bag of flour at the door of Smithy's study: and Bob inquired what the game was.

"Oh! You ass, you startled me!" stuttered Bunter. "I—I ain't doing anything—I mean, I ain't going to do anything with this bag of flour. I say, Cherry, did you know Smithy was out of the eleven? They're all talking about it in the Rag—hadn't you better cut down?"

"What are you up to, you fat chump?" asked Bob. "If it's a trick on Smithy, you'd better think twice. Smithy's had a spot of bother with Quelch, and he's not in a good temper."

"Fat lot I care for his temper!" said Bunter, disdainfully. "I'll jolly well show him whether he can buzz a dick at a fellow, who only came to give him a message from Quelch! Think I'm going to let a cad like Smithy buzz dicks at my head? I'll show him!"

"Where did you get that bag of flour?"

"I haven't been down the kitchen stairs, if that's what you mean, Bob Cherry. If Mrs. Kebble makes a fuss about a bag of flour, don't you get saying anything," said Bunter, anxiously. "She might think it was me——."

"She might!" chuckled Bob. "Better forget all about Smithy, old fat man, and take it back where it belongs."

"I'll watch it!" said Bunter. "Perhaps Smithy will be sorry for himself when he gets this on his nut! He, he, he!"

"Not so sorry as you'll be, when he gets on your trail," said Bob.

"Well, he won't know I fixed it up," said Bunter. "I say, Bob, old chap, lend a fellow a hand. I can't reach the door, see? You could, standing on your toes. I'm going to plant this bag on top of the door, to land on Smithy when he comes up—a booby-trap, you know—think he'll like it, when it comes down whop! He, he, he!"

"And suppose Redwing gets it instead? " asked Bob.

"Eh?" Bunter, in his schemes of vengeance, had apparently forgotten the existence of Tom Redwing, who shared that study with Smithy. "Oh! That would spoil the whole thing—I don't want to waste it on Redwing. If he came up first, he would get it, and not Smithy." Bunter wrinkled a fat brow in thought. "I say, Bob, be a pal—you go down, and keep Redwing back somehow when the fellows come up—you can pull his leg somehow——."

"Can I?" said Bob, rather grimly.

"Yes, old chap! Look here, his father, old Redwing, is at sea now—well, tell him you've heard that his father's been wrecked."

"What?" yelled Bob.

"That will keep him!" said Bunter. "You can tell him afterwards that it was only a joke, you know."

"You fat villain!" gasped Bob.

"Oh, really, Cherry——."

"If I could stand on my right leg, I'd jolly well boot you along the passage with the other," hooted Bob.

"Beast!"

"Now chuck it, you silly ass! Smithy will skin you alive if you play potty tricks in his study."

"Yah!" retorted Bunter. "Smithy's going to have it, I can tell you. I'll keep Redwing off somehow, when I've fixed it up: they won't be coming up yet, anyhow. I certainly ain't going to waste it on Redwing. You mind your own business, Bob Cherry—I—I mean, will you stick this bag of flour on top of the door for me, old chap?"

"No: I jolly well won't, and you'd better not, you fat ass," answered Bob: and he limped on down the passage, leaving the fat and fatuous Owl to his own devices.

"Beast!" snorted Bunter.

He blinked at the door again. The top of it was far—very far—out of his reach—Bunter was tall only sideways, as it were. He had to have something to stand upon: and the only resource was to fetch a chair out of one of the studies.

Having decided on that resource, and having blinked cautiously down the passage to make quite, quite sure that the Bounder was not in the offing, Bunter laid the bag of flour on the floor, and rolled along to his own study, No. 7, for a chair.

He emerged from No. 7 with that article of furniture, and, after another cautious blink towards the landing, rolled back to the door of No. 4.

There he planted the chair, and picked up the flour-bag. There was a fat grin on his face as he mounted the chair, with the bag of flour in his fat hands. This was going to be a surprise for Smithy—and quite an unpleasant surprise. It would show him that he couldn't buzz "dicks" at a fellow's fat head with impunity.

But it was not an easy task that the vengeful fat Owl had set himself. He was able to reach the top of the door now. But that big bag of flour was heavy, and the fat junior had to take both hands to it. Unluckily, in those clumsy fat hands, the bag bumped on the door-top and knocked it wider open—out of Bunter's reach.

"Blow!" hissed Bunter.

He was losing time, and he did not want to lose time. True, prep was not due yet: but the fat Owl was anxious to get through and get clear: at a safe distance from the booby-trap set for Herbert Vernon-Smith. The bare thought of being caught at it by the Bounder was terrifying.

However, there was no help for it: Bunter had to descend from the chair, and step into the study, to recapture the runaway door. He made a grab at it from where he stood on the chair, and almost toppled over with his bag of flour. Then he stepped down, and stepped into the study. He grasped the door to pull it back to the doorway: but stopped, suddenly, at a sound of footsteps and voices coming up the passage from the landing.

"Oh, crikey!" breathed Bunter, in a horrified gasp, as the strident tones of the Bounder fell on his ears.

He stood spell-bound, with one hand on the door, the bag of flour under the other arm. He was out of sight for the moment, from the passage: but Smithy was coming——!

"Oh, don't jaw, for the love of Mike!" He heard the Bounder's voice. "I've had enough of that from the fellows in the Rag——."

"You can't be surprised to hear what they think of you for cutting the match on Wednesday when you know how badly you're wanted!" came Redwing's quiet voice.

"Will you give a fellow a rest?" snapped the Bounder. "I've come up to get away from the jaw, and I don't want any more from you. Why, what the thump is this chair doing here, stuck outside our door?"

The Bounder, evidently, was not in a good temper, for there was the sound of a crash, as he kicked the chair across the passage. The next moment he was staring at Billy Bunter in the study.

"What the dickens—why—what—you fat owl, what are you doing here? Did you stick that chair there? What are you up to in my study, you potty porpoise?"

"Oh, crikey! N-n-nothing!" gasped Bunter. "I—I—I——."

The Bounder's eyes glinted at him. The big bag of flour under Bunter's arm immediately connected itself, in his mind, with the chair that had been standing outside the doorway. Smithy did not need telling what the fat Owl's intention had been: and that, had he arrived at his study a little later, he would have walked into a booby-trap!

"Why, you—you—you——!" he breathed.

"I—I—I say Smithy, I—I—I——!" stuttered the hapless Owl.

"What were you going to do with that bag of flour?" asked Vernon-Smith, grimly.

"Oh! Nothing!" moaned Bunter. "I—I mean, I—I was going to—to make a cake——."

"A cake?"

"Yes, old chap! I—I thought you'd like a cake for supper, and I was going to—to—to——!"

"You fat ass!" said Redwing, laughing. "Let him cut, Smithy—there's no harm done."

"Give me that bag of flour, Bunter."

"Oh, certainly, old chap! Here you are!" gasped Bunter. "If—if—if you'd like me to make you a cake, old fellow——."

"You meant this for my napper," said Vernon-Smith. "Well, you're going to get it on your own."

"Oh, crikey! I—I say, old chap——!"

"Hold him outside the study, Reddy—we don't want it all over the floor here. Hold him while I burst it over his fat head."

"Yarooooh!"

Billy Bunter had quite enjoyed the prospect of that bag of flour bursting on Smithy's head. But the prospect of it bursting upon his own was evidently far from enjoyable. He made a desperate bound to escape. Smithy, with the bag of flour in his hands, left it to Redwing to stop him: as Reddy could easily have done. Instead of which, Tom Redwing stepped aside, and Bunter bolted past him, and flew down the passage like a hunted hare.

"Stop him, you fool!" yelled the Bounder.

"Oh, rot!" snapped back Redwing. "Keep your rotten temper, and leave him alone, Smithy. There's no harm done."

Vernon-Smith gave him a savage look. For the moment, he seemed disposed to hurl the bag of flour at Redwing's head, as Bunter's was no longer available. However, he stopped short of that, and slammed it on the table instead.

"You fool!" he muttered. "You know what he meant to do with it."

"Yes, and I know that you tipped him over with a dick, for nothing. Serve you right if you'd got it!" retorted Redwing.

"If you're looking for a row, Tom Redwing——."

"Oh, dry up: you make me tired."

The Bounder stared at him. It was quite unusual for Tom Redwing to take such a tone with him: and there was no doubt that the Bounder, unconsciously perhaps, presumed upon his chum's quiet patience. But that patience seemed to have reached the limit now.

Tom Redwing came into the study and shut the door, and proceeded to sort out his books for preparation, the Bounder watching him with a sullen scowl. But the scowling face cleared, as his eyes fell again on the bag of flour on the table. A sudden idea seemed to come into the Bounder's mind. He picked up the bag, lifted it into the study cupboard, and shut the cupboard door on it. Redwing glanced at him in surprise.

"That fat ass must have snooped that flour from below stairs," he said. "Better get it back somehow."

"It's going to stay where it is," answered Vernon-Smith. "Just as well that I didn't burst it over Bunter's head.

There's somebody else's head I'd rather burst it over, if a chance comes my way."

Redwing jumped.

"You mad ass! If you're thinking of Quelch——."

"Why not?" said the Bounder, coolly.

"Look here, Smithy——!"

"Oh, dry up—you make me tired!" mimicked the Bounder. "Didn't I say I'd get level? If I get half a chance, Quelch has got it coming! Now shut up, and give a fellow a rest!"

Redwing compressed his lips: but he said no more. When a tramp of feet, and a buzz of voices, announced that the rest of the Remove were coming up to prep, there was one member of the form—the fattest member—who rolled into the passage in fear and trembling, with a pair of little round eyes, and a pair of big round spectacles, warily on the watch for Smithy. But Billy Bunter's fat head was no longer in danger from that bag of flour. It was destined, when opportunity knocked, for quite another head—a much more majestic "nut" than Billy Bunter's.

## CHAPTER 5

## UNPOPULAR!

BILLY BUNTER grinned.

It was in break the following morning.

It was a sunny morning, and the Owl of the Remove was sunning himself in the quad, leaning on the front of the tuck-shop, with his plump hands in the pockets of his tight trousers, idly blinking through his big spectacles at other fellows more actively engaged.

It might have been supposed that William George Bunter had little occasion for grinning that morning. He still had a twinge in his fat chin where a Latin dictionary had landed, hard, the previous day. In form, he had earned a hundred lines from Quelch for "skewing" in con. He had been disappointed about a long-expected postal-order: and being in his usual stony state, was outside the tuck-shop, instead of inside, where he yearned to be. Nevertheless, Billy Bunter did grin—a wide grin that extended almost from one fat ear to the other.

It was the sight of Herbert Vernon-Smith that made him grin. The Bounder was coming out of the tuck-shop. Outside that establishment, something was waiting for him, as Bunter knew if Smithy did not.

A number of Remove fellows had gathered there. Squiff, Peter Todd, Ogilvy, Russell, Morgan, and several other footballing fellows were in the little crowd. They had rather grim expressions on their faces: and they all made a movement as the Bounder came out of the shop.

Vernon-Smith, about to cross to the House, was stopped

by that little crowd barring his path. He stared at them in angry surprise.

"What's this game?" he snapped. "What do you fancy you're up to? Let me pass."

"Stop where you are!" said Squiff. "We've got something to say to you, Smithy—and something to do, if what we say isn't any use."

"What the dickens do you mean?"

"You're letting the team down to-morrow," said Peter Todd.

"I've had that from Wharton."

"Now you're getting it from us," said Russell. "What sort of a rotter do you call yourself, Smithy, to cut a match like that, letting down your skipper and the side?"

"Four men out of the team already, and you propose to walk off and leave us in the lurch," said Squiff. "Do you want that townie bunch to walk over us at Soccer?"

The Bounder did not answer, but his brow grew black. Ever since the list had been posted in the Rag, Smithy had been left in no doubt as to what the Remove footballers thought of him. He was at the lowest ebb of popularity in his form. It was not pleasant to Smithy: though it had made no difference to his determination to carry on in his own way.

"Now, look here, Smithy," said Squiff. The Australian junior spoke more amicably. "You're a footballer and a sportsman, and you don't want to play a dirty trick. Think it over again."

"I'm fixed up for Wednesday afternoon," muttered the Bounder.

"Well, what is it, if it's so jolly important that you can't play Soccer for your form when you're badly wanted?" asked Peter Todd. "Any secret about it?"

Smithy was silent. A fat chuckle came from a fat junior leaning on the tuck-shop window.

"He, he, he! I jolly well know what it is, you fellows! That Highcliffe cad Ponsonby is having a car to the races—he, he, he!"

The Bounder glanced round at Bunter with glinting eyes. He made a movement towards the fat Owl. Two or three of the juniors interposed.

"Is that it, Vernon-Smith?" asked Ogilvy, quietly.

"Find out!" snapped the Bounder.

"We seem to have found out," said Squiff, "and if that's why you're letting the side down to-morrow, Vernon-Smith, you're a measly rotter and a rank outsider."

"Will you let me pass?" muttered the Bounder, between his teeth.

"No!" answered Quincy Iffley Field, coolly. "We're giving you a chance, Smithy, to throw over your silly rot and play up for your side, as you jolly well know you ought to do. Will you come with us now and tell Wharton that you're playing?"

"No!"

"Is that final?" asked Peter Todd.

"Yes!"

"That does it, then! Collar him, and duck his head in the fountain."

The Bounder's eyes blazed, and he made a rush to break through the ring of juniors. He had expected dark looks and hard words, and did not care for them. But he had not expected a ragging. But it was a ragging that was coming to him, and he had no chance of escaping. Hands grasped him on all sides as he rushed, and in the midst of six or seven angry fellows, he was hustled away towards the fountain in the quad.

"He, he, he!" chuckled Billy Bunter. He rubbed a fat chin where a twinge still lingered. The fat Owl had raided a bag of flour from below stairs, for Smithy's special behoof, the previous day: but he had failed lamentably to catch Smithy in his booby-trap. Now, however, Smithy was booked for something even more unpleasant than a bag of flour on the "nut": and Billy Bunter watched the proceedings with great amusement and satisfaction.

The Bounder struggled savagely as he was hustled away. But he resisted in vain. The crowd of Removites came up to the fountain with a rush, the Bounder struggling in their midst.

"Will you let go?" panted Vernon-Smith. "I—I—I'll —Oh!"

"Tip him in!"

Splash!

The water in the granite basin rose almost in a water-spout, as the Bounder's head splashed in. It came out drenched and dripping, his cap floating away. He stood panting and spluttering, water running down his neck, and glaring at half-a-dozen faces in speechless fury.

"That's that!" said Squiff. "Now you know what the form thinks of you, Smithy, you rotter. Now clear off before you're kicked."

"Kick him anyway," said Ogilvy.

The Bounder looked, for a moment, as if he would rush on the whole crowd, hitting out right and left. But he did not want his head to go into the fountain a second time. Choking with rage, he turned and tramped away towards the House, dripping water as he went, and followed by a hiss from the Removites.

He passed Harry Wharton and Co. in the quad, as he went: and four of the five smiled at the sight of him.

THE WATER IN THE GRANITE BASIN ROSE ALMOST IN A WATER-SPOUT, AS THE BOUNDER'S HEAD SPLASHED IN

Harry Wharton did not smile: his look was coldly contemptuous. Vernon-Smith paused for a moment to give the captain of the Remove a watery glare.

"You're at the bottom of this," he muttered, thickly. "If you fancy you can rag me into jumping to your orders, Harry Wharton——."

"Not in the least," answered Wharton, coolly. "You're out of the football, Vernon-Smith, as I told you yesterday. You don't come in again at any price."

"Hadn't you better go in and look for a towel, Smithy?" grinned Bob Cherry. "You look damp!"

"The dampfulness is terrific, my esteemed Smithy," chuckled the Nabob of Bhanipur.

The Bounder included all the five in a savage glare, and tramped on. Certainly, a towel was what he chiefly needed, at the moment. Neither did he want to catch the eye of master or prefect, in his present state. But Wingate of the Sixth, the Greyfriars captain, caught sight of him, and called to him.

"Here, Vernon-Smith!"

Reluctantly Smithy came to a stop.

"What the dickens have you been up to?" exclaimed Wingate. "You're soaked with water! What——."

"Only some fellows larkin'," muttered the Bounder. "It was—was an accident, Wingate——." Smithy certainly did not want the captain of the school, and Head of the Games, to learn what the trouble was. Neither, to do him justice, did he wish the fellows who had ducked him to contact a prefect's ash.

"Um!" said Wingate, doubtfully. "Well, cut in and get yourself dry, you young ass, and don't have any more such accidents."

The Bounder cut in, glad to escape further inquiry.

At the door of the junior lobby, Skinner grinned at him. Harold Skinner was more or less friendly with the scapegrace of the Remove: they had tastes much in common. But Skinner was the kind of fellow to find something amusing in the misfortunes of his friends. He had witnessed the ducking, from a distance, and had been considerably entertained thereby.

"By gum, you look wet, Smithy," he said, grinning. "You—why—look here, what are you at—do you think you can shove a fellow over?" yelled Skinner, indignantly.

Apparently the Bounder thought that he could, for he did—and Skinner went sprawling. Vernon-Smith tramped in, leaving him to sprawl and splutter. In the lobby he grabbed a towel, and rubbed his dripping head, tearing off collar and tie and hurling them to the floor. He was still towelling wet hair and a crimson face, when Tom Redwing came hurriedly into the lobby.

"Smithy! What's up?" he exclaimed. "I've just heard that you——."

"Can't you see what's up?" snarled the Bounder. "I've had my head ducked in the fountain—can't you see, or are you blind?"

"But why——."

"Can't you guess why, you ninny?"

"Oh!" said Redwing, "I see! Well, you might have expected the fellows to cut up rusty, if it's that——."

"Oh, shut up!"

Tom Redwing gave him a look. It was not the friendly look that he usually had for his chum.

"Well, you asked for it, and it serves you right!" he said. "You're doing a rotten thing, and you've made fellows sick with you. You've got what you've asked for."

The Bounder clenched his hands.

"Look here, Redwing——."

But Tom Redwing did not "look there". He seemed as "sick" with the Bounder as the other fellows. He turned and walked out of the lobby without another word: and Smithy was left to do his towelling alone.

## CHAPTER 6

# SMITHY THINKS TWICE

BOB CHERRY came into the Rag after third school, limping a little. His friends were punting a footer in the keen air in the quad: but Bob, for once, had no use for strenuous activities. With severe twinges in his bruised knee, and the prospect of standing on one leg to watch other fellows playing Soccer on the morrow, life did not seem quite so bright to Bob as it usually did, and his ruddy face was not quite so sunny as was its wont. And a frown came over it as his eyes fell on Herbert Vernon-Smith, sitting at the table in the Rag, with a pen in his hand, and a sheet of notepaper on a blotter before him. Bob's feelings towards a fellow who let down his side were inexpressible in words: indeed, had his right leg been available for action, he might have been tempted to express them with the foot attached thereto!

There were other Remove fellows in the Rag, and they were all looking at Smithy. Redwing had a set face: Squiff, Ogilvy, Toddy, Morgan, and several other fellows looked openly contemptuous. The Bounder did not seem aware of their inimical stares. He was chewing the pen-handle with a meditative air, as if uncertain of what he intended to write. Only two words, so far, appeared on the paper: and several pairs of eyes had seen them—the words were "Dear Pon".

Why Smithy chose to write that letter to his associate at Highcliffe in the Rag, instead of in the seclusion of his own study, was rather puzzling. He was not the fellow to care much what other fellows thought of him: but the depth of unpopularity to which he had now fallen, could hardly have been a matter of indifference even to the Bounder. Yet he was almost ostentatiously writing to Ponsonby under a dozen pairs of eyes, rather displaying what he was doing than making any attempt to conceal it. Really he seemed to want the other fellows to see.

He glanced up as Bob, with a grim look, passed him at the table.

"Leg still bad?" he asked.

"If it wasn't, I'd boot you!" was Bob's answer. "Jolly glad they ducked your cheeky head this morning."

The Bounder laughed.

"Thanks!" he said.

"Oh, rats!"

"Like me to send your kind regards to Pon?" asked Smithy, blandly.

Bob came to a halt, staring at him.

"So you're writing to that Highcliffe rat?" he exclaimed.

"Just that!"

"About your jaunt to-morrow, I suppose?" said Bob, breathing hard.

"Exactly."

Bob Cherry glanced round.

"I can't use my leg," he said. "Isn't there a fellow here who will boot him? What about you, Squiff?"

"Just thinking of it," said Squiff, and he came towards the table, several other fellows following him. Tom Redwing made a movement, as if to interpose: but he checked it. For once, he was not disposed to stand by his chum. Smithy was asking for it, as hard as he could.

The Bounder did not seem alarmed. He smiled at the

lowering faces round him. He seemed to be in a strangely changed mood.

"Collar him!" said Bolsover major.

"Boot him!" said Ogilvy.

"Hold on," said Vernon-Smith, quietly. "Let me finish my letter before you fly off the handle: I want to catch the early post with it."

"He, he, he!" came from a fat Owl in an armchair. "I jolly well know what he's got on for to-morrow! I heard him telling Skinner——."

"I fancy we all know, now," said Peter Todd. "We'll jam that letter down your neck, Smithy, and then boot you round the room, see?"

"Good egg!" said Bob Cherry.

"Hold on, I tell you," said the Bounder. "I just must let Pon know I'm booked to play football to-morrow, and can't join up as arranged."

"Oh!"

"What?"

"Is that it?"

"Smithy!" exclaimed Redwing. His face was suddenly bright, as he came over to his chum. "Smithy, old chap, you've changed your mind—I knew you would—you couldn't do such a rotten thing—I jolly well knew——."

The Bounder laughed again.

"It's been changed for me!" he explained. "You'll be pleased to know that the sermons you've given me lately have produced a proper effect——."

"Oh, don't be an ass," said Tom.

"And there's nothing like ducking a fellow's head to help him change his mind," went on the Bounder, coolly. "Much obliged to you fellows for takin' the trouble."

The juniors eyed him dubiously. The Bounder,

evidently, was in a very changed mood. Probably he had realised that he had gone too far in his arrogance: and realised, too, that in point of fact he did not want to make his whole form "sick" with him. But it was probable, too, that on reflection his sporting instincts had prevailed: making him resolve, at long last, to do the right thing and not the wrong one. Certainly he was very keen on that "jaunt" with Ponsonby and Gadsby and Monson of Highcliffe School, and he had been extremely unwilling to abandon it. But that was what he had, at last, decided upon.

"Look here, Smithy, if you mean that——!" said Bob Cherry.

"I quite often mean what I say," answered Vernon-Smith.

"You're going to play for the Remove to-morrow?"

"Right on the wicket!"

"Good man," said Bob, heartily. "Never mind what you were going to do, so long as you wash it out and play up for Greyfriars."

"Hear, hear!" said Squiff.

"If he means it——!" said Peter Todd, doubtfully.

"Of course he does," said Redwing, hotly.

"Well, let's see what he says to Pon!" answered Peter. Toddy, evidently, had some doubts on the subject.

"O.K.," said Vernon-Smith. "Read what I write, if you like—and then you can take the letter down to the box, if you feel like a walk."

"I will!" said Peter, emphatically.

The Bounder shrugged his shoulders, dipped the pen in the ink, and began to write, a dozen pairs of eyes following the words as the pen travelled over the paper.

Dear Pon,

Sorry I shan't be able to join up for that motor-run to-morrow after all. There's a Soccer match on here: and the fellows seem to think I'm too valuable to be left out: an opinion in which I cordially concur. Hope you'll have a good time in pleasant scenery.

Cheerio,

H. Vernon-Smith.

It was quite a harmless letter, if it had met other eyes than those of the juniors. The Bounder was always cautious. Even Mr. Quelch, had he seen it, would never have guessed that the "motor-run" on a half-holiday had been planned to end up at a spot where there were horses and bookmakers!

Having finished the letter, the Bounder addressed an envelope to Cecil Ponsonby at Highcliffe, folded the letter, and placed it therein.

"Your move, Toddy!" he said, blandly.

Peter Todd picked up the letter.

"You really want me to post this?" he asked.

"Haven't I said so?"

"O.K. It goes into the box, then!" said Peter, and he walked out of the Rag with the letter in his hand.

Bob Cherry gave the Bounder a hearty smack on the shoulder: or rather, a bang!

"Good man!" he exclaimed.

"Ow! Don't crock me for the game to-morrow!" yelled Smithy.

"Ha, ha, ha!"

The Bounder rose from the table. His expression was very cheery. Probably the relief and pleasure in Tom Redwing's face helped to console him for the loss of the disreputable "jaunt" with Pon and Co. Anyhow he had made up his mind: and now that his letter to Ponsonby was posted, the die was cast. The juniors who had been on the very point of "ragging" him were all cheery and friendly now: and as the Bounder walked out of the Rag in the midst of a cordial crowd, no one could have guessed that a quarter of an hour earlier he had been the most unpopular fellow in the form.

## CHAPTER 7

## ADAMANT!

"WELL?"

Harry Wharton shot that word out like a bullet.

He was in the quad with Frank Nugent, when the Bounder came up to him. Five or six fellows came with Smithy: Bob Cherry among them. The Bounder, evidently, had come to speak to the captain of the Remove: but Wharton had no desire whatever to hear anything that he had to say.

If other fellows in the Greyfriars Remove were "sick" with Smithy, none was quite so "sick" as the captain of the form. With his team already weakened by unavoidable omissions, his best winger had let him down and left him in the lurch, and for a reason of which any decent fellow ought to have been ashamed. His feelings towards the Bounder, just then, were of the deepest scorn and aversion: neither was he disposed to make a secret of them.

After long cogitation, Wharton had made up his depleted team again. Smithy's place at outside right was assigned to Tom Redwing: a selection that Smithy had recommended, and which no doubt would gratify him. Harry Wharton certainly had no wish to gratify Smithy: but he had to do the best he could with what material he had, regardless of other considerations.

What Smithy had to say now, the captain of the Remove neither knew nor cared: but he did not want to hear it. His manner made that very clear, and brought a flush to the Bounder's cheeks.

"About the footer to-morrow——!" the Bounder began.

Wharton cut him short at once.

"You've nothing to say about that, Vernon-Smith! I suppose you know that Redwing's in your place—you've seen the list. If you've got any more advice to give me, you can keep it."

The Bounder breathed hard.

"I'm playing to-morrow," he snapped.

Wharton stared at him. If Smithy, and the other fellows, expected to see him look relieved and pleased, they were disappointed. His stare was cold, hard, and uncompromising.

"You're playing to-morrow?" he repeated.

"Yes."

"Do you mean football?"

"What else?" snapped Smithy.

"Well, so far I had supposed that you were playing the blackguard with Ponsonby, not football," said Harry. "If you've changed your mind, and would rather play football, I hope you'll get a game somewhere. Anything else to tell me?"

The Bounder's eyes glittered.

"I've come here to tell you that I've changed my mind, and thrown other things over, to play in the Courtfield match to-morrow," he said.

"How good of you!" said the captain of the Remove, sarcastically. "You throw your skipper over one day, and throw other fellows over the next—and by to-morrow, I suppose, you'll be throwing me over again. I think I told you in my study that you couldn't play fast and loose with Soccer. You walked out of the Remove eleven, and you stay out."

"Wharton, old man——!" began Bob Cherry, in dismay. It had not occurred to Bob, so far, that if the Bounder came round, there might be difficulties on the other side. Evidently, there were!

"Look here, Wharton——!" began Squiff.

"We want Smithy——!" said Peter Todd.

"Do we?" said Harry. "Do we want a man who may let us down any minute? Mightn't Smithy change his mind again? He seems rather given to changing his mind."

"You know I wouldn't," muttered the Bounder.

"I don't know anything of the kind," answered the captain of the Remove, coolly. "All I know is that you're not to be trusted. I told you plainly that if you threw us over, you were out of Remove Soccer, and that was that! I'd sooner play Bunter than you, Vernon-Smith: at least he could be trusted not to back out. If you've really changed your mind, and if you mean what you say, I'm sorry—but you don't play Soccer for the Remove while I am captain."

"You mayn't stay captain long at that rate!" snarled the Bounder.

Harry Wharton shrugged his shoulders.

"That's for the Remove to decide," he answered. "I'm not football captain in the Remove by right divine, like a jolly old Stuart King. If the fellows don't want me, they can say so, and I'll step down. But so long as I am captain, you're outside Remove Soccer."

Vernon-Smith clenched his hands, hard. He was strongly tempted to dash them into the cool, contemptuous face of his form-captain.

He had not expected this, or anything like it. Wharton, certainly, had told him, quite plainly, that if he cut the Courtfield match, he had to cut Remove footer. But he knew his value to the team—and, in point of fact, overrated it. Wharton might have his back up: he might be resentful and ungracious: but he simply could not exclude his best winger from a match of which the prospects were already very dubious. So it had seemed to Smithy. He was finding out his mistake now. The captain of the Remove had given him his chance, and he had chosen to disregard it. Now it was too late.

Harry Wharton turned to walk away, as if the matter was ended. There were exclamations from three or four fellows at once.

"Look here, Wharton——."

"That's rot!"

"Think again, old chap——."

"We don't want that bunch of townies to beat us over again."

Wharton turned back.

"Let's have this clear," he said. "Smithy was picked to play Courtfield. He threw us over, and was warned that if he did, he would not be asked to play again. He did so all the same. Now he says that he's changed his mind. I haven't changed mine. Is it the business of a football captain to chop and change from minute to minute, according to the fancies of one fellow in the team?"

"Of course not," said Bob. "But——."

"Well, Smithy was a silly goat," said Squiff. "But he's come round——."

"And am I to sit and wait and wonder whether Smithy will come round?" asked the captain of the Remove, contemptuously. "That isn't my idea of a football captain's job, if it's yours, Field."

"It isn't, fathead! But——."

"The fact is, we want Smithy in the team, and he's

willing to play," said Peter Todd. "That's the point, old bean."

"Not at all! His place has been filled."

"Redwing will stand out, and be glad to," snapped the Bounder.

Wharton gave another shrug.

"If Redwing ever captains the Remove, he can decide who plays at outside right," he answered. "Until then, not."

"You want that bunch of townies to walk over Greyfriars on our own ground to-morrow?" sneered the Bounder.

"Oh, chuck it," said Harry, scornfully. "You didn't care yesterday whether they walked over us or not. What's the difference to-day?"

"But——!" began Frank Nugent.

Wharton did not seem to hear.

"The matter's settled," he said, very distinctly. "Vernon-Smith walked out on us, and he stays out. I've no more to say about it."

And with that, the captain of the Remove did walk away, to put an end to the discussion.

Frank Nugent, with a rather troubled face, went with him: and Bob, looking still more worried, followed. The rest stayed in a group round Vernon-Smith. Other fellows joined them, and hot discussion followed. The Bounder's face was dark: but there was at least one glimmer of satisfaction for Smithy: it was very plain that all the footballing fellows were against Wharton in this. Whether he was in the right or in the wrong, they were thinking chiefly of beating Trumper's team from Courtfield: and to that end, there was no doubt Herbert Vernon-Smith was wanted in the team.

Harry Wharton, as he walked away, was silent: and neither Bob Cherry nor Frank Nugent spoke. He glanced from one to the other, with a slightly sarcastic expression.

"You fellows think that I ought to give in?" he asked, suddenly.

"Um!" said Bob, uncomfortably. "We don't want Trumper's gang to beat us twice running, old chap."

"Smithy's an irritating brute," said Frank, "but—I think I'd stretch a point, old fellow. All the fellows think the same—that's plain enough."

Harry Wharton nodded, slowly.

"I can see that," he said, "but I think I'm right, and I don't mean to give in an inch. I'd rather resign the captaincy—much rather, than let one cheeky tick run the show while I'm called captain. If the fellows choose to back up Smithy, they can elect him skipper if they like: and he can captain the side in all the matches this season: if he isn't in Extra School for smoking, or sacked for pub-crawling," added Wharton, satirically. "So long as I'm captain, he's out of Remove Soccer: so it's no use talking about it."

And—as it was no use talking about it—his chums said no more. The Bounder, in his arrogance, had gone over the limit: and the captain of the Remove was adamant. But they could not help feeling that that adamantine attitude would lead to trouble: and they were right.

## CHAPTER 8

# MAN WANTED

LORD MAULEVERER strolled into the Rag after class that day, with his hands in the pockets of his elegant "bags", and an unusually thoughtful expression on his placid face. He did not, as usual, make for the nearest armchair. He walked across to the football list posted on the wall, and stood regarding it for some minutes: and then slowly shook his noble head.

Mauly was no great man at games. Certainly, he never dodged a compulsory practice, as Billy Bunter, Snoop, Skinner, and other such slackers did whenever they could. But on other occasions he was seldom found urging the flying ball. Had he been asked to play for his form, the request would probably have filled him, not with delight, but with dismay. Indeed Mauly did not always remember the dates of the fixtures: though when he did remember, he would loyally turn up to cheer the goals. Soccer, as a rule, passed his lazy lordship by like the idle wind. But for once, it seemed that he was interested.

The list he was reading was not very impressive, considering that a hard match was due on the morrow. Had it been a game with Cecil Reginald Temple and Co. of the Fourth, it would have been more than good enough. But Dick Trumper and his friends of Courtfield were what Fisher T. Fish would have called a "tough bunch" at the winter game. "Townies" they undoubtedly were: many of them at work on week-days, with much less time for games-practice than fellows at Greyfriars School. But they played a good game and a hard game, and were not easy to beat. The list at which Mauly was looking was, like the curate's egg in the story, good in parts! In other parts it was not.

J. Bull.
S. Q. I. Field. P. Todd.
R. Russell. D. Morgan. P. Hazeldene.
F. Nugent. R. D. Ogilvy.
T. Redwing. H. Wharton. H. J. R. Singh.

Men like Tom Brown, Mark Linley, Dick Penfold, and Bob Cherry were unavoidably out. But a man like Herbert Vernon-Smith was, in the opinion of most of the Remove, avoidably out. One weak spot at least could have been avoided—if the captain of the Remove had so chosen.

Having read, marked, learned, and inwardly digested that unsatisfactory list, as it were, Lord Mauleverer glanced round at Harry Wharton, who was standing by the window, looking out. His eyes were on a group in the quad, who were talking together rather excitedly. What they were saying to one another he did not hear, but could guess. By this time, Wharton was left in no doubt that all the Remove were against his decision. It was possible that the knowledge only added to his determination.

But he glanced round, with a smile and a nod, as Lord Mauleverer joined him. He had noticed his lordship scanning the football list.

"Getting keen on Soccer, Mauly?" he asked.

"Well, yaas! Might a fellow speak a word?" asked Mauly.

"Two, if you like," said Harry, laughing.

"Well, a man doesn't want to butt in," said Mauly, "but——." He paused.

"Carry on!" said the captain of the Remove, encouragingly.

"Well, if you won't get your back up——."

"Not at all."

"Why not make a bit of a concession, and play Smithy?" asked Lord Mauleverer. "I know what a troublesome fellow he is, and that he treated you badly, and that he will crow his head off if he pushes into the team again after what he's done—I know all that, as well as you do. But after all, the game's the thing."

Wharton did not answer, but his face hardened.

"It's a bit awkward for old Redwing, too," went on Mauly. "He's in Smithy's place, and Smithy is his pal. He would stand out like a shot for Smithy. Couldn't you stretch a point, old man?"

Wharton shook his head.

"I dare say you're right," said Lord Mauleverer, "but there's such a thing as public opinion, you know: and all the form think that Smithy ought to be put back in the eleven. Even your own pals, I fancy."

"I shouldn't wonder."

"We want to beat Courtfield, you know."

Harry Wharton laughed.

"Come clean, old scout," he said. "What you really mean is that you think I'm riding for a fall, and that there's more trouble coming than I can handle. You'd like to steer me clear of it in time—isn't that it? You're a good chap, Mauly, and I'm much obliged—but there's nothing doing."

"O.K.," said Lord Mauleverer. "Excuse my buttin' in." And he strolled away to an armchair, as Tom Redwing came into the Rag.

Redwing had a flushed face, and his look was troubled.

He came directly across to the captain of the Remove at the window.

Wharton gave him a keen look. It was the Bounder himself who had suggested that Redwing should take his place, when he "walked out". But since he had changed his mind, and was prepared to walk in again, as it were, there was no doubt that he looked at the matter with a very different eye, and it was very probable that he was making things uncomfortable for his chum. Harry Wharton fancied that he could guess what Tom Redwing was going to say, before a word was spoken.

"Look here, Wharton——!" began Tom, awkwardly.

"Looking!"

"About the match to-morrow——!" stammered Tom.

"That's all cut and dried."

"I know Smithy acted badly," said Tom, in a low voice, "and I told him so plainly enough, more than once. But he's ready now to do the right thing, and all the fellows think that he ought to be given a chance——."

"All but one, I fancy," agreed Wharton.

"Who's the one, then?"

"Little me."

Redwing bit his lip.

"You've got right on your side, in a way," he said, "but I think you're pushing it too far."

"Thanks for your opinion."

"You've put me in Smithy's place——."

"Smithy's own suggestion."

"I know! I know! But it's different now. Look here, Wharton, I know you've got reason to have your back up, but——."

"But my back isn't up! I'm acting as I think a football captain ought to act—that's all."

"I know you think so," said Tom, "but with everybody against you, couldn't you think twice about it?"

No answer.

"Well, look here," said Redwing, after a long pause, "Smithy's ready to play, and keen to play, and every man in the Remove excepting you thinks that he ought to play. I can't take his place. I'm not half his form, as you know as well as I do. If you won't play Smithy, you must look for another outside right."

"I knew that was coming," said Harry, quietly. "Smithy will make things as tough as he can for me."

"I'm sorry——."

"You needn't be! This comes from Smithy, not from you. The hands are the hands of Esau, but the voice is the voice of Jacob!" said Wharton, sarcastically. "So you're going to let me down, Redwing?"

Tom Redwing crimsoned.

"I don't call it that," he said. "You've put me in the place of a better man, and you ought to change back. Everyone says so."

"Everyone can say what everyone likes!" drawled Wharton. "Leave it at that. You're out of the team, and I don't want to hear any more."

"If you'd play Smithy——!"

"I'm not asking for advice, thanks."

Harry Wharton took a pencil from his pocket, and walked across to the football list. He drew the pencil through the name of T. Redwing, and then stood for several minutes in thought. Tom Redwing, from the window, and Lord Mauleverer, from the armchair, watched him curiously. They knew that he was thinking out a name to write in the place of T. Redwing—and that that name most certainly was not to be H. Vernon-Smith.

Finally, he wrote in a name. Redwing and Mauly stared at it. The name was "Mauleverer".

"Oh, gad!" ejaculated Mauly. He sat bolt upright in his armchair. Tom Redwing compressed his lips.

"Do you really mean that, Wharton?" he called across the room.

Wharton looked round.

"Why not?" he asked.

"Mauly—in Smithy's place—you're mad."

"Thanks! Mauly won't walk out on me, at any rate," answered the captain of the Remove. "A man you can trust is worth half-a-dozen you can't! Mauly, old man, you'll have to pull up your socks to-morrow."

"Oh, gad!" repeated his lordship, evidently far from overjoyed at the prospect. "I'll do my best, old man, but——."

"No man can do more," said Harry, lightly, and he put the pencil in his pocket and walked back to the window, his manner cheerful and unconcerned.

Tom Redwing, with a look more troubled than when he had entered, left the Rag, with an unhappy consciousness of having made matters worse, instead of better as he had hoped. Lord Mauleverer sighed gently. A strenuous Soccer match was not exactly his lordship's line of country: and the most strenuous game of his lazy life lay ahead of him: for Mauly was loyal to the core, and was certainly going to back up his captain to the last shot in the locker. But what the Remove fellows would say when they found his name in the list rather worried him—though it did not seem to worry Harry Wharton.

## CHAPTER 9

## ULTIMATUM!

"I SAY, you fellows——."

"Oh, ring off, Bunter."

"Shan't!" retorted Billy Bunter, independently. "What are you jawing Wharton for, I'd like to know! You ought to be backing him up."

"Eh?"

"What?"

"I'm backing you up, Harry, old chap!" said Bunter, encouragingly.

Harry Wharton laughed.

The Famous Five were gathered in No. 1 Study at tea. It was not quite the usual cheery function in that study.

If the captain of the Remove was troubled by the parlous state of Remove Soccer, his face did not reveal it. He looked quite unconcerned. But Bob Cherry, Nugent, Johnny Bull, and the Nabob of Bhanipur were neither looking nor feeling unconcerned. They were thinking of the dubious prospects of the match on the morrow: but still more, of Wharton's own position. Like the amiable Mauly, they could not help feeling that he was "riding for a fall": and it worried them.

One after another, they had expressed their opinion across the tea-table that Smithy, in spite of all, ought to be put back into the eleven. A fellow who had made a false step could not do more than retract it: and that Smithy had done. Wharton's view apparently was that "what he had said, he had said": and that that was the end of it. For once there was a difference of opinion in the Co. There were fellows in the Remove, like Skinner and Snoop, who hinted that Harry Wharton regarded himself as a sort of Great Panjandrum, a sort of monarch of all he surveyed whose right there was none to dispute. For once, his friends could not help feeling that there was just a spot of truth in it.

Billy Bunter's opinion on the subject was valued by nobody. His announcement that he was backing up "Harry old chap" caused Harry old chap to laugh, and Johnny Bull to snort. Indeed it might have caused Wharton to feel a little doubt when he found that the only fellow in the form who backed him up was William George Bunter. But the fat Owl was quite serious about it.

"Don't you give in, old fellow," he said.

"I won't!" said Harry, laughing.

"That's right!" said Bunter. "Don't you let that cad Smithy throw his weight about. I'm backing you up, old boy. I'll play at outside right to-morrow if you want a better man than Mauly."

"Ha, ha, ha!"

"Blessed if I see anything to cackle at! You fellows can cackle, but I jolly well wouldn't walk out on Wharton and leave him in the lurch like Smithy," said Bunter, warmly. "Truest friend and noblest foe, as Shakespeare said—that's me, all over!"

"Did Shakespeare say that?" asked Frank Nugent.

"Well, it might have been Browning——," admitted Bunter.

"Not Tennyson?"

"No!" said Bunter, decidedly, "not Tennyson. It was either Brownspear or Shaking—I mean either Browning or Shakespeare. You don't learn much in English Literature with Quelch, Nugent. But never mind that," went on Bunter, "you stick to your guns, Harry, old chap: I'm backing you up all along the line."

"How did Bunter know that Wharton had had a cake from home?" asked Johnny Bull, sarcastically.

"I didn't!" yelled Bunter, indignantly. "I never saw Gosling take the parcel in, and how should I know there was a cake in it, if I did? Still, I'll have a slice of that cake, Harry old fellow, if you don't mind."

"Do!" said Harry.

Bunter did—without delay. It was quite a large slice, and left the cake looking rather a ruin. With a capacious mouth packed to capacity with cake, Bunter's entertaining conversation ceased for the moment: and Bob Cherry took up the tale again.

"I wish you'd think it over, old chap," he said.

"What is there to think over?" asked Harry. "If Smithy is to run Soccer in the Remove as he chooses, he ought to be elected captain. Do you think he would let any man in the team play fast and loose, if he were skipper?"

"Um! Not likely! But that isn't the point! A football skipper's business, after all, is to win matches. Smithy's the man for goals."

"And his captain is to eat his words?" asked Harry, with a curl of the lip.

"Well, no! But—but stretching a point——."

"The stretchfulness of the esteemed point is the proper caper," remarked Hurree Jamset Ram Singh.

"I don't think so."

"Well, a wilful man must have his way," said Johnny Bull, "but you're making a mistake, old man."

"You let Harry alone," Billy Bunter re-started, his fat

voice coming a little muffled through cake. "He's right! Smithy's a rotten outsider! Why, I've still got a pain in my chin where he buzzed a dick at me yesterday——."

"You fat ass!" roared Bob.

"Oh, really, Cherry——."

"There'll be a row about this," said Nugent.

"Looks like it," agreed Wharton.

"And you don't care?" asked Johnny, rather tartly.

"Couldn't care less."

That reply reduced the other fellows to silence. If that was the attitude of the captain of the Remove, argument evidently was wasted.

"You stick to it, old chap," Bunter filled up the pause. "It's about time that cheeky ass Smithy learned where he gets off. Buzzing a dick at a fellow——."

"Fathead," said Harry, politely.

"Oh, really, Wharton! I'm backing you up, you know. You needn't call a fellow names when he's the only man in the Remove backing you up."

"Ass!"

"Beast! I—I mean, do you mind if I have another slice of that cake, old chap?"

"For goodness sake, finish it, and roll away."

Billy Bunter blinked at him indignantly. Really, this was a little ungrateful from the captain of the Remove to his only supporter in the whole form! However, the fat Owl proceeded to finish the cake. First things came first, with Bunter.

"I say, you fellows," Bunter's voice came muffled again. "I say, they're jawing it over in the Rag, and I fancy they're coming up here to see you about it, Harry! Don't you worry, old fellow! I'm standing by you!"

There was a tramp of feet in the Remove passage.

Four fellows in the study looked perturbed. Harry Wharton did not heed. He looked, as he had said, as if he couldn't have cared less: though probably the fact that the fat Owl was standing by him did not add to his resolution.

Five members of the Remove eleven came into the study, in a bunch. They were Peter Todd and Squiff, the two backs; Russell, who had taken Bob's place at right-half; Morgan and Ogilvy. All of them were looking very uncomfortable, but at the same time determined.

"Oh, you're here, Wharton," said Peter.

"Adsum!" answered Harry, lightly.

"We've come here to talk about the footer," said Squiff.

"And we jolly well think——!" began Ogilvy.

"What we think is——!" said Morgan, starting at the same time.

"You see——," coincided Russell.

"What about talking one at a time?" asked Wharton, blandly. "Much easier to follow if you take it in turns."

"Harry, old fellow——!" murmured Nugent. Wharton did not heed that murmur. He was evidently in a quite uncompromising mood.

"Look here, Wharton——!" began Peter, Squiff, and Ogilvy together.

"O.K. Make it a chorus, if you like," said Harry. "Don't mind me."

Squiff's jaw set grimly.

"I suppose you guess what's coming," he snapped.

"It's an easy guess," agreed Harry.

"Well, we'll tell you, all the same. We all think that Smithy ought to be in the team. He's wanted, and he's willing to play. Will you play him?"

"No!"

"You won't, when every man in the Remove is against you?" exclaimed Ogilvy.

"Right in one: I won't."

"That's right—stick to it!" chirruped Billy Bunter. "I'm backing you up, old chap! And if you fellows want to know what I think of you, I can jolly well say, quite plainly—yarooooh! Leggo my ear, Toddy, you beast!"

Peter Todd did not let go the fat ear. It seemed that the opinion of William George Bunter, valuable as it doubtless was, was not wanted. Peter twirled the fat Owl out of the study by a fat ear, heedless of indignant howls from Bunter, and Squiff kicked the door shut after him. The captain of the Remove was left to face the music without his only supporter!

"Now, let's have this plain!" said Ogilvy. All the quintet were angry now: and indeed, Harry Wharton's manner was not calculated to conciliate. "You're going to chuck away a football match, and let a bunch of townies walk over us a second time, because you've got your back up with Smithy. Well, it's not good enough, see?"

"Either Smithy plays, or we don't!" said Peter Todd, "and you can put that in your pipe and smoke it."

"That's that!" said Squiff.

"Take it or leave it," said Russell.

"And we mean every word of it, look you," said Morgan.

Four fellows in No. 1 Study looked, as they felt, dismayed. No change was perceptible in Harry Wharton's face. He regarded the little crowd of indignant juniors thoughtfully.

"So this is a sort of ultimatum?" he remarked.

"You can call it that," said Squiff. "We mean every word of it."

"O.K. Shut the door after you, please."

Squiff and Co. looked at him. Perhaps they had not known precisely what to expect in reply to their "ultimatum". Certainly they did not seem to have expected this. Never had five fellows looked more taken aback.

"Did you say shut the door after us?" asked Peter, breathing hard.

"Yes! It's a bit draughty with the door open," explained Wharton.

"Is that all you've got to say?" roared Squiff.

Harry Wharton raised his eyebrows.

"Is there anything else to say?" he inquired. "You fellows have resigned from the team, and your resignations are accepted. Isn't that the lot?"

Squiff and Co. looked at him, and looked at one another. Then, in silence, but only too evidently with deep feeling, they backed out of the study: and Peter shut the door with a bang that sounded like a cannon-shot.

Silence in No. 1 Study followed that bang. Harry Wharton's friends looked at him, without speaking but with considerable expression. He did not seem to notice it. He drew a paper from his pocket: it was a copy of the football list posted in the Rag. He pushed his plate aside, laid the paper on the table, and proceeded to draw a pencil through five names in the list, one after another. His friends breathed rather hard as they watched.

"You can't do it, Harry," said Nugent, at last.

Wharton looked up.

"How do you mean?" he asked.

"You can't leave them out——!" said Bob.

"I don't quite follow! A football captain's powers are limited, you know—I can't make fellows play if they won't.

All I can do is to fill their places. Anything else to suggest?"

"Only getting off the high horse!" grunted Johnny Bull.

Harry Wharton shrugged his shoulders.

"My esteemed and absurd Wharton——," murmured Hurree Jamset Ram Singh.

"Better leave it at that," said Harry, quietly. "We don't agree, it seems: but I'd rather resign the captaincy of the Remove than let Vernon-Smith get away with this. Now I've got to think this out—I've five places to fill: so if you fellows have finished tea——."

His friends left the study without speaking again. The captain of the Remove was left to work out this problem of filling five places in the depleted team: a matter which certainly required some concentrated thinking.

## CHAPTER 10

## NEW PROSPECTS

HERBERT VERNON-SMITH smiled.

After third school on Wednesday, he strolled into the Rag with Tom Redwing, to look at the football list posted there. It was a list that had gone through many variations: and probably even Harry Wharton would have admitted that all the changes had been for the worse, from the Soccer point of view.

Billy Bunter, ensconced in an armchair in the Rag, gave the Bounder an inimical blink through his big spectacles as he came in. There was no longer a twinge in Bunter's fat chin, but it lingered in his fat memory. Gladly would the fat Owl have punched Smithy's head, had it been practical politics. As it was, he had to content himself with a devastating blink.

Heedless of the Owl and his blink, in fact not even observing him sprawling in the armchair, Vernon-Smith walked across the room, and stood looking at the list. Tom Redwing's face was glum: but the Bounder smiled. He seemed to see some cause for elation in what every other footballing fellow in the Remove regarded as disastrous.

"What a crew!" he remarked, derisively.

"Rotten enough," muttered Redwing. "You've been a lot to blame for this, Smithy. If you hadn't started the ball rolling——."

"Ancient history!" drawled the Bounder. "Don't begin your sermons all over again, old bean. The lost sheep returned to the fold, didn't he—and you know the welcome he got! Could I do more than throw over Pon, and tell our respected and revered skipper that I was ready to play?"

"Well, I suppose not: but——."

"The dear man's got his back up, and he's ridin' for a fall! What a crew!" repeated the Bounder, as he read out the names.

J. Bull.

P. Bolsover. M. Newland.

T. Dutton. W. Wibley. P. Hazeldene.

F. Nugent. M. Desmond.

Mauleverer. H. Wharton. H. J. R. Singh.

"Good man in goal," went on Smithy. "Two good men in the front line! Pah! What a crew to stand up to Trumper's gang this afternoon."

"Nugent's pretty good——."

"Pretty good isn't good enough."

"Dutton's a good half——."

"That deaf ass!" sneered the Bounder.

"And Wibley's not bad——."

"Not bad at amateur theatricals," jeered Smithy. "If we were playing Hamlet, Wib's the man! But isn't it Soccer to-day?"

"Well, it's not a laughing matter, if we get wiped off the ground by the townies to-day," said Redwing, sharply.

"No 'if' about it," said Smithy, coolly. "That crew could hardly stand up to Temple's fancy crowd in the Fourth. They haven't an earthly against Courtfield. I wonder Wharton isn't playing Bunter—he might as well!"

A fat junior in an armchair concentrated unlimited scorn and contempt in his blink at the Bounder. It produced no effect on Smithy who did not even see it.

"Or Coker of the Fifth!" went on Smithy, laughing.

Tom Redwing gave him a sharp look. The Bounder's exclusion from the team had made him savagely resentful: but he seemed to have got over that entirely now. Now he seemed satisfied and amused, and his chum could only wonder why. He could see nothing in the dismal state of affairs which Herbert Vernon-Smith could hope to turn to his advantage.

"Look here, Smithy, it's rotten, and you've done most to bring it about," he said. "If you think it's funny, you're the only man in the Remove that does. Wharton may be carrying things with a high hand: but it's you that put him in a tough spot——."

"And I'll keep him there," said the Bounder, with a glint in his eyes. "The fool is playing into my hands, though he doesn't know it—or doesn't care. What do you think the fellows will say, and do, if that bunch of townies beat us by six or seven goals, and go home laughing? Think he'll be able to ride off on the high horse after that?"

Tom Redwing made no reply.

"He will have to resign—or wait to be booted out," went on Smithy. "There will be a new captain of the form before long, Reddy."

"Oh!" Redwing caught his breath. "Is that what you've got in mind?"

"Why not?" The Bounder scowled. "I tell you, if Wharton would meet me half-way, I'd play up now, and forget the rest. But will he?"

"I suppose not! But——."

"Well, let him keep on as he's started, and take what's coming to him afterwards. That means a new election in the Remove: with H. Vernon-Smith as a candidate for the captaincy—the winning candidate, I fancy."

Smithy drew a deep breath, and his eyes danced. He had not envisaged this, or thought of it, when the trouble began. But now that the possible prospect opened before him, it attracted him irresistibly. Second place in anything always irked the arrogant Bounder. He was a rebel by nature: though, like most rebels, he was likely to come down hard and heavy on any other rebel, once power was in his hands.

"Captain of the Remove!" he said. "Like the idea, old bean? Little me, what?"

Redwing did not look as if he liked the idea over-much.

"You don't seem to enthuse!" jeered Smithy. "But you'll back me up, Reddy. You can't let down a pal: and every vote in the form will count."

"I hope it won't come to that!"

"It will!" said the Bounder, confidently. "It's coming to that, and I'm helping it on all I can. It's between Wharton and me now, and it's his choice, not mine. War to the jolly old knife, as that's what he chooses."

"But, Smithy——," muttered Redwing.

"Oh, have a little sense," snapped the Bounder. "I thought he was letting off steam in his study the other day: but he means every word of it, as he's shown now. I'm out of Remove Soccer, if he keeps on as captain. Think I'm going to look on at matches with my hands in my pockets, like that yawnin' ass Mauleverer, or sit it out in the tuck-shop like that fat ass Bunter? I'll watch it! This is my chance—Wharton is choosing to make a fool of himself, and I'm going to make the most of it."

He jerked a contemptuous thumb towards the list on the wall.

"That lot will go down in a heap this afternoon.

But——." He laughed. "If you've given proper attention to Quelch in English Literature, Reddy, you'll remember that there's such a thing as making assurance doubly sure, as jolly old Shakespeare said first, and jolly old Byron after him. That's what I'm goin' to do. I'm going to talk to some of those fellows——."

"But——!" exclaimed Redwing.

"But rats!" retorted the Bounder, and he turned away. Tom Redwing's face was clouded. Smithy's face was cheery: his step elastic. The captain of the Remove was, as he had said, playing into his hands: and it seemed to Smithy that everything was coming his way. A very attractive goal lay ahead: and only too well Redwing knew that his chum would have little scruple, if any, about the means he used to reach it.

Redwing did not speak again: but another voice made itself heard: a fat voice from an armchair.

"Yah! I'll jolly well vote against you, Smithy, and chance it. Yah!"

Vernon-Smith looked round, and for the first time observed William George Bunter. For a moment, a glint came into his eyes: and in that moment Billy Bunter was in danger of being hooked out of the armchair and bumped on the floor. But the next, the Bounder was smiling.

"That you, Bunter! Just the chap I wanted to see," he said, amiably.

"Well, the want's all on your side!" snorted Bunter. "I jolly well don't want to see your ugly mug, I can tell you. Buzzing a dick at a fellow's head when he comes up with a message from a beak——."

"Well, I didn't know it was a message, you know." Smithy's manner was very amicable, and Tom Redwing could only stare at him. Why the Bounder was taking the trouble to conciliate the fat and fatuous Owl of the Remove, was quite a puzzle: though a puzzle that was soon to be solved. "Look here, Bunter, old bean——."

"Yah!"

"There's going to be a spread in my study after prep——."

"Eh?" Billy Bunter sat up and took notice.

"I'd like you to come, if you feel that way."

Bunter beamed.

A dictionary banging on a fat chin was neither grateful nor comforting. A narrow escape from having a bag of flour bursting over his fat head was not enjoyable. Billy Bunter had been feeling extremely inimical. He had even been considering the possibility of recapturing that bag of flour from No. 4 Study, and letting Smithy somehow have it on his "nut". But all such thoughts vanished from his fat mind now. Bunter was not the man to bear grudges—not when there was a spread about!

"I'll come, old chap!" he said, affably. "I'll be there all right!"

"Right-ho, old fellow," said Smithy, and with a friendly nod to the fat Owl, he walked across to the door. Redwing followed him out.

"Look here, Smithy——!" he muttered.

"That's one vote, if there's an election, Reddy!" grinned the Bounder. "Lots of methods of electioneering. 'Feed the brute' is the method with Bunter. What!" He chuckled.

"If that's the sort of thing——!" began Redwing.

"Quite!" said the Bounder: and he laughed and walked out into the quad, leaving his chum frowning.

## CHAPTER 11

# THE LAST SHOT IN THE LOCKER

"WHARTON——."

Bolsover major and Hazeldene spoke together.

"Here," said Harry.

After dinner, the Famous Five had come out of the House, four of them not looking so cheery as was their wont, on a fine clear day, a holiday, with a football match in the offing.

Bob Cherry, generally the most exuberantly cheerful of the five, seemed peeved. A fellow who had to stand with a painful knee, watching second-rate players lose a Soccer match for the school, couldn't be quite expected to look or feel optimistic. Frank Nugent was glad to be in the team, and he was going to play the hardest game of his life in support of his captain and chum: but he had lingering doubts about the outcome. Johnny Bull, always a good man in goal, was booked for plenty of exercise therein, for he did not doubt that Trumper and Co. would come through the Remove ranks almost like scythes through corn. Johnny had often made wonderful saves: and that afternoon he was going to save all he could: but saving the match was another matter. Hurree Jamset Ram Singh, on the left wing, was as good a man as the Remove could put into the field: but Soccer was not a one-man game: nor a three-man game, if it came to that: and the sad fact was that in the Greyfriars eleven there were only three men up to the mark for such a match. Four fellows hoped for the best, but could not help expecting the worst: only Harry

Wharton, of the five, looked sedately cheerful. Perhaps he expected as well as hoped for the best: or possibly he was determined not to see what other fellows could see. At all events he was going on the way he had marked out for himself, never even thinking of yielding an inch.

But a shadow crossed his face, for a moment, as Bolsover major and Hazel came up together. He scented trouble at once: neither could he doubt that if trouble was coming, the wily Bounder was at the bottom of it. There was a bullying air about Bolsover, and a hangdog look about Hazel, which indicated very plainly that they had something unpleasant to say.

"Well?" said Harry, as they seemed in no hurry to speak.

"Well, you see——!" began Hazel, haltingly.

"Oh, get it out," said Bolsover major. "Look here, Wharton, you know what every fellow in the form is saying—you've turned Smithy out of the team——."

"Smithy turned himself out," said Wharton, mildly.

"And five other fellows——," muttered Hazel.

"Haven't you heard?" asked Harry, in the same mild tone. "They resigned. They came to my study yesterday to tell me so."

"Oh, come off it!" snapped Bolsover major. "The long and short of it is, Wharton, that it won't wash. If you like to play a Soccer match with a team of rags and tatters, and send the townies home laughing at us, we don't! If you're not playing Smithy, and Squiff, and Toddy, and——."

"I'm not."

"Then you're not playing me!" growled Bolsover. "And Hazel says the same."

"Do you, Hazel?"

"Yes, I do!" muttered Hazel, suddenly. "It's not good enough, as Bolsover said. Play Smithy——."

"I'm not asking for advice, thanks." Harry Wharton took a paper from his pocket, and a pencil, and crossed out two names in a list. "That's the lot! You can cut."

Bolsover major and Hazel looked at him. They did not seem to have expected that abrupt dismissal. Harry Wharton, however, appeared to have done with them, for he turned his back, leaving them to "cut".

With very expressive looks, they cut.

"Oh, my hat!" groaned Bob Cherry. "The jolly old team is getting curiouser and curiouser, as Alice said in Wonderland. You've got to find another back and another half now."

"Plenty of talent in the Remove," said Harry, lightly.

"Look here, old chap, the men would come round if you asked them. There's still time, and if you asked Toddy and Squiff——."

"Think it over again, Harry," said Nugent, anxiously.

"I've done all the thinking I'm doing about that, Frank." Two more defections from the team had evidently not softened the adamant!

"You're making a mistake, old man," said Johnny Bull.

"I've heard that one!"

Johnny grunted, and said no more.

"My esteemed and absurd chum," murmured Hurree Jamset Ram Singh.

Harry Wharton glanced up at the clock-tower.

"Kick-off at three," he said. "Not a lot of time to find two more men. See you fellows later."

He nodded to his friends and walked away, leaving them exchanging clouded and expressive glances. They were backing him up: and they admitted that firmness was a quality needed in a football captain. But they could not help feeling, like a good many other fellows, that the captain of the Remove was carrying firmness to the length of stubborn obstinacy. There could be little doubt that Squiff and Co., now that they realised that their move had not driven Wharton into playing the Bounder, would have come round, at a word, rather than have seen the home side walked over. Clearly, however, Wharton was not going to utter that word.

In fact, he passed Squiff, and Toddy, and Ogilvy, in a little group in the quad, when he left his friends: and they all glanced at him as he passed: perhaps expecting, or hoping, to hear the operative word. But he went on his way without a sign.

He came on Skinner, Snoop, and Stott, lounging idly by the elms with their hands in their pockets.

"Seen Elliott?" he asked.

Skinner grinned, and winked at his companions.

"Gone out on his bike," he answered.

Wharton compressed his lips.

"Seen Smith mi. about?"

"He went out with Elliott."

Skinner gave his friends another wink, and Sidney James Snoop giggled. On a half-holiday, a good many fellows had gone out of gates: which made Wharton's position more difficult than ever. It was not going to be easy to fill the vacant places even with third- or fourth-rate material.

He looked over Skinner and Co. Skinner and Snoop were of no use to him: but Stott was a footballer of sorts, and might, indeed, have been a good man at the game, had he consorted less with Skinner. The captain of the Remove was not in a position now to be too particular. He had to have players.

"Care to play this afternoon, Stott?" he asked.

Stott stared at him. It was a request that he had never expected to hear from the captain of his form.

"You've never asked me that before," he remarked, sarcastically.

"I'm asking you now."

"Because you're hard up for men, I suppose?"

"Exactly," said Harry, calmly. "I want a right back. Are you on?"

"Any port in a storm, what?" grinned Skinner. "The fact is, Wharton, we're going out this afternoon, and Stott's coming. Come on, Freddy."

But "Freddy" did not stir.

"Wharton's asked me to play," he said.

"Oh, rot."

"Well, I don't think it rot! I'm your man, Wharton, if you want me," said Stott.

Skinner frowned, and Snoop sneered. But the prospect of playing for his school seemed to have caused Stott to develop a will of his own for once. He looked at Wharton, disregarding his companions.

"Good man," said Harry. "Turn up in the changing-room on time."

"You bet!" said Stott.

Harry Wharton walked on, leaving Skinner and Snoop arguing with Stott, who ended the argument by walking away to the changing-room. But Wharton's further quest was very discouraging. Some fellows were out of gates: several others, probably not flattered by being called upon to fill up gaps at the last moment in a team booked for defeat, blankly refused. It was a singular and novel experience for the captain of the Remove, and the Bounder, who had a mocking eye on him from a distance, wondered whether he would, at long last, come down off his perch, as Smithy expressed it.

Nothing, however, was further from Wharton's thoughts. Not that Smithy, at this stage, was at all anxious for his form-captain to yield the disputed point. With such bright new prospects opening before him, Smithy was quite satisfied with the way things were going.

Wharton could hardly feel satisfied. Any minute now the men from Courtfield might arrive, and he was still a man short for his team, and no man was available. With all his adamantine determination, he could scarcely think of taking the field against Courtfield with ten men. In that curious state of affairs, his eyes fell on a fat figure lounging by the door of the changing-room, blinking at him through a pair of big spectacles.

He hesitated.

The Remove eleven was already what Bolsover major had called it—a team of rags and tatters. But such an addition as that would be the climax. Nevertheless, he had to play a Remove man, and Bunter was a Remove man, whatever else he was or wasn't. The fat Owl was the last shot in the locker. He hesitated: but his hesitation was brief.

"Bunter!" he rapped.

"I—I say, it wasn't me!" exclaimed Billy Bunter, in alarm. "I haven't been up to your study, old chap——."

"You fat ass!"

"Oh, really, Wharton—I—I tell you I haven't been near your study, and I never looked into the cupboard, and the chocs weren't there when I looked in——."

"Will you listen to me, you burbling owl?"

"Oh! Yes, old chap, but I expect it was Nugent had the chocs——."

"Like to play for the Remove?"

Billy Bunter gave so sudden a jump, that his big spectacles almost fell off.

"Eh?" he ejaculated.

"You offered the other day, you know," said Wharton, sardonically. "Well, now's your chance, old fat man."

"Oh, crikey!" said Bunter.

"Hazel's standing out," explained Wharton. "You're going to play left half."

"Oh!" said Bunter. He slowly assimilated the idea, and a fat grin of satisfaction overspread his plump visage. Bunter, at least, believed that he could play Soccer, if nobody else in the Remove did! "Well, it's taken you a jolly long time to spot a fellow's form, Wharton——."

"Fathead!"

"Still, I'll play," said Bunter, magnanimously. "You've got a rotten team, old chap: but one really good man in the side may pull it together——."

"Oh, my hat!"

"One jolly good man makes a lot of difference," said Bunter, sagely. "We'll jolly well beat that townies crowd. Rely on me, old man."

"Roll in and change," said Harry, laughing.

Billy Bunter rolled cheerily into the changing-room, greatly bucked. Harry Wharton was far from feeling bucked as he followed him in. But the fat Owl of the Remove was the last shot in the locker: and that was that.

## CHAPTER 12

## SEVEN—ONE!

BOB CHERRY groaned.

It was not a painful twinge of his damaged knee that evoked the groan. That knee was far from mended: and standing round watching football did not improve it. But Bob had forgotten that knee, and was insensible to twinges now. It was the game he was watching that made him groan.

A good many fellows had gathered to watch. Among them were the discarded members of the eleven, who looked on with grim or sarcastic faces. Vernon-Smith, though he made some attempt to conceal it, was in high feather—a feeling not shared by any other man in the Remove.

But not only Remove men watched that unfortunate match. Fellows in other forms had heard that there were "ructions" in the Remove, and that their football team was at sixes and sevens. And the news that Billy Bunter was playing for his form excited quite a lot of interest. Temple of the Fourth told Dabney and Fry that it would be as good as a circus: and his friends agreed that it was bound to be: so there were Temple, Dabney and Co. watching and grinning. Hobson and his friends in the Shell joined the crowd. Even Coker of the Fifth condescended to give the juniors a look-in: and he remarked sarcastically to Potter and Greene that that was what they seemed to call Soccer in the Lower School.

It was unlucky that while the Remove team was at its lowest ebb, the men from Courtfield were at the top of their form. Trumper and Grahame and Wickers and Solly Lazarus, and the rest, had come over expecting a hard game as usual, with victory on the knees of the gods. They found the game about as hard as a sharp blade might have found a chunk of cheese.

"Some game, Reddy," the Bounder murmured, as Trumper and Co. came down on the home goal for the umpteenth time, like wolves on the fold.

Redwing knitted his brows, without replying. It was not a happy day for him. He was far from satisfied with the line he had taken: still less satisfied with the line his chum had taken. He watched with a clouded face, aware of the Bounder's sardonic amusement, and irritated by it.

The game was worth watching: at least from the point of view of entertainment. Never had the Greyfriars Remove put up so rotten a show at Soccer. There were bright spots, but they were few.

Johnny Bull, in goal, had been performing miracles from the whistle. The halves and backs seemed nowhere. One of the halves, in fact—a very fat one—spent most of his time sitting on the ground and panting for breath. But contact with Mother Earth did not have the effect on Billy Bunter that it had on Antaeus of old. Every time he went down, the fat Owl was slower in getting up again.

But while halves and backs seemed almost to make a point of leaving goal open to attack, Johnny between the posts was a real marvel. Shots rained on him, and Skinner remarked to Snoop that the Courtfield men looked like playing a hundred up! But it did not work out like that. Johnny hopped and jumped like a kangaroo, tireless and ever on the alert: again and again, and yet again, the whizzing ball met a ready foot or a ready fist or a hard head, and came back into play. With almost everything else in their favour, Trumper and Co. did not find it easy to get past that sturdy son of Yorkshire's spacious county. But even Johnny could only keep down the margin.

Now Johnny performed another of his miracles, and the ball, whizzing in from Dick Trumper's foot, went back to midfield instead of into the net. It was another wonderful "save": though it did not, as the Bounder remarked, cut much ice, as the visitors were already three up to nil. And a minute or two later Courtfield were attacking hotly again, with the Greyfriars halves and backs looking rather like chaff before the wind.

Only in the forward line, apart from Johnny, were the Remove men showing any of their old quality. Harry Wharton was playing the game of his life, his face grim, as if determined somehow to snatch victory from the jaws of defeat. Hurree Jamset Ram Singh was at his very best—and it was a very good best. Frank Nugent was putting in all he knew, and displaying unexpected powers. But the surprise-packet was Lord Mauleverer at outside-right. Hardly a man had expected Mauly to put up a show much better than Bunter's. Indeed the sardonic Bounder had predicted that Mauly would forget the match, and be found taking a nap on his study sofa when the whistle went; instead of which his lazy lordship seemed to have forgotten that laziness was his besetting sin. He was keen, alert, untiring, and playing up as if Soccer had always been the delight of his heart. Loyalty to a friend in a jam was Mauly's long suit: and he was going to help Harry Wharton pull that game out of the fire if he could.

But a fourth goal for Courtfield, ten minutes before the interval, did not look as if the game would be pulled out of the fire. And again the whistle was followed by Trumper and Co. coming down like wolves on the fold: and shots

THE CAPTAIN OF THE REMOVE SLAMMED THE LEATHER IN

at goal came almost like hail. But Johnny Bull was equal to the test this time, as often before: and the ball came away with a whiz that would have carried it far, had it not met the fattest head at Greyfriars in transit. There was a frantic yell from Billy Bunter as he rolled over, with fat little legs kicking up in the air.

Dick Trumper was on the ball the next moment, and it shot back at goal: only to meet a ready fist that thumped it out again. Somehow, Tom Dutton cleared to midfield, and Harry Wharton pounced on the ball. Then there was a stir among the spectators: the Remove side were waking up at last! The ball went up the field with short passing, in spite of all the Courtfielders could do: and when Micky Desmond, in the excitement of the moment, miskicked, Hurree Jamset Ram Singh jumped in and saved it, and sent it across to Nugent, who let Mauleverer have it as he was rushed over: and Lord Mauleverer, with ease and grace, and an unerring foot which nobody had ever dreamed that his lordship possessed, centred to Wharton at the psychological moment, and the captain of the Remove slammed the leather in, beating William Wickers in goal all the way.

"Goal!" gasped the Bounder. And for the moment he forgot his ambition, and his scheming, and was a sportsman again. "Goal! Good man! Oh, good man! Goal!"

"Goal!" shouted Redwing, his face bright.

"Goal!" roared Bob Cherry. "Oh, good man! That's the stuff to give 'em! Goal! Goal!"

But the Bounder was himself again in a moment or two.

"Flash in the pan," he said to Redwing. "I'd like to see Wharton do that twice!"

He was not likely to see it. The whistle went for half-time with the score at four to one: and in the interval, a fat winded figure crawled away. Billy Bunter had been quite keen to play for School: he was much keener now to get off the ground before the game re-started. Bedewed with perspiration, with an ache in every fat limb, winded to the wide, the fat Owl crawled away, almost on his hands and knees, and was seen no more. He was not missed! The Remove lined up for the second half a man short: one or two of them perhaps inclined to follow Bunter's example.

In the second half, it was a case of "thus bad begins, but worse remains behind". If Harry Wharton had still hoped to snatch victory from the jaws of defeat, he had to part with that hope now.

He knew now that he had taken too long a chance. Even now, in the bitter moment of defeat, he did not and could not regret that he had refused to yield a point to the arrogant Bounder. But a friendly word to fellows like Squiff, or Toddy, or Ogilvy might have saved the situation: and he had not uttered it.

It was, however, too late to think of that now.

The game went on to a dismal finish: dismal for the home team, at all events, though the Courtfield men seemed to find it pleasant enough and even amusing.

All Harry Wharton's almost superhuman exertions, backed up strenuously by Nugent, the Nabob, and Lord Mauleverer, could do, was to keep down the margin. Except for Johnny Bull, the rest were nowhere in the second half. Luckily, Johnny in goal was still a tower of strength: and but for stubborn and untiring defence, the score would have been an absurdity. As it was, Trumper and Co. had taken their seventh goal when the final whistle went. A defeat by seven goals to one was a new experience for the Greyfriars Remove: in its way, that game had made history! Only the Bounder found cause for satisfaction in that dismal outcome of the "ructions" in the Remove.

## CHAPTER 13

# FACING THE MUSIC

"Boo!"

That was a very unusual greeting for the captain of the Remove.

It was not an elegant greeting. But it was very expressive. It showed very plainly what the Greyfriars Remove thought of their once-popular captain.

The Rag was crowded.

The Courtfield men had gone home victorious: some of them had been seen grinning as they departed. Greyfriars men—not in the Remove—had been seen grinning too. In the Remove feelings were deep. In the Remove they prided themselves that they played Soccer with the accent on the "play". They could take a beating: but this was the limit. Seven-one—from a bunch of townies! Not long ago the Bounder had been the most unpopular fellow in the Remove. Harry Wharton had now changed places with him.

The Famous Five "tea'd", not very happily, in No. 1 Study. After tea Harry Wharton came down to the Rag. His friends, guessing the kind of reception he was likely to meet there, would willingly have walked him off in some other direction. But if there was music to be faced, Harry Wharton, whether in the right or the wrong, was the man to face it. He headed for the Rag: and his friends went with him, with clouded looks.

The moment he appeared in the doorway, there was a roar.

"Boo!"

A faint colour came into his cheeks. But his face was quite calm as he walked in.

The Bounder, lounging by the window, winked at Tom Redwing. Up to the moment of Wharton's entrance, an excited and noisy discussion had been going on: Wharton the subject of it. There was no need for the Bounder to suggest that the fellow who had "chucked" away a Soccer match from sheer pride and obstinacy, and sent away a crew of townies grinning at Greyfriars football, should be turned out of the captaincy. That idea was already in almost every mind. The Bounder had, in fact, only to reap where Harry Wharton had sown.

"By gum!" Smithy murmured to Redwing. "Does he still think that he can carry it off with a high hand? He's got another guess coming, Reddy."

"It's rotten," muttered Redwing.

"Is it?" grinned Smithy. "Why, he's stiff-necked ass enough to take another team like that over to Rookwood to play Silver's crowd. Think anybody here would stand for that?"

Redwing made no reply. He was well aware that his chum was thinking much less of Soccer records, than of "cashing in" on the present state of affairs.

Lord Mauleverer, inert in an armchair, looked round. His lordship was quite overcome by his unusual and strenuous exertions that afternoon. But he sat up and bestowed a nod and a smile on Wharton as he came in. He was the only fellow there who had anything like a friendly greeting for the captain of the Remove. The rest, even fellows with whom Harry Wharton had always been on the best of terms, were hostile.

Bolsover major and several other fellows made a move,

as if disposed to adopt more active measures than "booing". Bob Cherry, Frank Nugent, Johnny Bull, and Hurree Jamset Ram Singh gathered round their leader. Nugent whispered to him.

"Look here, Harry——."

"Well?"

"What's the good of a row?" muttered Frank. "Let's get out of this."

Wharton smiled, and shook his head.

"I've something to say to the fellows," he answered.

"No good talking to them now," muttered Bob.

"No time like the present."

"Look here, Wharton," grunted Johnny Bull. "You've put everybody's back up—can't you leave it at that?"

"My esteemed and absurd chum," murmured Huree Jamset Ram Singh, "a stitch in time saves ninepence, as the English proverb remarks. Let us take a little walkfulness abroad."

Harry Wharton did not heed. Apparently he had come to the Rag with something to say, and was going to say it, though the skies fell.

He stood with his hands in his trousers' pockets, looking over a crowd of hostile faces, with a cool air of indifference that certainly did not produce a pacifying effect upon the angry Removites.

Squiff came forward, followed by Peter Todd and Ogilvy and Russell. Bolsover major and his friends contented themselves with a renewed "Boo!" which woke the echoes.

"Oh, shut up that row!" exclaimed Squiff, looking round. "Let a fellow speak! Look here, Wharton——."

"Looking," said Harry.

"You've chucked away a Soccer match——."

"And sent a crew of townies home laughing at us!" hooted Peter.

"Seven—one!" said Ogilvy. "Proud of it?"

"And all because you had your back up with Smithy!" exclaimed Russell.

There was a roar of voices, a dozen fellows speaking at once. Harry Wharton waited calmly for the hubbub to subside. His friends were looking, and feeling, uneasy: but the captain of the Remove seemed quite at his ease. The Bounder watched him curiously, wondering whether his rival was about to make a final mistake, and leave the game entirely in his hands.

As soon as he could make his voice heard, Harry Wharton spoke again.

"You fellows don't seem to be satisfied," he remarked quite casually.

"Satisfied?" repeated Squiff, staring at him. "You begin by turning out the best winger in the Remove——."

"You're losing your memory, old man. If you mean Vernon-Smith, he turned himself out."

"Wasn't he ready to come in again?" demanded Peter Todd. "Didn't you keep him out because you had your silly back up?"

"Not at all! Vernon-Smith was warned if he let us down, he was out of Remove Soccer, and would stay out. That still goes, if I stay captain of the form."

The Bounder smiled, and winked at Tom Redwing again. He could have asked for nothing better than this.

"You won't stay captain long at that rate!" said Peter.

Wharton shrugged his shoulders.

"I said 'if'," he remarked, lightly.

"Not much 'if' about it, if that's your line," said Squiff,

grimly. "Just before you came in, we were discussing turning you out——."

"I guessed that one. Get on with it," said Harry. "If I go out, I've no doubt that there's someone ready to take my place." He glanced across at the Bounder. "Chance for you, Smithy, if you're not sacked for pub-crawling before the next fixture."

The Bounder reddened, but affected not to hear.

"Let's have it clear," went on Harry. "I'm not sticking on where I'm not wanted. No need to yell your head off, Bolsover. I tell you fellows plainly that if I keep on as skipper, what I have said goes: Vernon-Smith stays outside Remove Soccer. Take it or leave it."

"Harry——!" muttered Nugent.

Wharton did not heed him. Evidently his mind was made up: on that disputed point he was not yielding an inch, or a fraction of an inch.

"That's what I've looked in to say," he went on. "I'm ready to resign the captaincy of the form on the spot—you needn't take the trouble to turn me out: I'm ready to save you the trouble. Want me or not? Yes or no!"

There was a roar.

"No!"

From Lord Mauleverer came a gentle "Yaas". It was drowned in the roar. There was no doubt about the feeling of the Remove on the subject. A good many fellows, probably, would have hesitated at an extreme step: but the cool indifference of Wharton's manner had the effect of putting up the backs of friends as well as foes. He was asking for it—and getting it!

"Is that clear enough for you?" snapped Squiff.

Harry Wharton nodded.

"Quite!" he answered. "Have it your own way, by

all means. I resign: and you can elect a new form-captain as soon as you like! That's the lot!"

And with that, Harry Wharton—no longer captain of the Greyfriars Remove—turned and walked out of the Rag, leaving the crowded room in a buzz behind him.

## CHAPTER 14

## BACK UP!

"I SAY, you fellows!"

Four fellows, in No. 1 Study in the Remove, were rather surprised.

It was tea-time, or rather past tea-time, on Thursday, the day following the unlucky Courtfield match. Four members of the Co. had gathered there: but they were waiting tea for the fifth. Bob Cherry, in his study up the passage, was giving some more attention to his crocked knee. That knee was still in a very unreliable state: and Bob was fervently anxious for it to be a going concern again when the Rookwood match came along.

Quite a handsome spread awaited him in Wharton's study, when he came. There was ham, there was jam; there were dough-nuts, there were several eggs, and Johnny Bull had contributed a cake of considerable dimensions which had arrived from home. Billy Bunter's eyes, and spectacles, might have been expected to turn, immediately, on the good things on the table: especially the cake and the jam. He might, indeed, have been expected to stretch out a fat paw to one or the other, or both, without delaying for the formality of an invitation so to do.

Instead of which, the Owl of the Remove did not direct a single blink at the well-spread board. For once, perhaps for the first time in his fat career, Bunter passed by an enticing array of edibles like the idle wind which he regarded not. Food, for once, did not seem to interest him.

He blinked at Harry Wharton, Frank Nugent, Johnny

Bull, and Hurree Jamset Ram Singh. He did not seem even to notice that the table was spread for tea at all. Really, it was surprising.

"I've just looked in——!" went on Bunter.

"Look out again!" suggested Johnny Bull.

"Oh, really, Bull——."

"And shut the door after you," said Nugent.

"Oh, really, Nugent——."

"Want anything, Bunter?" asked Harry Wharton. It was tea-time: but the fat Owl had apparently not looked in for tea.

Indeed, an attentive glance at Bunter's fat face revealed that he had already been somewhere where there was jam. There were sticky smears round the most capacious mouth in the Remove. The best-filled waistcoat at Greyfriars was spotted with crumbs, which indicated that Bunter had found cake where he had found jam.

Bunter, in fact, had fed already: and his fat and shiny look hinted that there had been ample supplies, and that he had over-done it a little: as he seldom failed to do when supplies were ample. For once, Bunter had had enough, and did not want any more!

He grinned at the former captain of the Remove.

"Not from you, old chap," he said. "You're not likely to vote for Smithy, after the rows you've had, what? He, he, he!"

The juniors observed now that Bunter had a crumpled paper and a pencil in hand. On the paper several names were scrawled.

"Vote for Smithy!" repeated Harry, his brow darkening a little. The discarded captain of the form had "taken the knock" with absolute indifference and equanimity, outwardly at least. Possibly he did not feel quite so equable within.

"That's it," said Bunter. "I'm canvassing for votes, Smithy's my candidate, see?"

"You fat ass!" said Nugent. "Buzz off."

"Well, the election's to-day," said Bunter. "There's been a meeting in Smithy's study——."

"With jam and cake?" asked Wharton, sarcastically.

"Eh? There were some light refreshments," said Bunter, with dignity. "That wasn't why I was there, of course. But you should have seen Skinner and Snoop and Bolsover guzzling the jam tarts! And Fishy, too! I say, you fellows, I jolly well saw Fishy slip some of the apples into his pockets. He, he, he!"

The fat Owl chuckled.

"Smithy's not a bad chap," he went on. "I mean, he's got his good points——."

"He didn't buzz a dick at you this time?" asked Nugent. "You've not pinched another bag of flour from below stairs for his napper?"

"Well, I'm not the fellow to bear grudges," said Bunter, loftily.

"Not when there's cake and jam about!" snorted Johnny Bull.

Billy Bunter disdained to reply to that!

"Well, about the votes," he said. "I told Smithy I'd do some electioneering for him. Not because he lent me half a crown, you know——."

"Ha, ha, ha!"

"Blessed if I see anything to cackle at! I think Smithy will make a jolly good captain," said Bunter, warmly. "Not so jolly high-and-mighty as you are, Wharton, if you don't mind my saying so."

"Not at all!"

"Smithy will go easy," said Bunter. "He won't always be rooting a fellow out for games-practice on compulsory days, when a fellow doesn't feel like it. You jolly well always did, Wharton, and you can't jolly well deny it."

"Guilty, my lord," said Harry, laughing.

"Well, nothing against you, old fellow, but I think it will be a change for the better, if Smithy gets in. Lots of fellows think so. I suppose you know Toddy's put up. A chap would like to back up a man in his own study: but it can't be done," said Bunter, shaking a fat head. "I told Toddy plainly that he couldn't expect it, when he's so jolly mean with food in the study. He kicked me——."

"Good!" said Johnny Bull.

"Beast! I—I mean, I hope you're going to rally round, old chap. As you fellows are my pals——."

"Are we?"

"—as you fellows are my pals, I thought I'd ask you. Shall I put your names down? Mind, Smithy's going to stand a tremendous spread to celebrate the election if he gets in. Of course that hasn't anything to do with the voting: still, every fellow who votes for him will be asked. You know what it will be like—Smithy's caked with oof," said Bunter, temptingly.

Harry Wharton laughed. Smithy, evidently, was not too particular in his electioneering methods: he had turned Bunter, at least, into a whole-hearted supporter!

"Well, you can cackle," said Bunter, "but I can jolly well tell you that one of Smithy's big spreads ain't to be sneezed at. Look here, Quelch has fixed the Form election for six o'clock in the Rag. Wingate's coming in to count the votes, as I dare say you know. There's not a lot of time to waste. I've got down Skinner and Snoop and Stott, and Bolsover major and Fishy on my list. Shall I put your name down, Bull?"

"I'll kick you if you do."

"Beast! What about you, Nugent?"

"Nothing."

"What about you, Inky?"

"The nothingfulness is terrific."

"I suppose it's no good asking you, Wharton?"

"Hardly."

"Well, look here, Smithy will make a jolly good form-captain," urged Bunter. "First-class footballer, if that's what you're particular about. He wouldn't play a team of duds and get whopped by a bunch of townies like Wharton: you can bank on that. Look at the gang Wharton played yesterday—only one really good man in it, if you ask me——."

"Ha, ha, ha!" yelled No. 1 Study.

"Oh, don't keep on cackling whenever a fellow opens his mouth," yapped Bunter. "I say, you fellows, you're not going to vote for a freak like Toddy. Smithy's the man—I'm plumping for him, and so are lots of fellows. Look here, you come in on the winning side, see? Back me up."

Johnny Bull rose from his chair.

"You want me to back you up?" he asked.

"Yes, rather, old chap! Back me up, old fellow——."

"Done!" said Johnny.

"Good!" grinned Bunter. "That's right, old fellow—you back up a pal—why—what—leggo—wharrer you at?" yelled Bunter, as Johnny Bull grasped him by both fat shoulders, and backed him up against the wall of the study, with a bang. "Ow! wow! Gone mad? Leggo! Wharrer you up to?"

"Backing you up," answered Johnny.

"Yow-ow! You silly idiot, stoppit!" shrieked Bunter. "If you back me on that wall again, I'll—yarooooooh!"

"Ha, ha, ha!"

"Leggo! Beast! Wow!"

"Ha, ha, ha!"

Billy Bunter squirmed out of Johnny Bull's grasp, and bounded out of the doorway. Apparently he had had all the backing-up he wanted in No. 1 Study. He rolled up the passage, his fat face red and wrathy.

But the frown disappeared from his plump brow, as he met Bob Cherry coming along from No. 13. Bob was limping a little, and there was a lingering scent of Elliman's about him. That knee was still troublesome. Billy Bunter came to a halt, his ample form almost blocking the passage. Four members of the famous Co. had been deaf to the voice of the charmer: but perhaps he still had hopes of the fifth.

"Hold on a minute, old chap!" he squeaked.

Bob shook his head.

"Nothing doing," he answered.

"Eh? Wharrer you mean——?"

"Stoney!" explained Bob.

"Oh, really, Cherry! Tain't that!" yapped Bunter. "I say, Cherry, I'm electioneering for old Smithy——."

"Old Smithy!" repeated Bob, staring. "Has Smithy grown 'old' since he buzzed that dick at your silly chin?"

"Old Smithy's my candidate," said Bunter, unheeding. "I'm getting votes for him, see? Jolly good chap, old Smithy! Don't you think he will make a better form-captain than Wharton ever did?"

"No, ass."

"Well, between ourselves, old fellow, I expect you're as

fed up with Wharton's high-mightiness as any other fellow what?" said Bunter, blinking at him.

"You blithering cuckoo."

"Beast! I mean, will you let me put your name down for old Smithy——?"

"Blow Smithy!"

"Look here, old chap, you let me put your name down, and I'll see that you're asked to Smithy's spread after the election——."

"You fat, frabjous, footling, foozling, flabby codfish, if this dashed leg wasn't crocked, I'd boot you down the passage," growled Bob. "Get out of the way and go and eat coke."

Billy Bunter gave him an inimical blink. Evidently, he was not going to secure the vote of that member of the Famous Five for his candidate. Bob gave a little wriggle, as his painful knee twinged: and the fat Owl blinked down at the damaged limb, a glimmer coming into the little round eyes behind his big round spectacles.

"That knee still crocked?" he asked.

"Yes, ass."

"Is it really bad?" asked Bunter. He seemed interested.

"Of course it is, fathead! Think I should be dotting-and-carrying-one for the fun of the thing?" hooted Bob.

"Well, you needn't yell at a fellow," said Bunter. "Only asking! I say, couldn't you even run up the passage if you wanted to?"

"Of course I couldn't! I couldn't run a yard," grunted Bob.

"Oh, crumbs!" said Bunter. "I say, if you couldn't run a yard, suppose a fellow smacked you on the nose for calling him names, you couldn't even run up the passage after him, could you?"

"Eh! No! What—why—what—wow!" roared Bob, as a fat paw suddenly reached out and smacked his nose. "Why, you—you—you—I—I—I—I'll——."

"He, he, he!" cachinnated Bunter.

He jumped back, grinning, and cut up the passage at a run.

"He, he, he!" floated back as he bolted.

Bob Cherry made a stride in pursuit. But he made only one! A fearful pang in his damaged knee brought him to a halt.

"Oh!" he gasped, "Ow!"

"He, he, he!" came melodiously from the distance.

Billy Bunter, chuckling, disappeared. And Bob Cherry, with feelings that were really too deep for words, limped onward to No. 1 Study and tea.

## CHAPTER 15

# THE ELECTION

"WHARTON!"

Harry Wharton glanced round.

"Walk this way!" called out Peter Todd.

The late captain of the Remove did not reply: neither did he "walk that way". Possibly he had not forgotten that Peter was one of the fellows who had delivered the "ultimatum" in No. 1 Study a few days ago with such dire results on the football field.

The Rag was crowded when Harry Wharton and Co. came in shortly before six o'clock, the hour fixed for the Form election. Almost every man in the Remove was in the room. Three were unavoidably absent: Tom Brown in "sanny", and Mark Linley and Dick Penfold away. But almost everyone else had turned up. The Remove was a large form: and few were likely to miss the election of a new form-captain. Even Billy Bunter was there: rounded up to vote by the Bounder's not very scrupulous electioneering methods.

A little crowd surrounded the Bounder: and it was composed not only of slackers like Skinner and Co. and the fat Owl. It included fellows like Squiff, and Russell, and Ogilvy, and Tom Redwing. Smithy had a good following, and he was feeling fairly confident.

But Peter Todd, the rival candidate, also had his group, though so far much less numerous than Smithy's. Tom Dutton, Wibley, Monty Newland, and three other fellows formed it. And as the Famous Five came in, a lazy figure emerged from an armchair, and ambled over to join Toddy's party. The addition of Lord Mauleverer brought the number up to seven—and Peter was in optimistic hope of further recruits. He waved a welcoming hand at the Famous Five, and called to their leader—with no result. Five votes in a bunch were quite likely to turn the scale, if they came Peter's way. But Wharton merely glanced at him, and looked away again. His face was indifferent.

Four members of the Co. were quite willing to join Peter's crowd. If they were not particularly enthusiastic for Toddy, at all events they were opposed to his rival. Harry Wharton might have been expected to be still more strongly opposed to Smithy. But Wharton did not always react as expected.

"Toddy's our man, old chap!" hinted Bob Cherry.

Wharton raised his eyebrows.

"Is he?" he asked.

"Well, perhaps he won't be any great shakes as form-captain: but we want to keep Smithy out, don't we?"

"Do we?"

"Well, don't we?" demanded Johnny Bull, warmly. "Didn't Smithy start all the trouble—and isn't he cashing in now on the trouble he started?"

"Oh, quite!"

"Well, then——!" said Frank Nugent.

Wharton shrugged his shoulders.

"If the Remove want Smithy, they can have him!" he said. "Why not?"

"The whyfulness is terrific, my esteemed and absurd chum," murmured Hurree Jamset Ram Singh. "The estimable Toddy may be no great shakefulness, but the disreputable Smithy is the limit. Let us go over and plump for the ridiculous Toddy. A stitch in time saves ninepence, as the English proverb remarkably observes."

"Plump away," said Harry. "I'll look on."

"You're going to vote?" exclaimed Nugent.

Wharton shook his head.

"No! You fellows do as you like: leave me out."

"But——!" began Bob Cherry and Johnny Bull together.

"My dear chaps, I'm not interested," said Harry. "If you want to keep Smithy out, go and vote for Todd."

"Don't you want to keep him out?" demanded Bob.

"Why should I? The Remove are welcome to him, if they want him," answered Wharton, indifferently. "You fellows get to it, and I'll watch the show."

"But——!" said Nugent.

"Leave it at that," said Harry: and to end the argument, he walked away to the armchair Lord Mauleverer had vacated, and sat down there: evidently intending to be only a spectator of the proceedings, without taking part in them.

His friends exchanged glances, and Johnny Bull grunted. Then, leaving him to his own devices, they walked across to Peter Todd's party, and joined up there. Toddy greeted them with a cheery grin.

"You fellows backing me up?" he asked.

"We is—we are!" answered Bob.

"The backfulness is terrific, my esteemed Toddy," assured the Nabob of Bhanipur.

"What about Wharton?" asked Peter.

"Sitting it out," grunted Johnny Bull.

"Every man to his taste," said Bob. "How many have you got, Toddy?"

"Eleven, with you fellows," said Peter. "I fancy one or

two more may join up. Smithy isn't getting it all his own way, at any rate."

Bob looked round over the crowded room, and began to count heads.

"Nearly everybody's here," he said. "Let's see—twenty-three—twenty-four—do you make it twenty-four, Franky?"

"Twenty-five," answered Nugent. "No, twenty-six."

"That's it—twenty-six!" said Johnny, "and two being candidates, that leaves two dozen to vote."

"Not quite, with Wharton sitting it out," said Bob. "Twenty-three—you've got as good as half already, Toddy."

Peter made a grimace.

"Not quite," he said. "If Smithy gets a dozen, he will beat me by the odd man. Look here, if Wharton would join up, that would give me half, at any rate. Go and talk him over."

"Fat lot of good that would be," said Johnny. "Might as well argue with a mule."

Peter cast a rather anxious glance round. A dozen fellows had gathered round the Bounder; one more than Toddy's crowd.

"One or two may come over," he remarked, hopefully.

"Hallo, hallo, hallo! there goes six!" exclaimed Bob, as there was a chime from the clock-tower. "Not much time left. I say, Squiff, old man!" Bob bawled across the Rag. "You're on the wrong 'bus, old chap—come over here."

"Bow-wow!" was Sampson Quincy Iffley Field's reply to that.

"Hallo, hallo, hallo, Bunter!" roared Bob. "Roll over

here, old fat man, and I'll cash your next postal-order, if it isn't for more than tuppence."

"Yah!" was Billy Bunter's elegant retort.

"Here comes Wingate," said Nugent, as the door of the Rag opened, and the captain of Greyfriars came in.

Wingate of the Sixth was to count the votes: and keep order if necessary. A prefect's presence was sometimes necessary on such occasions.

To the Remove, this occasion was one of tremendous importance. Wingate's look did not quite indicate that he regarded it as such. Still, the great man of the Sixth was kindly prepared to see the proceedings through.

He glanced round over an excited crowd of juniors, and shut the door. The Removites were sorted out into two opposing groups now, which looked about evenly divided between Toddy and Smithy. But they were not quite evenly divided: Smithy, so far at least, had the odd man.

Harry Wharton, in the armchair at a little distance, looked on imperturbably. Peter gave him an appealing look: Smithy, a scowl. Neither produced any perceptible effect on the late captain of the form.

"The rotter!" Vernon-Smith muttered in Tom Redwing's ear. "This is pie to him."

Tom looked at him.

"What do you mean, Smithy? Wharton looks like cutting the voting——."

"Oh, don't be a goat!" snarled the Bounder. "Think he isn't going to join Todd's crowd at the last minute? That will make it a tie."

"If the votes tie, there will have to be another election later," said Tom. "Some of Toddy's men might come over——."

"Or some of mine might go over!" hissed Smithy.

"Wharton's vote will make it a tie, and goodness knows what may happen next time. He's sitting there to keep me on tenterhooks——."

"I don't think he would——."

"Oh, you're a fool."

Redwing made no reply to that. The Bounder clenched his hands, and his look at the imperturbable figure in the armchair was black and bitter. A tie in the voting meant a postponed election, with the result very much on the knees of the gods. Supporters might fall away from either side—or there might be a third candidate in the field next time: and the Bounder, who had banked on success, might find his chance gone, never to recur. So far he had been successful: Harry Wharton was down and out: but he wondered savagely whether it was a case of "thus far and no farther". His look at the junior in the armchair was one of sheer evil: and Wharton, meeting it, smiled: a smile that added to the Bounder's suppressed fury.

The buzz of many voices in the Rag died down. Wingate was speaking.

"All ready? Now let's get to business."

There was no delay in getting to business. Herbert Vernon-Smith was proposed and seconded, amid cheers from his party. Counter-cheers for Toddy, in his turn, sounded as loudly. If the Bounder had hoped that one or two of Peter's party might stray across, he had to forget it now. All the voters had made up their minds by this time. Only the fellow sitting at ease in the armchair remained an uncertain quantity. But that the late captain of the Remove intended to weigh in, at the last moment, on Toddy's side, the Bounder had not the slightest doubt.

"Hands up for Vernon-Smith!" said Wingate.

Twelve hands went up: one of them rather in need of washing. Then another was added, equally in need of a wash. There was a rap from Wingate.

"Bunter, you young ass, what are you putting up both hands for?"

"Oh!" gasped Bunter, "I—I—I——." One of the grubby paws went down again in a great hurry.

Wingate counted, and announced the result.

"Twelve!" he said. "Now hands up for Todd."

Eleven hands went up.

Harry Wharton, in the armchair, looked on without making a sign. He seemed mildly interested in what was going on, but not concerned in it.

The Bounder caught his breath.

"By gum!" he breathed. "Reddy, is that fathead really sitting it out——?"

"Looks like it!"

"By Gad! Sulkin' in his tent, like jolly old Achilles, what?" The Bounder could hardly control his excitement. The moment had come now: and still Harry Wharton did not stir. Wingate was counting.

"Eleven!" he announced.

Many eyes were turned on Harry Wharton. He did not seem aware of it. His look was calm and unconcerned.

There was a buzz in the Rag. The Bounder's eyes danced. The counting was completed, and Harry Wharton had not voted. Smithy could hardly believe in his good luck. Wingate's voice was heard over the hubbub.

"Vernon-Smith, twelve votes. Todd, eleven votes. Vernon-Smith is elected captain of the Remove!"

## CHAPTER 16

# NOTHING FOR BUNTER

BILLY BUNTER sneered.

It was quite a large and expressive sneer.

He curled a fat lip. He turned up a little fat nose, which came easy, as Nature had started it on the way. His little round eyes blinked scorn through his big round spectacles.

He was standing in No. 7 Study, regarding the tea-table. It was the aspect of that not very festive board that appeared to evoke the fat Owl's scorn.

Bunter was not usually scornful of meals: even frugal meals. No. 7 Study never flowed with milk and honey like the Bounder's or Lord Mauleverer's or Monty Newland's. Peter Todd and Tom Dutton were not wealthy: and though, according to Bunter, his palatial home at Bunter Court was inundated with wealth, none of it ever travelled as far as Greyfriars School. But howsoever little might be going, Billy Bunter was, as a rule, the fellow to annex the lion's share thereof. Now, on the day following the Remove election, he seemed in quite a different mood. He did not take his seat at the table. He did not reach out fat hands to the supplies before his study-mates had a chance at them. He regarded them with a tremendous sneer.

"That all you've got for tea, Toddy?" he asked derisively.

"That's the lot!" assented Peter. "Like more?"

"I jolly well should!" said Bunter, emphatically.

"Well, cut down to the tuck-shop, and cart it in," suggested Peter. "We'll wait tea till you get back."

"Oh, really, Toddy——."

Tom Dutton, the deaf junior, stared at Bunter.

"What are you making faces for, Bunter?" he asked. Apparently Dutton had mistaken Bunter's look of ineffable scorn for "making faces".

"Oh, you go and eat coke," was Bunter's reply to that question.

"Joke? Silly sort of joke, I think," said Dutton. "I'd give you something to make faces for, if I were Toddy—voting against a man in your own study at the election yesterday."

"I voted for the best man," said Bunter, "and I jolly well got him in, too. I'm pally with Smithy—he's a jolly good sort. Look at the spread he stood after the election! Smithy will make a tip-top skipper."

"Eh?" Dutton glanced at the table. "Where?"

"Where what?" yapped Bunter.

"Where's the kipper? We haven't got a kipper for tea, have we, Toddy?"

"Oh, crikey! I didn't say kipper," howled Bunter. "I said skipper."

"Well, if you said slipper, what do you mean? What about a slipper?"

"Oh, dry up, for goodness sake."

"There isn't a cake," Dutton pointed to the table. "Can't you see what we've got, or do you want new specs, you owl? There's no kipper, and no cake either. If you want kippers and cakes, you'd better stand them. It's about time you stood your whack in the study, if you ask me."

"Hear, hear!" grinned Peter Todd. "Get to it, Bunter."

"I've been disappointed about a postal-order,"

answered Bunter, with dignity. "I told you I was expecting a postal-order, Peter——."

"You did!" assented Peter. "Lots of times! Don't tell me again."

"Well, if that's all you've got for tea, I'm not teaing in this study," said Bunter, with another scornful blink at the table. "Bread and marger, and a few sardines and a spot of cheese—yah! I'm going to tea with Smithy."

"Shut the door after you!" said Peter: apparently not in the least downcast at the prospective loss of Bunter's company at the tea-table.

"Yah!"

Billy Bunter rolled out of No. 7, and shut the door after him, with a bang. He rolled down the passage to No. 4.

There was an anticipative grin on his fat face as he arrived at the door of the Bounder's study. He could afford to despise the short commons in his own study—now. He was pally with Smithy—at all events, the Bounder had been very pally the day before. Bunter had voted for him: indeed in his enthusiasm he had even tried to vote with both hands—he had helped Smithy to get in: and it had not yet occurred to his fat brain that, having done so, he had now out-lived his usefulness, so to speak. The fat Owl had a happy vision of spreads in Smithy's study: and Smithy had had no scruple whatever in leaving him in that happy dream—till after the election. Bunter was now due to wake up, as it were: though he was not yet aware of it.

He tapped at the door of No. 4, and pushed it open, and blinked in. Smithy and Redwing were seated at the table, which was spread for tea—in the Bounder's usual lavish style. The fat grin expanded on Bunter's plump visage. This was rather a change from the frugal board in No. 7.

The Bounder was looking very cheery. His success in the Form election had "bucked" him tremendously. He was captain of the Remove now: Harry Wharton, who had left him out of the Soccer, was a back number. Triumph was like meat and drink to Smithy. His victory had been by a narrow margin, but victory was victory, and he enjoyed it to the full. He was speaking as Bunter blinked in, and he went on, regardless of the fat face at the doorway.

"Looks good, Reddy, what? We shall take a jolly good team over to Rookwood—with yours truly captaining it, old man! Linley and Browney and Penfold will be back in the ranks by then, and Cherry's knee will have mended. We shall be right at the top of our form. Jolly good beginning, what?"

"I say, Smithy——," came a fat squeak at the door.

The Bounder glanced round.

"Shut that door," he said.

"Oh, really, Smithy——."

"Want anything?" snapped the Bounder.

Billy Bunter blinked at him in indignant surprise. There was really no need for Smithy to inquire whether he wanted anything. When the fat Owl rolled into another fellow's study at tea-time, what he wanted was easily guessed.

"I—I thought I'd give you a look in, Smithy——."

"Did you? Well, now look out again, and shut that door."

"I—I say, I'm jolly glad you pulled it off yesterday, Smithy! You're the man we want, you know."

"Thanks! Now shut that door."

"I—I jolly well voted for you, Smithy! I—I'd have given you two votes, too, if Wingate hadn't spotted me——."

"You fat ass!"

"Well, we jolly well got you in, Smithy, old chap! Wharton's nose is out of joint now, ain't it? He, he, he! I—I say, I—I haven't had my tea——."

"I guessed that one." The Bounder rose to his feet. "Wait a minute, Bunter, till I get something out of the cupboard."

"Oh, good! What is it, Smithy—a cake?"

"No—a bag of flour!"

"Wha-a-t?"

Billy Bunter was rolling in. He suddenly ceased to roll. He blinked at the Bounder, stepping across to the study cupboard: and it was an alarmed blink. Bunter had forgotten that bag of flour. Now he was reminded of it.

"I—I—I say, Smithy, what do you want that bag of flour for?" he gasped.

"Guess!" answered Smithy, over his shoulder.

"Smithy, old man——!" exclaimed Redwing.

The Bounder did not heed him. He groped in the cupboard.

"Look here, you beast—I mean, look here, old chap!" squeaked Bunter. "Didn't I jolly well vote for you in the election? If I'd jolly well voted for Toddy, you'd never have got in at all. You jolly well only scraped in on one vote, and you jolly well know it! And if you jolly well can't ask a fellow to tea, when you've jolly well got lots, I can jolly well say—keep off, you beast!"

Billy Bunter made a sudden backward jump into the passage, with the activity of a fat kangaroo, as the Bounder turned from the cupboard with a large bag of flour in his hands. He came towards the fat Owl, lifting the bag. Bunter was outside the study in a twinkling.

Bang! The study door closed quite suddenly after

Bunter. A red and wrathful Owl breathed indignation in the passage.

"Beast!" howled Bunter, through the keyhole.

Then he sadly departed, his vision of spreads in Smithy's study fading out like the mirage in the desert. Evidently Smithy, now that the election was over, and he was duly elected captain of the form, had no further use for William George Bunter. It was quite a painful discovery for the fat Owl, and it was an indignant Bunter that rolled back to No. 7. There was nothing in No. 4 for Bunter, unless it was a bag of flour on his fat head: and the frugal tea in No. 7, at which he had turned up his fat little nose, was his only resource.

Peter Todd grinned at him, as he rolled into No. 7 again.

"Not teaing with Smithy?" he asked.

Snort from Bunter.

"I'm done with Smithy," he snapped. "Smithy's a cad! Rotten outsider! I jolly well wish I'd voted for you, Toddy. After all, we're pals, ain't we, old chap? I'm going to tea here, Peter."

"Are you?" asked Peter. He seemed to doubt it.

"Yes, old chap! I——." Billy Bunter paused, as he turned his spectacles on the table.

His absence had not been long. But the frugal supplies in No. 7 had not taken two hungry juniors long to deal with. There was still half a loaf on the platter: but the margarine had disappeared, and Peter was finishing the last sardine, and Dutton the last spot of cheese.

"Oh, crikey!" said Bunter.

"Pile in, old fat man," said Peter, encouragingly.

"I—I say, Peter, is there anything in the cupboard?"

"Oh! Yes."

"I can have it, I suppose?"

"Certainly."

"What is it, Peter?"

"A bottle of Elliman's, and a tin of shoe polish. Help yourself."

"You silly ass!" yelled Bunter. The fat Owl was ready for tea—more than ready—but he did not seem disposed to help himself either to a bottle of Elliman's or a tin of shoe polish. Neither did he seem to feel like piling into what was left of the loaf.

He gave Toddy a devastating blink, and rolled out of the study again. Again a bang woke the echoes of the Remove passage, as the door closed on him: and a dismal and hungry fat Owl rolled away disconsolately to tea in hall.

## CHAPTER 17

# THE NEW BROOM

"LITTLE Side at three! Don't be late."

Herbert Vernon-Smith threw those words across his shoulder, as he passed Harry Wharton and Co. on the Remove landing, after dinner on Saturday.

He did not wait for a reply.

He walked on into the Remove passage, leaving the Famous Five staring after him, and then looking at one another.

Bob Cherry frowned. Nugent breathed rather hard. Johnny Bull grunted. The Nabob of Bhanipur shrugged his slim shoulders. Harry Wharton smiled faintly. Such were the various effects of the brusque command from the new captain of the Remove.

"Cheeky ass!" said Bob.

"The cheekfulness is terrific," remarked Hurree Jamset Ram Singh. "Put a beggar on horseback, and he will go longest to the well, as the English proverb remarks."

"Does the silly ass think we want to slack about like Bunter or Skinner?" growled Johnny Bull.

"Hardly," said Nugent. "What he wants is to throw his weight about. I've a jolly good mind to walk out and leave him to stew in his own juice."

"Compulsory day," said Bob.

"I know: but all the same——."

"Nothing doing," said Harry Wharton. "Every man has to turn up on compulsory days, or be reported to the Head of the Games for slacking. We don't want to go up to Wingate for that."

"After all, Smithy's got to round the men up," said Bob. "Might be a bit more civil about it. But he likes giving orders."

"He was not nicknamed the Bounder for nothing," said Harry, contemptuously, and the Famous Five, not feeling in the least pleased with their new captain, went down the stairs, and headed for the changing-room.

Smithy, evidently, was enjoying his new importance. His view seemed to be that he spoke as one having authority, saying "Do this!" and he doeth it! No doubt he found a relish in giving orders to the late captain of the form, who had left him out of the Soccer. Games-practice was compulsory on certain days, and there were fellows in the Remove who dodged when they could: but the Famous Five were too keen on the strenuous life to require "rounding up". But it pleased the new captain to address those strenuous youths as Wharton in his time might have spoken to slackers like Skinner and Bunter.

Well aware that he had left irritation behind him, and rather amused by it, the Bounder walked up the Remove passage, and looked into No. 14. Fisher T. Fish was sitting at the table there, with a pen in his hand, a wrinkle in his brow, and a paper covered with figures before him. Apparently the business-man of the Remove was doing his accounts. He glanced up irritably as the door opened.

"Games-practice at three," said Smithy.

"Say, whatyer know?" snapped Fisher T. Fish. "I guess I'm busy. Look here, big boy, I voted for you on Thursday——."

"Six, if you don't turn up on time," interrupted the Bounder, and he turned away without waiting for an answer, leaving Fisher Tarleton Fish breathing very hard through his long Transatlantic nose. Evidently, the circumstance that he had helped to elect the new captain was not getting Fishy off!

Smithy's next visit was to No. 12. In that study, Lord Mauleverer was stretched elegantly on a cushioned sofa, gazing meditatively through the window at a blue sky.

"Turn up at three, Mauleverer."

His lordship glanced round.

"Is it a compulsory day?" he inquired.

"Don't you know it is, fathead?"

"How should I know?" asked Mauly, innocently. "Can't remember little things like that!"

"Don't be late, anyhow."

"I'm feelin' a bit tired, old bean—Oh, gad, where did that outsider pick up his manners?" murmured Lord Mauleverer, as the bang of the study door interrupted him. Smithy was gone, and his lazy lordship slowly and reluctantly gathered up his elegant limbs from the cushions.

No. 11 was Smithy's next port of call. Skinner, Snoop, and Stott were in that study, and they gave the Bounder a welcoming grin as he appeared in the doorway.

"Trot in, old top," said Skinner, amicably. "I say, we were just talking about a little run this afternoon—care to come?"

"Can't be done—games-practice at three."

Skinner laughed.

"Well, I suppose you could hardly cut it, now you're captain of the form," he agreed. "Not all beer and skittles to be form-captain, Smithy! I suppose Wingate or the games-master would sit up and take notice, if you cut."

"Hard cheese, Smithy," said Snoop.

"Tough!" agreed Stott.

Vernon-Smith looked at them, with a curl of the lip.

Skinner and Co. had undoubtedly had an impression that things were going to be easier for them under a form-captain like the scapegrace of Greyfriars. Under that impression they had plumped for Smithy in the election. Now they were, perhaps naturally, expecting a "quid pro quo": their votes had got Smithy in as captain, and it was up to Smithy to go easy in return. That was how Skinner and Co. looked at it. They were about to discover that the Bounder's view was very different. No master is quite so masterful as a rebel who finds power in his hands. The new broom was going to sweep clean.

"I've looked in to tell you——!" began Smithy.

"Oh, that's all right," said Skinner. "Wish you could come, but I suppose it wouldn't do. We're going——."

"You're going to the changing-room, and you're turning up on Little Side at three sharp."

"Eh?"

"What?"

"That's all!" The Bounder turned to go.

Snoop and Stott stared at him, Skinner rose to his feet, with a very unpleasant glitter in his eyes.

"Hold on a minute, Smithy," he said.

"Well?" Smithy turned his head.

"I suppose you're joking——."

"Nothing of the kind. Where's the joke?"

"Look here, Smithy, come off it," snapped Skinner. "You can jolly well let us off if you like, now you're skipper. We've banked on it."

"That's your look-out."

"Think we should have taken the trouble to vote you in as skipper, if you'd told us you were going to carry on like Wharton?" demanded Skinner. "You let us believe——."

"You as good as said——!" began Snoop.

The Bounder interrupted him.

"Little Side at three," he snapped. "Every man who doesn't turn up will be reported to the Head of the Games for slacking. Is that plain enough for you?"

"Look here——!" yelled Skinner, furiously.

The Bounder did not "look there". The new captain of the Remove had no more time to waste on Skinner and Co. He slammed the door and departed, leaving Snoop and Stott scowling, and Skinner almost green with rage.

The Bounder had one more call to make. That was to No. 7 Study, where he found the fattest member of the form sitting, or rather sprawling, in an armchair, with his fat little legs resting on another chair, happily travelling through a jam tart.

Billy Bunter ceased to masticate jam and pastry, and blinked round in alarm as the door opened.

"I say, Russell, I never—Oh! Is that you, Smithy?" The fat Owl was relieved. "I—I thought it was Russell —I—I haven't been in his study, you know, but he might think this jam-tart was his, if——."

"Get a move on."

"Eh?"

"Games-practice at three. It's close on now."

"I—I say, Smithy, old chap, you can let a chap off, you know, now you're form-captain. I jolly well voted for you, you know. You ain't the fellow to go round bothering chaps like Wharton, are you, old fellow?"

"Yes!"

"Oh, really, Smithy——."

"Get moving!"

"Look here, I—I ain't fit to-day," howled Bunter, "I've got a pain——."

"You'll have another if you don't shift."

"An awful pain in my leg!" gasped Bunter. "I think it's pneumonia, Smithy! I—I'm going to ask Quelch to let me see the doctor about it—I—I am really! I—I say, Smithy, you'll let a chap off, won't you, when he's got a fearful pain in his arm—I mean his leg—we're pals, ain't we, old chap——?"

"Not at all."

"Look here, you beast—yaroooh! Leggo my ear, will you?" yelled Bunter. "If you don't leggo my ear, I'll—wow! wow! wow! Leggo! I'm going, ain't I?"

And Bunter went.

There was quite a full attendance at games-practice that afternoon. Willing or unwilling, the Removites turned up as one man: some of them, who had voted Smithy in, with very deep feelings, now that they found how clean the new broom was going to sweep!

## CHAPTER 18

# CORNERED!

"BETTER leave him alone," said Snoop, sagely.

"Much better," said Stott.

Skinner scowled blackly.

On Wednesday afternoon, a half-holiday, most Greyfriars fellows were finding life rather enjoyable. Skinner was an exception.

That afternoon, Skinner and Co. would gladly have gone on the little excursion out of bounds, which had had to be cut out on Saturday, owing to the unexpected and disconcerting clean-sweeping of the new broom. But there was, so to speak, a lion in the path: or to be more exact, two.

In the first place, Skinner, who slacked in form as in games, had been awarded an hour in Extra School: and was booked to turn up in Monsieur Charpentier's class-room at three o'clock. In the second place, an hour of games-practice had been fixed for four o'clock, which Skinner had no hope of escaping, under the heavy hand of the new captain of the Remove. So Skinner's afternoon, divided between French, which he loathed, and football, which he detested, was likely to be a dismal one. His feelings were bitter—the bitterness about equally divided between his form-master, who had given him Extra School, and his form-captain, who had no mercy on slackers.

Very gladly Skinner would have "hit back" at either. Mr. Quelch was far too formidable a personage to hit back at. But Smithy, after all, was only a Remove fellow, and within reach of retaliation. That was Skinner's idea: which, however, evoked no enthusiasm whatever in his study.

"What are you afraid of?" he snapped. "Smithy can't eat us, I suppose, even if he found out——."

"Might catch us at it," said Snoop, shaking his head.

"No danger of that! I've had my eye on him—he's in the quad with Redwing——."

"Quelch might come up," said Stott. "I've heard that he came up suddenly the other day and caught Smithy smoking, and gave him six."

"I know where Quelch is! He's taking his trot in the quad—if you look out of the window you can see him on the path down there."

"Um!" said Snoop.

"Um!" said Stott.

"Look here, don't be funks," snapped Skinner. "It's as safe as houses—not a fellow about the studies. Smithy took us in—you know he did! Didn't he as good as say that things would be easier than they were with Wharton? And how have they turned out ? He's set up to be a high-and-mighty panjandrum more than Wharton ever did. He wouldn't have pulled our leg to get our votes, either. Didn't Smithy?"

"Well, yes, but——."

"I tell you it's as safe as houses. We're going to ship his study—and how's he to know that it was us? There's a good many other fellows with their backs up, since Smithy started throwing his weight about. It won't take the three of us five minutes—then I go down to Extra, and you fellows get off somewhere——."

"I'm getting off somewhere now, thanks," said Stott: and without waiting for a reply, he walked out of the study.

Skinner scowled after him as he went. Then he looked at Sidney James Snoop.

"You're coming, Snoopey?"

Snoop shook his head.

"I'm not having any rows with Smithy," he answered. "If you're keen on it, get on with it, and I wish you luck. But leave me out."

"Oh, go and eat coke!" snapped Skinner, and he swung out of the study, leaving Snoop shrugging his shoulders.

Stott, at the end of the passage, was just disappearing across the landing. He disappeared: and Skinner, like Moses of old, looked this way and that way, to make sure that no one else was in the offing. He went quietly down the passage, and stopped at the door of No. 4.

There he hesitated a little. Skinner was not a fellow to take risks, if he could help it: and no more than Snoop did he want a "row" with the hard-hitting Bounder. But it seemed, as he had said, as safe as houses. Vernon-Smith and Tom Redwing were out in the quad: Quelch was taking his walk on the path under the study windows: there was nobody about the studies on a half-holiday. Skinner would have preferred his comrades with him: but it seemed safe enough to "go it" alone: and he made up his mind.

He turned the door-handle, pushed open the door, and stepped quickly into the study. The next moment he was startled by a sudden squeak:

"Oh, crikey!"

"Oh!" gasped Skinner, taken quite aback. He stared across the room, at a fat figure looking round from the study cupboard, which was wide open. A pair of startled eyes blinked at him through a big pair of spectacles.

"Bunter! You fat fool!" panted Skinner, his eyes

fairly glittering at the Owl of the Remove. He had been so very, very careful to make sure that he was not seen entering Smithy's study. It had not occurred to him that that study might be already tenanted. But, as it happened, Skinner was not the only fellow who was taking advantage of the fact that there was "nobody about the studies". Billy Bunter had preceded him on the scene.

"Oh! Is that you, Skinner?" gasped the fat Owl. "I say, Smithy ain't here, if you want him—I saw him out in the quad before I came up——."

Skinner breathed hard. He did not want to be seen in Smithy's study—very much indeed he did not. And there was the fat Owl, blinking at him through his spectacles! Skinner was strongly inclined to rush at the fat junior and boot him all round the study. But second thoughts, proverbially the best, prevailed: and with an effort he cleared the enraged scowl from his face. Bunter took it for granted that he had looked in to speak to Smithy: and it was judicious to leave Bunter with that impression.

"Oh!" Skinner tried to speak casually. "I looked in to ask Smithy to let me off games this afternoon, as I've got a spot of Extra——."

"He, he, he! Bet you he won't!" grinned Bunter. "He jolly well won't let me off, though I've asked him three times. Rotten cad, you know—chucking his weight about now he's skipper. I jolly well wish we had Wharton back! He's a beast, but not such a beast as Smithy." Bunter gave Skinner a fat wink. "I say, old chap, you ain't pally with Smithy now—now he's turned out such a beast. I say, have a go at this cake! There's lots."

There was a wedge of cake in Bunter's fat hand. Crumbs spotted his fat waistcoat, and littered the floor round him. He had been very busy when Skinner's sudden entrance interrupted him.

"You fat frump!" said Skinner. "Sure Smithy's in the quad?"

"I jolly well made sure he was, before I came up. I say, this is a jolly good cake, Skinner, and I tell you there's lots——."

"I'll mention to Smithy that you're scoffing it," said Skinner, and he turned and walked out of the study, and shut the door after him.

He did not head for the stairs, however. The door of the next study was open, and no one was there. Skinner slipped into No. 5, half-closed the door, and remained on the watch. After what he had said, he did not expect Bunter to linger long in No. 4.

He was right: hardly a minute later, the door of Smithy's study opened, and Billy Bunter emerged. He had a large wedge of cake in either fat hand now, and he was in haste. The possibility of being caught by the Bounder in that study, "scoffing" the cake, was alarming: the fat Owl had lingered only long enough to take another cut at the cake. Skinner, from behind the door of No. 5, watched him emerge, roll hurriedly down the passage, and disappear across the landing.

All was clear once more!

Skinner, in his turn, emerged, and cut back to No. 4. In a few seconds he was in the Bounder's study again, with the door shut.

He stepped across to the window, which was open, and keeping carefully out of sight, glanced down into the quad.

There were plenty of fellows to be seen there. Among them he could see Vernon-Smith and Tom Redwing, at a little distance, occupied in what looked like a very earnest talk—Smithy's brows were knitted, and Redwing's face seemed clouded and anxious. What they were discussing Skinner neither knew nor cared: he was satisfied to see them still safe off the scene. He had a glimpse of a mortar-board on the path below: and was aware that Mr. Quelch was pacing there. But he was not, just then, interested in Quelch. Satisfied that the Bounder and his study-mate were still at a safe distance, he stepped back from the window.

Then he set to work. He was there to "ship" the study: and his first proceeding was to pick up the inkpot, and pour its contents over the books and papers on the table. His next was to open a bottle of gum, and stream the sticky fluid over Smithy's expensive leather armchair. He grinned sourly as he worked. He had been more or less "pally" with Smithy: and the Bounder, when he came back to his study, would have reason to regret that he was no longer pally! Grinning, he stepped to the grate, and picked up the poker, with the intention of raking down soot from the chimney, to scatter about the study.

But he stopped, suddenly.

In the Remove passage, hitherto deserted and silent, there was a sudden sound of running feet.

Someone was coming up the passage from the stairs, evidently in a hurry.

If it happened to be Smithy——!

Skinner turned quite cold, at the bare idea of being caught in the study, after what he had done. If it was Smithy, he was fairly caught!

The next moment he knew that it was Smithy: for he heard a calling voice: the voice of Tom Redwing.

"Smithy! Stop!"

There was no answer to that call: the running feet came

on. Skinner's face was almost white with terror. He had planned this carefully, and planned it well: he had felt himself perfectly safe: and now—in a few moments Vernon-Smith would be in the study, and he was cornered. And when Smithy saw what he had done——! The wretched fellow fairly cringed with fear. He seemed already to feel the angry Bounder's hard knuckles crashing on him.

"Oh!" panted Skinner. He stared round him like a hunted animal. Hardly stopping to think, he backed into the corner of the room behind the armchair, and crouched. To avoid immediate discovery: to keep out of sight, and hope for a chance of dodging away: that was all that was left.

He was barely in time. Hardly had he crouched into cover, when the door was flung open, and Herbert Vernon-Smith ran into the study.

## CHAPTER 19

## STOP IT, SMITHY!

"SMITHY!"

Redwing's voice called again from the passage.

The Bounder did not heed.

He came into the study breathlessly. Skinner had feared that, the moment he entered, he would see what had been done. But Vernon-Smith did not even glance at the table or the armchair. He cut across to the study cupboard, and groped in it. He did not seem even to notice the denuded condition of the cake on which Billy Bunter had been busy a short while ago, though it was almost under his eyes. The Bounder was in a state of hurry and excitement: why, was a mystery to the scared fellow crouching behind the armchair in the corner. Skinner could not see him: but he could hear: and he could only wonder what had brought Smithy to the study in such a hurry, and why he was groping in haste at the back of the cupboard.

Vernon-Smith found what he was seeking: and turned from the cupboard with a large bag of flour in his hands. He was turning towards the open window, when Redwing came breathlessly in.

"Smithy! Stop!"

"Don't be a fool——!"

"I tell you, stop——!"

"Don't meddle, you fathead. You've jawed me enough in the quad, and I don't want any more!" snapped the Bounder, savagely. "Mind your own business."

"Put that bag of flour back in the cupboard——."

"Oh, shut up!"

Unheeding his anxious chum, the Bounder stepped towards the window. But Redwing was not to be unheeded. He caught Vernon-Smith by the arm, and dragged him back by main force.

There was almost a yell of rage from the Bounder.

"Let go my arm!"

"Smithy, you mad ass, stop it!" panted Redwing. "If you chuck that down on Quelch——."

"No 'if' about it: I'm going to."

"It's a rotten trick, Smithy——."

"Oh, pack that up!"

"If you don't care for that, Smithy, have a little sense! There will be a fearful row——."

"I know that!" jeered the Bounder. "Quelch will be hopping mad! That's what I want. Remember that six he gave me?"

"You asked for it, and deserved it too!" exclaimed Redwing. "But never mind that. Have a little sense! You'll be found out——."

"Think Quelch will know where the flour came from, you fool? Think I shall let anybody see me chuck it? Don't be a goat—and let go my arm, I tell you. I've been waiting for a chance like that—ever since that fat fool Bunter brought that bag of flour here to fix up a booby-trap. Now Quelch is fairly asking for it—trotting up and down the path right under the window——."

"They'll trace it to you——."

"How come?" sneered the Bounder. "That bag's been parked here, out of sight, more than a week. And it wasn't I that snooped it from below stairs. I shall clear off the minute I've dropped it—far away, innocent as a babe, knowing nothing of what's happened. There isn't a spot of risk, and you know it."

"I know it's a rotten disrespectful trick——."

"Oh, ring off."

"Have a little sense!" breathed Redwing. "You've just been elected captain of the Remove—is that your idea of how a form-captain ought to carry on?"

"Rot!"

"You're in Wharton's place now, and it's a responsible place. You can't carry on like some mad fag——."

"I can do as I jolly well choose."

"Do you want to start your captaincy with a fearful row with Quelch, and perhaps going up to the Head——?"

"Quelch won't know a thing—unless you tell him!" sneered the Bounder. "Now let go my arm, before I punch your head, Tom Redwing. Quelch won't be trotting up and down that path for ever, and I'm going to get him while I have the chance——."

"You're not!" said Redwing, angrily.

"Will you let go my arm?" hissed Smithy.

"No, I won't. If you haven't sense enough to stop, I'll stop you," said Tom Redwing. "You're not going near the window with that bag of flour."

"By gad! I—I'll——." The Bounder wrenched savagely at his arm. Skinner, behind the armchair, heard a scuffle—then a fierce exclamation from the Bounder.

"You fool! Let go! You've split the bag—you'll burst it all over the place——."

"I don't care! Put that bag of flour back in the cupboard, Smithy! I tell you you're not going to drop it from the window. I won't stand for it."

"Mind your own business."

"Will you put it back?"

"No!" yelled the Bounder.

"If you don't, I'll punch it, and burst it. You can have it scattered over the carpet, if you like—you're not going to chuck it from the window."

The Bounder breathed fury. No one could have guessed that Tom Redwing was his best chum, from the look he gave him.

But he ceased to wrench and struggle. The paper bag already had a split in it, and flour was trickling out of the opening. It needed only one punch from Redwing to burst it, and scatter the contents in the study. And Redwing evidently meant every word he said. Whatever became of that flour, it was not going down from the study window to land on Henry Samuel Quelch.

"Oh, you rotter!" breathed Smithy. "I tell you this is my chance—it may never come again——."

"All the better——."

"I could get him now, easy and safe——."

"You can't and shan't."

"You meddlin' fool——."

"You can call me all the names you like, Smithy. But you're not going to play that rotten mad trick on Quelch. Are you going to shove that bag back in the cupboard, or do you want me to burst it?"

Vernon-Smith gritted his teeth in helpless rage. It was, as he had said, his chance, which might never recur. It had been in his mind ever since that "six" from Quelch's cane in the study. The Bounder had an unforgiving nature: and a long memory for grievances, real or fancied. The circumstance that he was now captain of his form, of whom some sense of responsibility was expected, made no iota of difference to him: he was still the Bounder of Greyfriars, wild and wayward, reckless and mutinous. But he was powerless to carry on now, if Redwing was determined to stop him. And Redwing's determination was fixed. His grip on the Bounder's arm was like iron, and did not relax for a moment.

Slowly, savagely, but inevitably, the Bounder gave in. He stood panting, the flour from the split in the bag trickling over his clothes.

Then in silence, but with a black brow, he moved back to the study cupboard, and slammed the bag of flour into it.

"Now leave me alone," he muttered.

"Coming out?"

"No!"

"I shall stay here if you do."

The Bounder looked at him, with smouldering eyes. Redwing did not intend to leave him—and leave him a chance of carrying on. In savage silence, he crossed to the door, and left the study.

Tom Redwing followed him into the passage. Skinner heard his voice, almost in pleading tones:

"Look here, Smithy, old man——."

There was no reply, and the footsteps died away down the passage.

They were gone: and Skinner, at last, was able to crawl out of his cramped hiding-place. Neither of them had dreamed for a moment that anyone was in the study—neither had noticed, in their excitement, the inky and gummy state of the table and the armchair. Skinner, immensely relieved, emerged from his corner, breathing hard, with spots of perspiration on his forehead. He was safe now—safe and unsuspected—free either to clear off, or to carry on with "shipping" the study.

But he was not thinking of either. There were quite other thoughts in Skinner's mind now.

## CHAPTER 20

# TWO BIRDS WITH ONE STONE

SKINNER stood in the Bounder's study, breathing hard—and thinking hard. Spots of flour, on the study carpet, glimmered in the sunshine from the window. Skinner stood listening.

No sound reached his ears. Smithy and Redwing were gone—the former in a towering rage, Redwing troubled and distressed by the quarrel with his chum. Skinner knew now why the Bounder had cut up to No. 4 so hurriedly: and he knew, too, that but for Redwing's intervention, Mr. Quelch, pacing in a stately manner on the path below, would have stopped a falling bag of flour with his majestic head. Skinner, certainly, would not have been sorry had it happened, and had Smithy been sent up to the Head for it: his feelings towards both were bitter. But it had not happened—yet! There was a cat-like gleam in Skinner's eyes, as he stood there, thinking hard.

For a long minute he stood: then he stepped towards the open window, and, taking even more care than before to keep out of sight, peered down.

He glimpsed a mortar-board below: Quelch was still pacing there, blissfully unconscious of the narrow escape he had had. Possibly he was thinking out a new chapter in his celebrated "History of Greyfriars", a work which had been the companion of his leisure for many years, and to which he was able to give attention when he was done with his form. A half-holiday for the Remove was a half-holiday for the Remove master also. Anyhow, there was

Quelch, pacing on the path under the study windows high above his head—pacing to the corner of the building, and then turning back to pace again. Of whatever Henry Samuel Quelch was thinking, as he paced, assuredly he was not thinking that a member of his form might drop a bag of flour from a study window to land on his mortar-board!

Skinner's eyes gleamed down at that mortar-board.

Quelch had given him "Extra" for that afternoon: in a few minutes he was due in the French master's class-room. Smithy had taken him in over the election, and let him down afterwards with contemptuous indifference. After Extra, Smithy was going to put him through it on Little Side. Both of them were the objects of Harold Skinner's malicious resentment: and if that bag of flour descended, after all, on Quelch's "nut", who was likely to be suspected? Not Skinner!

He breathed a long, deep breath.

The thing was safe—it could not have been safer or easier. But Skinner's nerve was not equal to his malice. It was a case of "willing to wound, and yet afraid to strike". He hesitated.

And then, as if to favour the design, Mr. Quelch stopped in his walk, fairly under the window of No. 4 Study far above his head. Wingate of the Sixth was coming across to speak to him: and Quelch stopped as the Greyfriars captain came up. Skinner backed from the window.

His mind was made up now.

He stepped across to the study cupboard, and reached into it for the bag of flour. He picked it up, handling it very carefully: with the split in the paper bag, it needed careful handling. Flour trickled out, and, careful as he was, it powdered his sleeves with white. As he lifted it across to the window, he left a floury trail on the carpet.

Then, once more, he hesitated.

The Bounder had the nerve for such things: Smithy would have taken accurate aim, and watched the bag fall upon its target, with perfect coolness. But Skinner lacked the Bounder's nerve. He was half-scared at what he was going to do: half-inclined to fling the bag across the study, scattering the flour over the room, and leave it at that.

But he braced himself. It was safe, absolutely safe, and it was killing two birds with one stone: Quelch would get the flour, and if anyone was suspected, it would be Smithy, certainly not Skinner. He hesitated: but once more he made up his mind.

He dared not take the slightest risk of being seen at the window. But he knew exactly where Quelch was standing. He could hear, faintly, the murmur of the Remove master's voice from below, speaking to Wingate. He set his lips, and tossed the bag from the window.

He did not stay to hear it fall. The instant it had left his hands, he turned and bolted across the study, and ran up the passage.

In a matter of seconds he was back at his own study. He had need for haste: for he had to get rid of the traces of flour on his clothes without delay, and to do it unseen by other eyes. After what had happened, any fellow observed with a spot of flour on his clothes was as good as "booked". He ran breathlessly into No. 11, and shut the door after him hurriedly.

A startled exclamation greeted him. Snoop stared at him blankly.

"Skinner! What the dickens——."

"Don't shout, you ass."

"But what——."

"Quiet! Get a clothes-brush—quick."

"You're smothered with flour," said Snoop, staring. "You've got it all over you. Some fellow been chucking flour at you, or what?"

"Shut up and find me a clothes-brush."

"All right—but what——?"

"Quick, you ass! If I'm seen like this I'm for it! Where's that dashed clothes-brush? Oh, here it is." Skinner grabbed a clothes-brush from the table drawer. "Brush me down, Snoopey—don't stand there gaping, fat-head! I'm due for Extra, and I've got to get every speck of this off first——."

"Oh, all right!"

Snoop took the clothes-brush, and proceeded to brush off the specks of flour. Skinner watched that proceeding, anxiously. Not the tiniest fleck was to remain on him, to tell its own tale.

But anxious as he was, he was grinning. He had "got away" with this and he was safe: there was not a clue, except the flecks of flour that were disappearing under Snoop's vigorous brushing.

"There you are," said Snoop, at last, "but you might tell a fellow——."

Skinner chuckled.

"You'll hear soon enough! If you see Quelch looking like a miller who's upset his own stock over his napper——."

Snoop jumped.

"Quelch!" he stuttered.

"Quiet! Sure it's all off?"

"Clean as a whistle! But—but—but you haven't——," gasped Snoop.

"Keep it dark! Not a word even to Stott! Can't keep a thing like this too dark," said Skinner. "Sure there's none left on me?" Skinner scanned his clothes, twisting rather like a cat chasing its tail, to make sure that every spot was gone, and gave a final rub or two with the brush. "By gum! There goes three!"

There was a chime from the clock-tower. Skinner threw down the clothes-brush, and grinned at Snoop's startled face.

"Mind, not a word—not a syllable——."

"Of course!" gasped Snoop. "But—but—if you got Quelch!—oh, crikey! There'll be a fearful row."

"That won't hurt me," said Skinner, coolly. "Mind, if anybody asks you, I never left the study till I went down to Extra—I was with you here all the time. Not that you're likely to be asked: if they get on a trail, it won't lead to this study. You can take that from me! Now I've got to cut! Mind, not a syllable about this, even to Stott! Mum's the word!"

"O.K. But——."

Skinner gave a last glance down at his clothes, opened the door, and left the study. Snoop was left staring.

Skinner lost no time on his way. The last stroke of three was booming out as he joined the other luckless individuals booked for Extra at the door of the French master's class-room, and went in with them. And during that Extra class, Harold Skinner grinned a good many times, and chuckled once or twice: really as if he found something quite entertaining in French irregular verbs!

## CHAPTER 21

# BY WHOSE HAND?

"HALLO, hallo, hallo!" ejaculated Bob Cherry.

"Oh, my hat!"

"Look!"

"Great Pip!"

Harry Wharton and Co. were not the only fellows in the quadrangle who exclaimed and stared. Fifty other fellows, at least, did the same.

It was a startling and amazing occurrence that had occurred. It was enough, more than enough, to make any Greyfriars fellow jump.

The Famous Five were sauntering in the quad, discussing the Rookwood match, due the following week. That match was to be played under the captaincy of Herbert Vernon-Smith: a very considerable change, especially for Harry Wharton. The topic was one of great interest to the chums of the Remove. But they forgot the Rookwood match, and Smithy, and Soccer, when that sudden, startling, amazing occurrence occurred!

They had noticed, as they strolled, that their stately form-master, Mr. Quelch, was pacing up and down the path under the study windows. Likewise they had noticed that he had stopped to speak to Wingate of the Sixth. But they were quite uninterested—till it happened!

Something suddenly whizzed downwards through the air, apparently from one of the junior study windows high above. It missed Mr. Quelch's mortar-board by an inch, and dropped between him and Wingate.

It struck the ground with a thud, and burst! Something white and powdery flew in clouds as it burst there. Mr. Quelch's gown, and Wingate's trousers, were instantly powdered white.

Mr. Quelch gave a startled jump. Probably it was the first time in history that the serious and sedate master of the Remove had been seen to jump, in the quad, like a kangaroo. Wingate fairly bounded. Both of them were utterly startled. Either might have received that unlooked-for missile right on the "nut". Luckily it had fallen between them. But it was very startling indeed.

Had that bag of flour come from the Bounder's hand, assuredly it would not have missed its target. But Skinner had been too hurried and nervous for accurate aim. Still, he had missed only by an inch: and Quelch, undoubtedly, had a shock as it shot past his majestic nose and crashed on the ground. Clouds of scattering flour flew on the wind.

"What——!" stuttered Mr. Quelch.

"Oh, gad!" gasped Wingate. "What——."

Equally amazed, they stared at the burst paper bag and the scattering flour. A crowd of fellows stared from all sides.

"It—it—it is—is—is flour!" articulated Mr. Quelch.

"Flour!" repeated Wingate, blankly.

"A b-b-bag of fuf-fuf-flour!" Quelch seemed afflicted with a stammer. "A bib-bub-bag of fuf-fif-flour!"

"But how—what——?" exclaimed Wingate.

He stared down at his floury trousers, and then stared up. That bag of flour had not, and could not have arrived horizontally. Obviously it must have come from above. It must have come from a study window. But if that bag had been thrown from a window, there was no sign to be seen of the thrower. All the windows above were blank.

IT STRUCK THE GROUND WITH A THUD, AND BURST!

"Bless my soul!" Quelch quickly regained his accustomed calm, and recovered from his stammer. "Some boy—some utterly foolish and thoughtless boy—has thrown that bag from a window——."

"That's it, sir! But——."

"It might have fallen upon either of us——."

"It very nearly did, sir——."

"Such carelessness—such thoughtlessness——." Quelch broke off, suddenly, and his gimlet-eyes glinted. It dawned upon him that a bag of flour could hardly have fallen from a window from mere carelessness. A fellow at a window might perhaps drop a book carelessly. But hardly a bag of flour! What could any fellow be doing at a study window with a bag of flour? The look that came over Quelch's face, as he realised this, was positively terrifying. That bag of flour must have been intended for a head—either his or Wingate's. It was a prank: a most reckless and outrageous prank.

"Upon my word!" breathed Mr. Quelch. He stared at the burst bag, and then up at innumerable blank windows. "That was no accident, Wingate——."

"Hardly, sir."

"It was thrown—intentionally——."

"Must have been, sir——."

Neither the Remove master nor the captain of Greyfriars could doubt that. Neither could any of the spectators: the only doubt in any mind was whether the missile had been intended for Wingate or for Mr. Quelch.

"By gum!" murmured Bob Cherry. "Somebody's up for a row over this! Does Henry look fierce?"

"The fiercefulness is terrific," murmured Hurree Jamset Ram Singh.

"What mad ass——?" muttered Nugent.

Bob gave a sudden start, as a recollection flashed into his mind.

"Oh, suffering cats! That blithering ass Bunter——."

"Bunter?" repeated Harry Wharton.

"He was larking with a bag of flour the other day—I remember—could that howling ass——?"

"Bunter wouldn't have the nerve," said Johnny Bull.

"I know he had a bag of flour—and it's not the sort of thing a fellow would be likely to have handy. Know where the fat ass is?"

"Frowsting over the fire in the Rag, most likely," grunted Johnny.

"Well, let's go and see."

"Oh, all right."

More and more excited spectators were arriving on the scene. Prout, Capper, Hacker, and other masters arrived: Loder and Walker and other prefects of the Sixth: Coker and Co. of the Fifth: a crowd of the Shell, the Fourth, the Remove, and fags of the Third and Second. It was a spot of quite unwonted excitement in the old quad at Greyfriars. There was a hubbub of voices: and in the midst of the crowd, Quelch, with a grim set face, was dusting flour from his gown. Wingate was scanning study windows: particularly interested in that of No. 4 in the Remove, which was open, and almost directly overhead.

Leaving that scene of excitement behind them, the Famous Five cut into the House, to look for Bunter. If the fat and fatuous Owl of the Remove had done this, they could not help feeling concerned about him.

"I say, you fellows."

A fat squeak greeted them as they came hurriedly into the Rag.

That apartment had only one tenant, who blinked at

the chums of the Remove through a pair of big spectacles as they came in. Bunter, as Johnny Bull had predicted, was frowsting over the fire in the Rag, his plump limbs sprawling in the roomiest of the armchairs there.

"Hallo, hallo, hallo! So you're here!" exclaimed Bob Cherry.

"Eh?" Billy Bunter blinked at him. "Yes! I say, you fellows, that beast Smithy has fixed an extra practice for four. Look here, it ain't a compulsory day, and I ain't jolly well going to turn up! You fellows back me up, and we'll tell Smithy where he gets off, what?"

Bunter, apparently, was thinking about matters quite other than bags of flour!

The Famous Five scanned him. If Bunter had been handling flour, he was likely to have traces about him. But there were no such traces to be seen.

"How long have you been in here, Bunter?" asked Harry.

"Eh? Ever since dinner," answered Bunter, promptly.

"You haven't been up to the studies?"

"No fear! I never went into Smithy's study, if that's what you mean. I never knew he had a cake! How should I?"

"You fat ass!" roared Bob Cherry. "How long is it since you were up in Smithy's study?"

"Eh! About half-an-hour, I think. I mean, I never was in Smithy's study—I've been sitting here ever since I came down—I mean ever since dinner——."

"Did you chuck a bag of flour from the study window?"

Bunter sat bolt upright.

"Eh? What? No! Wharrer you mean?"

"You had a bag of flour last week," said Bob. "You

were going to fix up a booby-trap in Smithy's study, but it never came off. What did you do with it?"

"I never did anything with it! That beast Smithy took it away from me, and he was going to bash it over my napper only Redwing stopped him——."

"Smithy!" exclaimed Harry Wharton.

"Did he keep it?" asked Bob.

"Yes, he jolly well did! I jolly well saw it in his study cupboard when I was sampling the cake—I—I—I mean, I never sampled the cake, and if Smithy kicks up a fuss, I don't know anything about it——."

"Fathead!"

"Beast!"

The Famous Five left the Rag: satisfied that Bunter was not the flour-hurler, and with little doubt of the culprit's identity. An anxious fat squeak followed them as they went:

"I say, you fellows, about that extra practice this afternoon——."

But the fat squeak passed unheeded.

"Smithy!" said Bob, in a low voice, as the juniors went out into the quad again. "If he kept that bag of flour in his study, he must have meant to do something with it—and we can guess what, now."

"Looks like it," said Harry.

"The lookfulness is terrific."

Johnny Bull and Frank Nugent nodded. Not one of the Famous Five had any doubt about it. And it soon transpired that the same idea was in other minds: for shortly afterwards, Herbert Vernon-Smith was being inquired for by the prefects up and down the school. Skinner, sitting in Extra, grinning over French verbs, was feeling quite safe: and had reason so to feel.

## CHAPTER 22

## SMITHY IS WANTED

"SMITHY!" panted Tom Redwing.

The Bounder gave him a black scowl.

After the "row" in No. 4 Study, Smithy had flung out of the House in a savage temper, more angry and exasperated with his friend than he had ever been with an enemy. Tom had not seen him since—till now! Now he had found him in a secluded corner of the old Cloisters. Smithy was leaning on the old ivied wall, a cigarette in his mouth and bitter anger and resentment in his face: and he scowled as Tom came panting up.

"What do you want?" he snarled.

"I've been hunting for you——."

"Hunt for somebody else, then, and leave me alone. You meddlin' fool—you interferin' ninny—get out!"

"For goodness sake, Smithy——."

"Oh, shut up!"

"Put that cigarette out of sight, Smithy! There may be a prefect along any minute. Loder and Carne and Walker and Gwynne are looking for you."

"Rot! Why should they?"

"Why should they?" repeated Redwing, staring at him. "Can't you guess, after what you've done?"

"I've done nothing, you fool, as you know as well as I do, as you stopped me," snarled the Bounder. "I shall get away with it all right another time, when you can't butt in and meddle."

Tom stared at him blankly.

"What on earth do you mean, Smithy? You've got away with it all right—except that the bag missed Quelch's head, and dropped at his feet. Thank goodness it did——."

"Bag?" asked the Bounder, staring in his turn. "That bag's still in the study cupboard, where I left it."

"Smithy!" gasped Tom. He fairly blinked at the Bounder. "Smithy! Do you mean to say that it wasn't you chucked the bag down?"

"Oh, gad! Did anybody?"

"Oh, Smithy! If it wasn't you——."

"It wasn't, you gibbering ass, if it's happened. Has it?"

"I tell you the bag of flour was thrown down at Quelch, while he was standing talking to Wingate under the study window. It dropped between them, on the ground, and both of them got some of the flour."

Vernon-Smith stared at him, as if unbelieving, for a long moment. He dropped the cigarette. If looks revealed anything, the Bounder was startled and astonished by what Redwing told him. Yet Tom could hardly believe that it was news to him. After what had occurred in No. 4 Study, he could hardly have helped taking it for granted that it was Smithy's act.

"Let's have this clear," snapped the Bounder. "You say that a bag of flour was chucked down at Quelch——."

"Yes, yes——."

"Well, if it was, I know nothing of it." His eyes glinted, as he read the doubt in Redwing's troubled face. "You fool! Didn't you stop me, in the study—didn't you follow me downstairs, and see me go out of the House?"

"Yes, but—didn't you cut back afterwards, Smithy?"

"No, I didn't."

"You mean to say that you've been outside the House ever since?" exclaimed Tom.

"Yes, I mean to say exactly that: and if you can't take my word on it, you can do the other thing."

Tom looked at him, and he could not help it if his look was doubting. Not for a moment had it occurred to him that the missile might have been thrown by any other hand than Smithy's.

The Bounder eyed him almost malevolently.

"So you don't believe me?" he sneered. "You call yourself a pal, and you can't take my word! Oh, get out, and leave me alone."

"I—I do believe you, Smithy, if you say so!" stammered Tom, "but—but I only just stopped you, in the study, and soon afterwards it happened, and I'd lost sight of you, and—and—oh, Smithy, if it was not you——."

"I've said so," snarled the Bounder. "I know nothing whatever about it—less than you do. So far as I know, the bag's still in the study cupboard, where I left it after you meddled. I haven't been near the House since. I came here to smoke a cigarette, if you want to know—and to cool down, if you want to know that too—I came jolly near punching your cheeky head——."

"Never mind that! If you were here when it happened——."

"I was, if it's happened at all."

"Well, it's happened," said Redwing, "and Quelch must think that it was you, as the prefects are looking for you——."

"And why for me specially?" sneered Smithy. "Give a dog a bad name and hang him—Is that it? Sure they're looking for me?"

"I heard Walker and Gwynne asking fellows if they'd

seen you—and of course I knew why—so I started hunting for you, to tip you—it's no good keeping out of sight—that only makes things worse——."

The Bounder laughed harshly.

"You thought I'd done it, and was skulking out of sight afterwards, is that it?" he sneered.

"Well, what was I to think?" exclaimed Redwing, hotly. "You would have done it if I hadn't stopped you, and I thought——."

"Well, as it happens, I didn't! I wonder who did! Some cack-handed ass, if he missed Quelch, as you say," said Smithy, shrugging his shoulders. "Pity he didn't get the old bird!"

"Thank goodness he didn't, Smithy! That would have meant a Head's flogging if he's found—and—and they think it was you——."

"They can think what they like!" sneered Smithy. "I expect they're just groping around in the dark and don't know a thing. Anyhow they can't fix it on me as I was out of the House at the time."

There was a sound of footsteps on the old stone flags, before Redwing could reply. Loder of the Sixth came up, frowning.

"Vernon-Smith! You're wanted! Did you come here to dodge out of sight, you young ruffian? I've been looking for you for a quarter of an hour, or more."

"No, I did not," answered Vernon-Smith, calmly. "A chap can stroll in the Cloisters on a half-holiday if he likes, Loder."

"Well, your form-master wants you," snapped Loder. "Come with me at once. You too, Redwing, as you're in the same study."

"Very well, Loder," said Redwing, quietly.

"Is anything the matter, Loder?" asked the Bounder.

Loder stared at him.

"I suppose you know what's the matter, as you pitched a bag of flour at your beak's head!" he answered.

"I did nothing of the kind."

"News to you, what?" said Loder, sarcastically.

"It was news, when Redwing told me a few minutes ago. I was nowhere near the House——."

"You can tell Quelch that!" said Loder. "Now come along. I've wasted more than enough time on you."

Loder turned and stalked away, and Vernon-Smith and Redwing followed him. The Bounder was quite cool. He had been at a distance, out of sight of the House, when the incident occurred, and he saw no cause for alarm. But Redwing was deeply troubled. He believed Smithy's denial—he forced himself to believe it—but he knew that the same was not to be expected of Quelch. It was not merely a case of a "dog with a bad name": Quelch must have had something to "go" upon, before he asked the prefects to find Vernon-Smith and send him in.

Many eyes turned on Vernon-Smith, as he followed Loder to the House. All Greyfriars, by this time, knew what had happened: and that Vernon-Smith of the Remove was under suspicion.

"I say, you fellows, here he is!" squeaked Billy Bunter, in great excitement. "I say, they've got Smithy."

Harry Wharton and Co. glanced curiously at the Bounder as he passed. They had no doubt that the right man was being taken to Quelch's study. They did not speak: but Squiff had something to say.

"You howling ass, Smithy!" said Squiff. "You thumping fathead, can't you learn to behave yourself now you're captain of the form? Think we elected you to chuck flour at Quelch's nut? What sort of a footling ass do you call yourself?"

The Bounder scowled at him.

"I know nothing about it, you cuckoo," he snapped.

"Eh? You didn't do it?"

"No, I didn't."

Squiff whistled.

"He, he, he!" came from Billy Bunter. "Didn't you, Smithy? What were you keeping that bag of flour in your study for, then? He, he, he!"

"You fat frump——."

Loder looked round irritably.

"Don't hang about there, Vernon-Smith! Follow me in at once."

"Come on, Smithy," muttered Redwing.

The Bounder followed them into the House. He left unbelief behind him.

## CHAPTER 23

## GUILTY!

MR. QUELCH was looking grim.

Indeed, his expressive countenance could hardly have looked grimmer.

He sat looking at the two juniors, after Loder had marched them into his study and retired, closing the door as he went.

But though he looked at both, it was obviously Herbert Vernon-Smith upon whom he was concentrating. The gimlet-eyes glinted at the Bounder.

Why No. 4 Study was picked upon, Smithy did not yet know. But he could see at a glance that Quelch had made up his mind, and his brow grew sullen. Redwing was there simply because he belonged to the same study: Quelch was not likely to suspect so quiet and steady a fellow of so wild and reckless a prank. But Smithy was the scapegrace of the form—a dog with a bad name. If either of the occupants of No. 4 Study had pitched that bag from the window, Quelch scarcely needed telling which of the two it was. At all events, he began with Vernon-Smith, Tom looking on in troubled silence.

"Vernon-Smith! You are aware of what happened a short while ago, under the windows of the Remove studies——?"

"Redwing told me ten minutes ago, sir."

Quelch's eyebrows lifted a little.

"You did not know until Redwing told you?"

"No, sir."

"Where were you at the time?"

"Strolling in the Cloisters, sir."

"Was anyone with you?"

"No, sir."

"I imagine not!" said Mr. Quelch, drily. "Do you deny being concerned in what happened, Vernon-Smith?"

"I know nothing about it, sir."

"Very well!" Mr. Quelch compressed his lips. "The bag was thrown from the window of your study——. That is ascertained beyond doubt——."

"I don't see why, sir," muttered the Bounder, sullenly. "If it was thrown from a Remove study, it might have come from any window——."

"If you do not see why, Vernon-Smith, I will tell you. I have myself examined your study, and found a considerable quantity of flour spilled over the carpet."

The Bounder started. This was news to him, and to Redwing too. In the scuffle in No. 4, the bag had split, and some spots might have escaped—Smithy had had to brush some off from his sleeves. But certainly nothing like a "considerable quantity" had been spilled.

"I never spilled any flour there, sir," muttered Smithy. "Any fellow could have gone into my study while I was out of the House——."

"You do not deny, Vernon-Smith, that a bag of flour was in your study cupboard, to your knowledge?"

The Bounder paused before he replied. For once, if for once only, he was "up" on a charge of which he was guiltless. But he sensed the net closing round him. What had been done, was what he had intended to do: the evidence against him was of his own manufacture.

"Before you reply, Vernon-Smith," went on Mr. Quelch, grimly, "I will tell you that the plainest possible traces have been found in your study cupboard, leaving no doubt that the bag of flour had been kept there. The bag had apparently been damaged, and some of the contents spilled."

Vernon-Smith breathed hard.

"There was a bag of flour in my study cupboard, sir," he admitted. "I do not deny that."

"Why did you keep it there?"

"I did not throw it from the window, sir! I never knew till Redwing told me that it had happened——."

"I am asking you why you kept so unusual an article in your study cupboard, Vernon-Smith."

"I—I took it away from a silly fellow who brought it to my study to play a silly trick, sir."

"Indeed! When did this occur?"

"One day last week, sir! Redwing was there—he will tell you the same."

"That is so, sir," said Tom Redwing, quietly.

"Quite!" said Mr. Quelch. "But that only explains how the bag of flour came into your possession, Vernon-Smith. It does not explain why you kept it in your study, putting it to no use. To what use did you intend to put it?"

"None, sir!" said the Bounder, hardily. "I put it in the study cupboard, and then forgot all about it."

Redwing made no sign, but the colour came unconsciously into his cheeks. To the Bounder, "telling the tale" to a beak was a mere trifle. But to Tom it was bitterly painful to hear a falsehood roll so glibly from the lips of his chum, whom he liked, and would have been glad to respect.

Silence followed.

The Bounder was outwardly calm: but his heart was beating. It was not he who had thrown the bag from the window: he at least knew that. Someone—he could not begin to guess who—must have entered his study after he had left it, and done the trick—spilling flour from the split bag over the carpet. That was the only explanation he could think of. Was Quelch likely to believe that? Even Tom Redwing found it hard to believe anything of the kind.

Quelch's face grew, if possible, still grimmer.

"I warn you to be careful what you say, Vernon-Smith," he said. "Do you venture to deny that you took the bag of flour from your study cupboard this afternoon?"

"Yes, sir!"

The Bounder's voice did not falter. He felt that it was a case of "in for a penny, in for a pound". One falsehood led naturally to another.

"Upon my word!" exclaimed Mr. Quelch, and the angry disgust in his face struck the Bounder almost like a blow. It dawned upon him that Quelch knew! How did he know?

The gimlet-eyes were scanning Smithy, as he stood before his form-master. It did not occur to Smithy, for the moment, that those gimlet-eyes, which nothing escaped, had picked up a clue.

"Upon my word!" repeated Mr. Quelch. "Vernon-Smith, you deny that you handled the bag of flour this afternoon——?"

"Yes, sir!" muttered the Bounder.

"Then how," said Mr. Quelch, in a very deep voice, "how do you account for the flecks of flour that I can see on your clothes?"

"Oh!" gasped Smithy, involuntarily.

His glance shot down at his clothes. He had brushed spots of flour from his sleeves, after the scuffle in No. 4. But he had never dreamed of what was going to happen--

that someone else might handle that flour bag, causing him to be called before Quelch. If a few floury specks remained, he had not heeded them. But Quelch, looking for exactly that, heeded them!

Redwing could have groaned. If the Bounder was innocent, as he hoped and tried to believe, the truth would have served him better than prevarication. But he had done it now. There were flecks of flour on his trousers—almost invisible: no one would have noticed them, unless looking for them. The Bounder himself had not noticed them. Quelch had!

"Well?" rapped the Remove master.

"I—I—I——!" Smithy could only stammer.

"You have been handling flour very recently, Vernon-Smith. You do not, I presume, persist in your denial?"

"I—I never threw it from the window, sir. I—I—I did take the bag from the cupboard—I own up to that—but—but—I put it back again, sir, without doing anything with it—I—I was going to—to lark with it, but Redwing persuaded me to put it back, and I—I did so——."

Mr. Quelch raised his hand.

"I can attach no weight whatever to any statement you make, Vernon-Smith. You have already answered me untruthfully. Did this occur, Redwing?"

"Yes, sir, certainly," said Tom. "The bag was back in the cupboard when Vernon-Smith went out of the study, and I followed him out."

"I think I can guess the nature of the 'lark' to which Vernon-Smith refers," said Mr. Quelch, grimly. "Can you say, Redwing, that Vernon-Smith did not return to the study, and carry out his intention, whatever it was?"

Redwing was unhappily silent.

Had he remained in his chum's company, after the

"row" in No. 4, he would have been a witness in his favour—if Smithy was innocent! But the Bounder had flung away in a savage temper, and he had left him to himself. Not for the first time, Smithy had reason to repent the indulgence of an ungovernable temper.

"Redwing! Answer me! Did Vernon-Smith remain in your company?" rapped Mr. Quelch.

"No, sir!" muttered Tom, reluctantly.

"You lost sight of him?"

"Ye-es, sir."

"Quite so!" said Mr. Quelch. "The matter is now settled beyond doubt. You may leave my study, Redwing."

"But, sir——!" stammered Tom.

"I said that you may leave my study, Redwing," said Mr. Quelch, raising his voice a little.

Tom, in silence, left the study. He could do nothing to help his chum. Vernon-Smith remained. He was judged guilty: as he had very nearly been in actual fact. He had dug for his own feet the pit into which he had fallen. It was futile to speak: Quelch had no use for anything further from him, true or false.

"I shall now deal with you, Vernon-Smith," said Mr. Quelch. "You threw the bag from the study window, intending it to fall upon either myself, your form-master, or Wingate of the Sixth Form, the captain of the school. If it had done so, you would be reported to your head-master for a public flogging. Fortunately for you, it did not, and I need not take so extreme a step. For your act in throwing the bag from the window, Vernon-Smith, you will go into Extra School for all the remaining half-holidays this term. For your untruthfulness, I shall cane you." Quelch rose to his feet, and picked up the cane from his table. "Bend over that chair."

In savage, sullen silence, the Bounder bent over.

That part of his sentence, even Smithy could not deny, was just. He had lied, and he was to be caned for lying. The heavy sentence of "Extra" for the rest of the term was due, not to him, but to the unknown person who had pitched the bag of flour at Quelch. But that did not help him, as Quelch was quite convinced that he was the person: and, indeed, could scarcely have believed anything else. His own actions and his own words had condemned him. Who was to believe that his own intention had been carried out by another, utterly unknown, hand?

"You may go, Vernon-Smith!" said Mr. Quelch, as he laid down the cane.

And the Bounder went, savage and sullen.

Tom Redwing was waiting for him anxiously at the corner of the passage. He would have spoken: but the Bounder brushed roughly past him, and tramped out into the quad by himself, in the blackest temper ever.

## CHAPTER 24

# SMITHY WANTS TO KNOW

"WHARTON!"

"Well?"

"I want a word with you."

"Two, if you like," said Harry Wharton, politely.

His manner to the Bounder was civil, but quite indifferent. That, indeed, had been his manner to the new captain of the form, ever since the election a week ago. If he was irked by the new state of affairs, and resented it, he gave little or no sign of anything of the kind. His quiet acquiescence rather surprised his friends: and certainly Smithy had not expected it: he had expected his ousted rival to give him all the trouble he could. But Wharton had given him no trouble at all, nor shown any desire to do so.

Vernon-Smith stood in the doorway of No. 1 Study, looking in. Wharton and Nugent had come up to their study for prep, and were getting out their books, when Smithy stopped in the doorway to speak. Frank Nugent gave his lowering face a rather curious glance, perhaps wondering whether Smithy had come there for a "row". He looked in a mood for one.

Neither of them asked Vernon-Smith to come in, but he came in. He fixed his eyes on Harry Wharton, taking no notice of Nugent.

"You're glad of this!" he said, in a low bitter voice.

Wharton raised his eyebrows.

"Of what?" he asked.

"You're out, and I'm in," said Vernon-Smith, savagely. "You've been lying low, but do you think I don't know how you feel about it?"

"I don't suppose you do," answered Harry. "I made a mistake, and you cashed in on it. But I'm not blaming you for my own mistakes."

"Oh! You admit that you made a mistake?" sneered Smithy.

"Why not? We all make mistakes at times," answered Wharton, carelessly. "You seem to have made a pretty considerable one yourself, this afternoon."

"That's what I came here to speak about. You know that I'm booked for Extra for the rest of the term?"

"I've heard so."

"That washes out football for me—I mean the matches."

"Quite."

"You'd like me to believe that you're not glad of it?" muttered the Bounder.

"Not at all: you can believe what you like."

"Well, never mind that! I'm captain of the Remove, and I'm barred from Soccer if this goes on. Have you any idea who buzzed that rotten bag of flour at Quelch's head this afternoon?"

Wharton and Nugent stared at him.

"Certainly I have," answered Harry.

"Who, then?"

"You!"

"Any use telling you I did not?" asked Vernon-Smith, between his teeth.

"Not much."

"I'll tell you all the same. I did not."

There was no reply to that. Plainly neither Harry Wharton nor Frank Nugent believed that statement, any more than Mr. Quelch had believed it. The Bounder's dark brow grew darker.

"I'll tell you what happened," he said.

"I fancy we know already," said Wharton, drily.

"Will you listen to me?" hissed Smithy.

"Oh, run on if you like. Don't make it too steep," said Harry, with a touch of contempt. "We all know that you had that bag parked in your study cupboard, and that it was chucked at Quelch from your study window. What else were you keeping it there for? Not to make cakes, I suppose!"

"That much is true," said Vernon-Smith. "I kept it for Quelch: and I was going to let him have it, this afternoon, only Redwing butted in and stopped me. I left it in the study cupboard, and never saw it again."

Again there was no reply.

"You don't believe that?" asked Smithy.

"Does Quelch?"

"You know he doesn't."

"Well, I don't, either, if you want an answer."

"It's true!" breathed Vernon-Smith. "And I want to know who went into my study, after I was gone, and chucked that bag from the window. It must have been very soon afterwards. Do you know anything about it?"

"What on earth should I know about it, even if what you say is true?" exclaimed Wharton, staring at him.

"This has dished me for the Soccer. I know who would like to see me dished," said the Bounder, savagely. "Whoever did it left a lot of the flour about my study: that was how Quelch got on to it. It was done to land me in a row, and dish me—and it's come off. A good many fellows are already saying that you will have to captain the side next week at Rookwood. That's where you come in."

"Why, you rotter——!" exclaimed Frank Nugent, red with anger. "Are you trying to make out that Wharton would——."

"I'm not making out anything: I want to know!" snarled the Bounder. "I'm going to find out, before next Wednesday, who did it, and I'm beginning here."

"If you want to be booted out of this study——!" Frank Nugent's eyes flashed at the Bounder, and he made a step towards him.

"Oh, let him run on, Franky," said Harry Wharton. He gave a scornful laugh. "Carry on, Smithy! It seems that you didn't do it, and that you think I did, to dish you over the Soccer. Is that the big idea?"

"I've not said so. I want to know, and I'm going to know, who did it. If it doesn't come out, what sort of skipper am I going to make, kept out of all the matches? It's got to come out."

"Well, if it will interest you, I was in the quad when it happened, and saw it happen—and Nugent was with me, as well as Inky and Bob and Johnny. But perhaps you think we were all in it together?" said Wharton, ironically.

The Bounder stood silent. Savagely suspicious as he was, prepared to suspect anybody or anything, even he could not carry suspicion to that length.

"You're the man who stands to gain by it," he said. "It couldn't have happened better for you. But—well, the idea came into my mind, but I couldn't half-believe you the sort for such a dirty trick." Smithy spoke half-apologetically. "But some pal of yours——."

"Thanks! But I'm not pally with the kind of fellow who would think out a scheme for landing another fellow in a row."

"You've no idea who the man was?"

"None at all—if it was not you."

"Or you, Nugent?" The Bounder's eyes turned on Frank. "You know nothing either?"

Nugent shrugged his shoulders.

"You want to see the man who chucked that bag at Quelch's nut?" he asked.

"Of course I do."

"Well, there's a looking-glass over the fireplace."

"What do you mean by that, you ninny?"

"Look in it! You'll see the man you want to see."

The Bounder clenched his hands, hard. Harry Wharton laughed.

"Nothing doing here, Smithy," he said. "You'd better try some other study. If what you say is true, there's some precious rotter in the form, and I wish you luck in rooting him out. Sorry I can't help."

"You're glad of it, at any rate," snarled Smithy.

"We've had that! Now, if you don't mind my mentioning it, it's prep, and we can't enjoy your conversation any longer."

The Bounder gave him an evil look, tramped out of the study, and slammed the door after him. Possibly he was satisfied that the Remove man who had most to gain by the affair had had nothing to do with it. But that left him groping wholly in the dark: absolutely at a loss.

Harry Wharton's face was thoughtful, as he sat down at the study table. The Bounder's angry suspicions he dismissed with contempt: but those very suspicions put the matter in a new light.

"I wonder——!" he said, slowly.

"It was Smithy!" said Nugent.

"I suppose it was! But—I wonder! He seemed in

earnest about suspecting me—and if he was the man himself, he couldn't, of course—after all, he's put a good many backs up in the form, since he became skipper. If it's as he says, he's getting a raw deal."

"If!" said Nugent.

"I wonder!" said Harry, again.

And it was left at that, and they settled down to prep.

## CHAPTER 25

# A PROBLEM

"PREP, old man!" said Tom Redwing, mildly.

"Oh, don't be a fool!"

The Bounder of Greyfriars, evidently, was not thinking of prep.

In No. 4 Study, Redwing sat at the table with his books. Vernon-Smith, with his hands thrust deep into his trousers' pockets, and a deep line in his brow, moved restlessly about the study. "Prep" was the last thing of which the Bounder was likely to be thinking, just then.

"No good getting into a row in the form-room in the morning, Smithy," said Tom. "It won't improve matters to have another row with Quelch."

"Hang Quelch!"

The Bounder came to a halt, and stared at his chum across the study table. That he had quarrelled with Redwing that afternoon, and that they had come very near to punching, he seemed to have forgotten. Tom was glad enough to forget it. Smithy's mind was full of the disaster that had fallen upon him, and that looked like making his captaincy in the Remove nothing but a farce—so long as it lasted. It could hardly last, if present circumstances continued unchanged.

"Look here, Reddy, we've got to work this thing out!" he said. "Can't you help? Look how I'm fixed. Lots of the fellows are saying already that it was a mistake to chuck Wharton. Anyhow he will have to captain the side if I'm out of it. It all goes his way, leaving me high and dry. All that I've won, thrown away—because some rotter has played a rotten trick! Who was it?"

Redwing made no reply to that: and the Bounder eyed him evilly.

"Are you still thinking that I did it?" he snarled.

"No!" said Redwing, slowly. "I take your word about that, Smithy! But—nobody else in the school will."

"I know that—unless we get the facts out." The Bounder clenched his hands. "It's Wharton who scores all along the line if I'm dished—you know that! I can't quite think that he had a hand in it——."

"For goodness sake, Smithy, don't be a fool," said Tom, sharply. "Wharton has his faults—you wouldn't be captain of the form now if he hadn't—but you ought to be ashamed of suspecting him of this for a moment——."

"Well, I don't suspect him, if it comes to that. But some pal of his might have put it through, on his account. I can't see any other reason for it. It seems that the whole gang of them were out of the House when it happened—Wharton himself, Nugent, Cherry, Bull, and the darkey. But he's got other friends in the form—any one of them might have—You don't think so?" snapped Smithy, as Redwing shook his head.

"No! And you wouldn't, if you were cool."

"It was somebody, wasn't it?" hissed Smithy.

"Yes, I suppose so. But——."

"I've thought of Todd. Only Wharton standing out of the voting beat him in the election. It was a close thing. He might think——."

"Toddy would no more do it than Wharton would! You'll get nowhere by silly suspicions like that."

"Well, who was it, then? You know what happened here. Somebody must have come in after we went down—

and jolly soon after, too. Might have had an eye on us, I shouldn't wonder. Whoever it was, came for a rag—you know we found gum and ink chucked about the room, when we came up later. He inked our books, and gummed the armchair, and chucked the bag of flour from the window. Isn't that clear?"

"I suppose so. Some fellow with his back up, and a pretty rotter at that," said Redwing. "Not a fellow like Wharton, or any of his friends. So far as a rag goes, you've asked for that——."

"What?"

"I may as well speak plainly, Smithy! You as good as diddled some of the fellows for their votes in the election. And you've been a good deal on the high horse since. You've put a good many backs up."

The Bounder breathed very hard.

"A rag's a rag," he said, "but landing me in a row with Quelch is quite another matter. You think it has nothing to do with the captaincy, or the Soccer—only some skulking rat hitting back in an underhand way——."

"That's what it looks like to me."

"But who?" muttered Smithy.

"I can't guess that."

"And I can't, either, if you're right." The Bounder resumed his angry pacing of the study. "Might have been anybody—even a fellow in another form, for all I know—if it was just a case of personal enmity. That doesn't make it so easy to spot him. But he's got to be spotted, Reddy."

Redwing was silent. He believed Smithy, though it required an effort. Some other fellow, utterly unknown, had done what Smithy had planned to do, and what only Redwing's intervention had stopped him from doing. But who the fellow was Redwing had not the remotest idea.

Smithy came to a halt again, staring at him across the table with a black brow.

"I tell you he's got to be spotted," he repeated. "Look how the matter stands. I'm captain of the Remove—Wharton down and out. It's the Rookwood match next Wednesday, and everything was going my way, for a score on the Soccer field to put me right at the top. I'm captaining a first-class team—Browney and Linley and Penfold are back in the ranks, and Cherry's knee's mended—I shall lead as good a side as the Remove has ever put into the field. Fellows who are still backing Wharton won't have much to say when we've beaten Rookwood on their own ground under my lead. And now—this!"

Vernon-Smith gritted his teeth.

"Extra next Wednesday, and Wharton captaining the side at Rookwood! I'm not standing for that, Reddy—not at any price! I'm going over to Rookwood with the team next Wednesday, if the skies fall."

"You can't, Smithy! Not unless we find out in time——."

"We must! But if we don't, I'm going all the same," said the Bounder, with savage determination. "I shall cut Extra, and I don't care if it means a Head's flogging when we get back."

"Keep cool, old chap! You can't flout Quelch like that——."

"I can—and will!"

"You can't! Do you think he wouldn't guess where you'd gone, and put a stop to it?" exclaimed Redwing.

"Think he would hike across to Hampshire to fetch me back?" sneered the Bounder.

"He might! Quelch isn't a man to be defied by any

fellow in his form. At least he would phone Rookwood, and where would you be, then?"

"Oh!" muttered Smithy. "If he did that——."

"He would do that, or anything else, rather than let you get away with it," said Redwing, quietly. "Have a little sense, Smithy. It's hard, I know: but you have to toe the line like any other fellow——."

"Isn't it rotten injustice?" hissed Smithy. "I'm booked for a term's detention for what I never did! Is a fellow to stand that?"

"You asked for it," answered Tom. "It was what you planned to do, and Quelch could only act on the evidence, which wouldn't have been there, if you hadn't——."

"Oh, give us a rest."

"Be reasonable, old chap! I know it's rough luck, but——."

"Oh, don't jaw."

Smithy paced the study again, evidently in no mood for sweet reasonableness. The fact that it was his own reckless and mutinous folly that had landed him in this disaster was no comfort to him.

Redwing sighed, and began, at last, on prep. But the Bounder did not join him. Trouble in the form-room the next day was nothing to him now.

He had to pull out of this somehow if his captaincy in the Remove was not to be a mere farce, destined to fizz out like a spent squib. While Redwing worked, Smithy moved about the study, thinking and thinking, with knitted brows.

He was going over to Rookwood for the match there. On that he was passionately determined. It was fixed and unalterable in his mind. But how he was to contrive it was another matter.

There was but a faint chance of discovering who had

played that wretched trick in No. 4: still less chance of the unknown culprit owning up. Smithy was ready to take any risk, to face any consequences. But what was the use of "cutting", and going over to Rookwood without leave, if Quelch intervened—and he could not doubt that Quelch would, as Redwing had said. A phone call to the headmaster at Rookwood would be sufficient, asking for a truant to be sent back. Quelch certainly would not hesitate at that, rather than allow a mutineer in his form to get away with mutiny.

In such an event, obviously Smithy could not play Soccer at Rookwood, and might as well be sitting in Extra at Greyfriars.

Nevertheless, somehow, anyhow, he was going to carry on, Quelch or no Quelch. He was going over to Rookwood on the following Wednesday to captain the Greyfriars side there. Nothing should stop him! But—but——.

There was a large size in "buts" in the way! He was going to do it—but how? That was the problem the Bounder had to think out. It looked like an unanswerable one: and it was no wonder that Smithy had reached no solution by the time prep was over, and the juniors went down from the studies.

## CHAPTER 26

# GIVE SMITHY A CHANCE!

"SOMEBODY looks as if he's enjoying life!" remarked Bob Cherry.

His friends smiled.

Bob's remark was mildly sarcastic. He was referring to the new captain of the Remove: and Herbert Vernon-Smith really did not look in the very least as if he were enjoying life that Saturday afternoon.

The Famous Five were standing at the window of the Rag, looking out into the quad, after dinner. They were all looking cheerful, under the influence of fine clear weather and the prospect of football that afternoon. Their cheerfulness was far from being shared by the fellow pacing moodily in the quad.

Vernon-Smith's brow was dark, and his eyes glinted. It was rather a rule at Greyfriars that a fellow did not display his feelings too obviously, especially in the way of discontent and bad temper. But the Bounder was already a law unto himself. If Smithy's temper was bad, he cared nothing if all the school observed it: in fact, as Harry Wharton had remarked, it was not for nothing that he had been nicknamed the "Bounder". Everyone at Greyfriars, from the majestic Dr. Locke, the head-master, down to the smallest fag in the Second Form, and Trotter the House page and Gosling the porter, was welcome, if he liked, to note that Vernon-Smith of the Remove was in a sullen and savage temper.

"The enjoyfulness does not seem to be terrific,"

remarked Hurree Jamset Ram Singh, with a dusky grin.

"Some skipper!" grunted Johnny Bull. "A Form match on this afternoon, and the jolly old skipper booked for Extra while we play it."

"Smithy all over!" remarked Nugent.

Harry Wharton did not speak. His glance dwelt thoughtfully on the moody fellow in the quad. And it was not wholly unsympathetic. Smithy, in his new position as captain of the form, was severely up against it: there was no doubt of that.

That afternoon, a Form match was scheduled: Remove v. Upper Fourth. A game with Temple, Dabney and Co. of the Fourth, was no great matter. But the new captain had intended to put his men through their paces, as it were, in that game, preparatory to the big fixture at Rookwood the following week. Instead of which, he was going to sit it out in Extra School: with the same bleak prospect before him on Rookwood day. If, as Harry half-believed, Smithy had not done what was laid to his charge, undoubtedly he was getting hard measure.

"It won't go on," said Bob. "A skipper who gets himself barred from Soccer by playing mad tricks on his beak can't carry on. A dozen fellows have told Smithy it's time he resigned."

"I can see him doing it!" grunted Johnny.

"It's that, or being chucked out."

"The chuckfulness is the proper caper," remarked Hurree Jamset Ram Singh, "and the soonerfulness is the betterfulness."

"The men are fed up," went on Bob. "I've heard Squiff say that he'd rather have punched Smithy's head than voted for him, if he'd known how it was going to turn out. Toddy says that if there's another election, he wouldn't dream of standing against you, old bean. You'd get in in a walk-over."

Wharton shook his head.

"Give Smithy a chance," he said.

"He's had his chance, and chucked it away," said Bob. "It was on the question of barring him from the Soccer that you had to get out. Well, now he's barred himself from the Soccer, so that question doesn't arise any longer. You don't need to bar him now he's barred himself, see?"

"He would never have had a chance at all, if Wharton hadn't been an obstinate ass with his back up," remarked Johnny Bull. Johnny was an almost painfully plain speaker, at times.

"Thanks," said Harry.

"Draw it mild, Johnny," murmured Nugent.

"Rot!" said Johnny. "Everyone thinks the same, including you fellows. What's the good of beating about the bush? Wharton was pig-headed——."

"Shut up, all the same, old chap," said Bob.

Harry Wharton smiled faintly.

"Johnny's right," he said. "I've thought it over a bit—more than a bit—and I can see it. I was right to begin with, but I'm rather afraid that I let Smithy put my back up a little too much—and—and—well, pride goeth before destruction, and a lofty spirit before a fall! I asked for it, and got it, and I've no kick coming."

"Oh!" said Johnny, rather taken aback. "Well, that's sense. Mean to say you'd play Smithy at Rookwood next week, if you were still skipper?"

"Quite!"

"Good man," said Bob. "What rotten luck that you're out, and that Smithy's ragged Quelch into giving him

Extra. Anyhow, there's nothing to stop you getting back, old man, now that Smithy's made such a muck of it."

Wharton shook his head again.

"Give a man a chance," he said. "Smithy was elected captain of the Remove, whether we like it or not——."

"And what's the good of a skipper who plays tricks like a mad fag, and gets himself Extra for the rest of the term?" demanded Johnny Bull.

Wharton paused before replying.

"I'm not sure that Smithy did," he answered. "He denies it——."

"His word's worth a lot!" grunted Johnny. "Don't be a goat, old chap. Everyone knows that Smithy kept that bag of flour specially to chuck at Quelch, and that settles it. He owned up that he was going to do it, only Redwing stopped him. Well, he cut back after he'd dodged Redwing, and did it."

"I know it looks like it. But——."

"But rats!" said Johnny.

"Hallo, hallo, hallo, what do you fellows want?" exclaimed Bob Cherry. Quite a little crowd of Removites poured into the Rag, and came across to the Famous Five at the window.

Squiff appeared to be the leader. He was followed by Peter Todd, Russell, Ogilvy, Penfold, Tom Brown, Mark Linley, and several other fellows.

"Oh, here you are, Wharton," said Squiff.

"Adsum!" said Harry.

"We've come to speak to you," said Peter.

"Carry on. Not another ultimatum, I hope?"

"Never mind that," said Peter, rather hastily. "Look here——."

"Look here——," said Tom Brown.

"About the Soccer," said Squiff. "Smithy can't carry on, now that he's made such a benighted fool of himself. You'll have to captain the side this afternoon, while that fathead is in Extra. Well, what about Rookwood next week?"

Harry Wharton raised his hand.

"Stop at that!" he said. "I shall play at Rookwood if I'm wanted, and that's all it's got to do with me. Smithy's skipper."

"I know that! But——."

"Never mind the 'buts'," said Harry. "It's up to you to back up the man you voted in."

"Think we'd have voted him in, if we'd known what was coming?" exclaimed Russell. "Look how it's turned out."

"A mad ass stuck in Extra for playing fag tricks!" said Squiff. "Smithy will have to go."

"That's not a matter for me to butt into!" said Harry, quietly. "Give Smithy a chance. Fair play's a jewel."

"Oh!" said Squiff, rather blankly.

"Look here——!" began Peter Todd.

"You fellows look here," interrupted Wharton. "Smithy says he never played that mad trick on Quelch, and I believe him for one——."

"Rot!"

"Rubbish!"

"We all jolly well know——."

"Quelch thinks so, at any rate, and that's that!" said Ogilvy. "Whatever we think about it won't get Smithy off."

"No," said Harry, "unless the facts come out. The fellow who did it may have the decency to own up. That would see Smithy through. Give the man a chance."

With that, Harry Wharton turned to the window,

leaving Squiff and Co. with a view of his back. That was a plain intimation that the interview was at an end: Squiff and Co. looked at one another rather uncertainly, stared at Wharton's back, and then retired, evidently considerably disconcerted. This was not what they had expected from the late captain of the Remove.

Bob Cherry winked at his friends. Johnny Bull grunted.

"Smithy wouldn't be so jolly particular, in your place, Harry!" remarked Bob.

"Very likely not," answered Wharton, drily. "I hope I'm a little more particular than Smithy, in some things."

"Wharton!"

It was the Bounder's voice, under the open window. The Famous Five put their heads out, and looked down. Vernon-Smith was standing under the window, and they could guess that he had heard what had been said in the Rag. He did not heed the Co.: his eyes were fixed on Harry Wharton, and there was a somewhat curious expression on his face.

"I heard the lot," he said. "I don't know what your game is, Wharton——."

Harry Wharton laughed.

"You wouldn't!" he said. "But if you heard the lot, you heard me say that fair play's a jewel. That's all."

The Bounder stared up at him, hard. Had the position been reversed, he knew, as the other fellows knew, that he would have taken advantage of it, and pushed his advantage to the limit. It was not easy for him to believe that Wharton was sincere.

"You'll captain the side this afternoon," he muttered, "and—and if I can't go over to Rookwood next Wednesday, you'll have to captain the side there. But——."

"It mayn't come to that," said Harry. "It may come

out who bagged Quelch the other day, and that would see you clear."

"You fancy the fellow might own up?" The Bounder could not help sneering, as he asked that question.

"Any decent fellow would," answered Harry.

"Any decent fellow wouldn't have landed me like this! No chance of that. But—I don't know what your game is, but I'll tell you this: I'm going over to Rookwood with the team next Wednesday, and whether you mean what you say or not, you can put that in your pipe and smoke it!" said the Bounder, savagely: and with that he turned and walked away, without waiting for a reply.

CHAPTER 27

# THE SPIDER AND THE FLY

"BUNTER!"

"Beast!"

That exchange of remarks took place in the Remove passage, after class on Monday.

Billy Bunter was lingering suspiciously near the door of No. 4 Study when Vernon-Smith came up. He was, in fact, debating in his fat mind whether a surreptitious visit to that study would be consistent with "safety first".

Bunter was hungry: which was not uncommon with Bunter. He had tea'd in No. 7 with Peter Todd and Tom Dutton: but it had been, as was often the case in that study, a frugal meal. Frugal meals were not of much use to the fat Owl. And, with the selfishness which Bunter so often and so sadly encountered, Toddy and Dutton had consumed their share of what was going, heartlessly regardless of the fact that Bunter could, and willingly would, have demolished the whole lot.

After which, Bunter had rolled hopefully up the passage to Lord Mauleverer's study, like a lion seeking what he might devour: only to find that his lordship was out, teaing elsewhere. After which again, he had rolled down the passage to No. 1 Study, where he found Mauly teaing with the Famous Five. But it seemed that there was no room for a fat Owl to wedge in: and a football boot whizzing across the study having apprised Bunter that he was superfluous, he had retired rather hastily.

So there was William George Bunter, blinking at the door of No. 4 through his big spectacles, and weighing pros and cons: whether to risk it, or to roll down and join the scramble in hall before it was too late.

He was rather glad that he had not risked it, when the Bounder came up the passage.

He blinked morosely at Smithy.

Billy Bunter's feelings towards the new captain of the Remove had rather chopped and changed of late. A dictionary thudding on a fat chin had roused him to vengeance with a bag of flour. But Smithy's electioneering methods had quite won him over, and turned him into an enthusiastic supporter. After the Form election, however, came another change. Bunter could hardly have loathed his lessons more than he loathed a form-captain who had no mercy on a fat slacker!

Certainly, a spread in Smithy's study would have brought him round again: right round like a fat humming-top. But having no expectations now of that kind, Bunter continued in a state of loathing. So when Smithy, coming up the passage, said "Bunter," he answered "Beast!"

The next moment he wished that he hadn't: for Smithy, to his surprise, gave him an affable nod.

"Looking for you, Bunter," he said. "Had your tea?"

"Oh! Eh? Yes! No! I mean——."

"Care to tea with me? I've got rather a spread."

Billy Bunter could hardly believe his fat ears. Smithy, contrary to all expectation, was asking him to tea! That was an invitation that Wiliam George Bunter was never known to refuse.

Once more the fat Owl's feelings veered round. He ceased to loathe Smithy on the spot! In fact he beamed upon him.

"I say, Smithy, old fellow, I'll come with pleasure," he gasped.

"Trot in, then," said Smithy, and he opened the door of No. 4.

Billy Bunter lost no time in "trotting" in. Indeed, he almost galloped!

Why Smithy was so pally all of a sudden, Bunter did not know. There was no election pending now! But he was prepared to make the most of it while it lasted.

His fat face beamed as he helped to sort out good things from the study cupboard. Only a few minutes ago, he had been contemplating a raid on those good things, at the risk of being caught at it and booted down the passage. Now he was requested, indeed pressed, to dispose of them at his own sweet will! He did not require much pressing.

Tea was soon going strong in No. 4 Study.

Smithy could not have been more affable. The fattest member of the Greyfriars Remove was feeling that life, after all, with all its vicissitudes, was really and truly worth living. So far from loathing Smithy now, Billy Bunter almost loved him as a brother.

"Isn't Redwing teaing here?" asked Bunter, presently. Having eaten enough for three or four fellows, and so taken the keen edge off his appetite, he had leisure to remember Redwing's existence.

Smithy shook his head.

"No: he's teaing up the passage, with Ogilvy." Smithy did not add that he had asked Redwing to tea out that day. It did not dawn on Bunter that Smithy had something to say to him which he did not want Redwing to hear.

"All the more for us," said Bunter, agreeably. "I say, Smithy, this is a jolly good cake! Not up to the cakes I get from Bunter Court: but jolly good. Mind if I finish it?"

"Do!" said Smithy.

Bunter did.

"Try the jam-tarts," went on Smithy, hospitably.

Billy Bunter was only too willing to try the jam-tarts. In fact they went down almost like oysters. It was a happy and sticky Owl.

"Jolly good, old chap," said Bunter, breathing rather hard. "I say, I'll stand you a spread like this, Smithy, when—when my postal-order comes——."

"Glad you like it," said Smithy. "I hope you'll come again, Bunter."

"What-ho!" gasped Bunter.

"You can have the run of the study if you like, for the rest of the term," added Smithy.

"Oh, crikey!" said Bunter. He blinked across the table at Vernon-Smith. Visions of unlimited tuck floated before his dazzled eyes. He wondered how he could ever have disliked Smithy!

"Only I want you to do something for me," added Smithy, casually.

Bunter, obtuse as he was, had already surmised that much, though he had not the remotest idea of what Smithy wanted. But he was undoubtedly prepared to do anything he could for a fellow who stood a spread like this, with the prospect of more to come!

"Anything you like, old chap," said Bunter, effusively. "Fellows are saying there's going to be another election in the Remove—if there is, I'll jolly well vote for you again, Smithy."

The Bounder's brow darkened for a moment.

"There's not going to be another election," he snapped. "I'm taking care of that."

"Well, I'm your man, whatever it is," said Bunter. "I'll play football at Rookwood if you like——."

"You howling ass."

"Oh, really, Smithy——."

"I—I mean—never mind—look here, Bunter, I'm rather in a jam over the Soccer," said Vernon-Smith. "You know Quelch thinks that I buzzed that bag from this study window the other day——."

"Didn't you?" grinned Bunter.

"No!" said Smithy, quietly, "I didn't! Some rat did it to land me in the soup. Quelch has got the wrong man."

"Um!" said Bunter. Like almost everyone else, the fat Owl had had no doubt that Quelch had "got" the right man. But Smithy's earnestness impressed him a little: and that handsome spread was undoubtedly a point in Smithy's favour!

"Rough luck, old man, if that's the case," said Bunter. He was helping himself from a large box of chocolate-creams. The chocolate-creams were good. Bunter was prepared to be sympathetic.

"Well, it's so," said Smithy, "and it's dished me over the Soccer. You can help me out if you like."

"Jolly glad to, if I could," said Bunter. He did not see in the least how he could help Smithy out: but he was willing to do anything he could, if a free run of the lavish study cupboard in No. 4 was to be the reward.

"If the fellow who did it owned up, that would see me clear," said the Bounder, eyeing the sticky fat Owl narrowly.

"Bet you he won't," said Bunter, sagely. "It's nearly a week ago, and he hasn't so far, at any rate."

"It would be all right if any fellow owned up to it."

"Eh?" Bunter's little round eyes widened behind his big round spectacles. "Only the fellow who did it could own up to it, I suppose."

The Bounder breathed rather hard. He was coming to the point now, the fat Owl little dreaming of the extraordinary scheme that had formed in his mind. Over the week-end, Smithy had been doing some very hard thinking.

Nothing whatever had come to light concerning the affair in No. 4 the previous week. Redwing, and rather unexpectedly Harry Wharton, believed the Bounder's denial: other fellows gave no heed to it. Skinner and Snoop, certainly, could have let in light; but they had been very careful to keep their own counsel.

What Remove fellows might think or believe, Smithy cared little. It was what Quelch believed that mattered. Only the discovery of the real culprit could change Quelch's belief: and of that, Smithy had given up hope by this time. And he had never had any hope that the fellow, whoever he was, would own up.

His sentence stood: and so long as it stood, he was captain of the Remove in little more than name. Even that could not last long. Harry Wharton had captained the Remove side in the Form match on Saturday: and if he had to captain the side at Rookwood, he would practically be back in his old position: and it could hardly be long before he was officially there also. Even if he was, as the cynical Bounder could not believe, willing to give the new captain a chance, the Remove would not stand for it. Smithy had to get out of that jam or go!

And he had, at long last, thought of a way out: which was why he was feeding William George Bunter up to his fat chin. The obtuse fat Owl was certainly the only fellow in the Remove to whom he could have put up the proposition he had in mind. Even with Bunter he had to be wary. It was in fact a case of "will you walk into my parlour, said the spider to the fly". Smithy could not feel quite sure yet of his fat fly.

Bunter was blinking at him curiously, as he did not speak. Smithy took the plunge at last.

"Somebody might do it, to do me a good turn," he said, slowly. "So long as a fellow owned up, that would be O.K. by Quelch! He couldn't guess that the fellow was pulling his leg."

"No fear," agreed Bunter. "Nobody's likely to pull Quelch's leg like that, and get landed in Extra for his trouble."

"A pal might," said Smithy.

"Um!" said Bunter. He seemed to doubt it.

"Look here, Bunter, suppose you own up to it?"

Billy Bunter almost jumped off his chair.

"Me!" he ejaculated.

"Yes, you."

"But I never did it!" gasped Bunter.

"I know that! And I never did it, either. Quelch has got the wrong man anyway, and he might as well have one wrong man as another."

"Oh, crumbs!" gasped Bunter. He understood now why he had been asked into No. 4 for that lavish spread, with the promise of more to come. Smithy wanted a "quid pro quo": and this was it! "I—I say, I—I don't care whom Quelch gets, so long as it ain't me, Smithy. But—but——."

"Be a pal," said Smithy.

"Oh! Yes! But—but—but a fellow who owned up would get what you got—and a chap doesn't want to stick in Extra every half-holiday——."

"It wouldn't come to that! Quelch would go easier

with you than with me," muttered Smithy. "He's down on me—he's not down on you. He would go easy."

"Um!" said Bunter.

"He would think it jolly decent of you, owning up to get another fellow out of a row, see?"

"Oh! Yes! There's that!" said Bunter, thoughtfully. "But——."

"Might let you right off."

"Um!"

Vernon-Smith watched the varying expressions on the fat face anxiously. Between impenetrable obtuseness, and a remarkable facility for fibbing, Bunter was just the man he wanted—if Bunter would play up.

"After all, it's only a leg-pull," he said.

"Oh! Yes! But——."

"Rather a lark to pull Quelch's leg."

Bunter grinned.

"Yes, rather," he agreed. "But——."

"Be a pal, old chap, and do your best for me," said Smithy.

Billy Bunter hesitated. Unlimited spreads in that well-provided study were a tempting prospect. But they were not to be had for nothing. The fat Owl hesitated.

But it was said of old that he who hesitates is lost.

"After all, it's only a leg-pull!" said Bunter.. "Only a lark, really, stuffing old Quelch——."

"That's all," said Smithy.

"I—I—I——."

"Well?"

"I'll do my best for you, old chap," said Bunter. "I say, is there any more cake in the cupboard?"

Herbert Vernon-Smith drew a deep, deep breath. The spider was sure of his fat fly now!

## CHAPTER 28

## BUNTER'S BEST

MR. QUELCH frowned.

"Bunter!" he rapped.

"Oh!" Billy Bunter came, apparently, out of the depths of a brown study, and jumped. "Yes, sir!"

"Are you paying attention, Bunter?"

"Oh! Yes, sir! I—I heard every word you were saying, sir!" gasped Bunter.

At which Mr. Quelch's frown deepened, and some of the Remove fellows grinned.

They were doing English History in the Remove form-room on Tuesday morning. There were fellows in the Remove who were interested in the annals of their native land. There were others who weren't. Billy Bunter was one of the latter.

At the best of times, Bunter was not a very attentive pupil. Sometimes a glare from a gimlet-eye, or even a rap of a pointer on fat knuckles, was required to cause him to sit up and take notice.

But never had even Bunter been so inattentive as he was on this particular morning. It might really have been supposed that the fat Owl had something on his fat mind, which quite excluded our island story from his plump thoughts.

Many times he had blinked anxiously at Mr. Quelch, though without paying the slightest attention to the words of wisdom that fell from his form-master's lips. Twice, thrice, he had opened the widest mouth in the Remove, as if to speak. But each time there seemed to be some impediment in his speech, for he closed it again without utterance.

A good many fellows had noticed it, and wondered what was the matter with Bunter. Peter Todd had nudged him, several times. Bob Cherry had given him a friendly hack under the desk, to remind him that he was in class, and that it behoved him to remember that circumstance. The Bounder glanced at him time and again. In all the Form, only Smithy knew what was in the fat Owl's mind, and that the worried Owl was endeavouring to screw up his courage to the sticking point.

Now Quelch's gimlet-eye was fixed on him, and he rapped. Really, Bunter had been asking for it ever since the lesson began.

"I trust, Bunter, that what you state is correct," said Mr. Quelch, with a rasp in his voice. "I shall now ask you some questions on the subject of the lesson, Bunter."

"Oh, lor'!"

"What? What did you say, Bunter?"

"Oh! Nothing, sir!" gasped Bunter. "I—I——."

"You will tell me, who led the Norman forces at the battle of Hastings."

"Smithy, sir——."

"WHAT!" Quelch almost shouted. Quelch had received some remarkable answers from Bunter, at various times: but never so remarkable an answer as that.

"Oh, my hat!" murmured Bob Cherry. All eyes in the Remove fixed on Billy Bunter. The Bounder gave him a black look.

"O! I—I—I didn't mean Smithy, sir!" stammered Bunter. "I—I mean—I—I—I meant—oh, crikey!"

Really, Billy Bunter could have answered that simple

question, if his fat mind had not been preoccupied. Even Bunter knew about 1066 and all that! But evidently he had been thinking of Smithy, and that name had popped out, as it were.

"What do you mean, Bunter? What——?"

"I—I—I mean—oh, lor'!—I didn't mean—oh, crumbs! —I—I——."

"If you do not answer my question immediately, Bunter——."

"Oh! Yes, sir! I mean, no, sir! But—but—but——."

"But what?" snapped Mr. Quelch.

"I—I—I——I've got something to tell you, sir, if—if you'll let me, sir," stuttered Bunter.

"If you have anything to say to me, Bunter, you may come to my study after class. You may not interrupt a lesson."

"Oh! Yes, sir! I—I was going to tell you before we started, sir, only—only—only——."

"Only what?"

"Only—only I—I—I didn't, sir," gasped Bunter.

"Upon my word!" said Mr. Quelch. He gazed at the fattest member of his form. Perhaps it dawned on Quelch, as it had dawned upon most of the Remove already, that the fat Owl had something on his mind. "I fail to see, Bunter, what you can have to say to me, of sufficient importance to interrupt a lesson. However, you may proceed. What is it?"

"I—I—I——!" stammered Bunter. Now was his chance to get it out. It had been quite easy to fix it up with the Bounder, in No. 4 Study, over a gorgeous spread, with the dazzling prospect of more such spreads to come. But it seemed far from easy under a gimlet-eye in the form-room.

"Well?" rapped Mr. Quelch. "What is it, Bunter?"

"Oh! Nothing, sir!" gasped Bunter. "I—I—I mean I—I mean—n-n-nothing, sir."

"Suffering cats!" murmured Bob Cherry.

Skinner winked at Snoop.

"Jevver hear a man ask for it like that, Snoopey?" he whispered. And Sidney James Snoop giggled.

"Bunter!" The thunder was rolling. "Bunter, you are deliberately wasting time, as it appears that you cannot answer a simple question. Now answer that question at once. Who led the Norman forces——?"

"It was me, sir."

"Eh?"

"Me, sir!" gasped Bunter.

Quelch gazed at him. The whole form gazed at him. This answer, even more remarkable than the former one, brought down the house, as it were. Not that Bunter, of course, meant it as an answer to Quelch's question. He was not thinking of Norman forces, or any sort of forces: he was thinking of his compact with Smithy, and desperately getting it out before his fat courage failed.

"It—it—it was me, sir!" groaned Bunter. "Me all the time, sir! I—I—I—I own up, sir!"

"Must be crackers," murmured Frank Nugent.

"The crackerfulness is terrific."

"Silence in the form! Bunter—you utterly absurd boy——."

"Oh, really, sir——."

"Explain at once what you mean, Bunter." Quelch realised that Bunter could not possibly mean that he had led the Norman forces at the battle of Hastings. He was alluding to some other matter of more recent date.

"I—I—I—I did it, sir!" mumbled Bunter.

"I—I—I—I DID IT, SIR!" MUMBLED BUNTER

"You did what?"

"I—I mean, it was me—me all the time! I—I—I chucked it, sir——."

"You what?"

"I—I mean, I—I threw it, sir——."

"You threw what?"

"The bib-bub-bib-bub—bob——." Bunter seemed afflicted with a stutter. "The bib-bub-bob-bag, sir."

"The bag!" repeated Mr. Quelch, blankly.

"Yes, sir!" gasped Bunter. He gasped with relief. He had got it out at last. "I—I—I'm sorry, sir—I—I—I—I chucked it—I—I mean I throwed it—I mean I threw it out of the window, sir——. I—I own up, sir."

Mr. Quelch gave quite a jump! All the Remove jumped. It was plain now what was on Billy Bunter's fat mind. He was owning up to that reckless prank in No. 4 Study of which Herbert Vernon-Smith had been found guilty and sentenced to a term's Extra.

History, in the Remove form-room, was forgotten. Even Quelch forgot it. The Battle of Hastings, at that moment, was something for which form and form-master couldn't possibly have cared less.

In blank amazement they gazed at Bunter. The Bounder drew a deep breath. He was the only fellow in the form who was not surprised. Most astonished of all were Skinner and Snoop. Skinner, really, could not quite believe his ears. His eyes fairly bulged at Bunter.

"Upon my word!" Quelch found his voice. "Bunter! Are you alluding to the outrageous act that was perpetrated on Wednesday last week, when a bag of flour was flung from the window of a Remove study?"

"Oh, dear! Yes, sir!"

"It was you!" exclaimed Mr. Quelch. "You confess,

Bunter, that it was you who threw that bag from the window of Vernon-Smith's study?"

"Oh, lor'!"

"Answer me, Bunter."

"Yes, sir!" groaned the fat Owl. He was "for it" now, and there was no retreat.

"Upon my word!" repeated Mr. Quelch. "You confess, Bunter, that it was your act, and that you have allowed another boy to bear the blame all this time—that you have caused your form-master to administer an undeserved punishment? Upon my word! I hardly know what to say to you, Bunter."

"I—I—I——."

"You need say no more, Bunter. You will come to my study after this class, and I shall consider how to deal with you."

"I—I——."

"Silence!"

There was deep silence in the Remove form-room. Skinner was still gazing at Bunter like a fellow thunderstruck. But almost everyone else looked at the Bounder. The fellows who had believed his denials could have been counted on the fingers of one hand. And now another fellow had owned up! Nobody in the Remove was likely to guess how and why that had come about. Even Quelch, wary as he was, was not likely to guess that.

"Vernon-Smith." Quelch broke the silence.

"Yes, sir."

"It appears that the act for which you were punished was not your act. I must point out to you, Vernon-Smith, that you have only yourself to blame for the error that was made, as there is no doubt that you kept the bag of flour in your study for some reckless purpose, and you answered

N

untruthfully when questioned on the subject. Nevertheless, it now appears that you were not guilty of the lawless act. Your punishment is, therefore, rescinded."

"Thank you, sir!" said the Bounder.

"We shall now resume!" said Mr. Quelch. With that the matter was dismissed, and English History resumed the tenor of its way in the Remove form-room. But after that dramatic interlude, few fellows found it possible to give much attention to English History: and the hour of dismissal, when it came, had never been so welcome to the Greyfriars Remove.

## CHAPTER 29

# ALL RIGHT FOR BUNTER

"I SAY, you fellows——."

"So it was you!" said Johnny Bull.

"Eh? Oh! Yes! But I say——."

"And you left it on Smithy all this time?" exclaimed Frank Nugent.

"Eh! You see—I—I—I mean——."

"We thought it might have been Bunter," said Bob Cherry. "You remember we looked for him and found him frowsting in the Rag——."

"Oh, really, Cherry——."

"The esteemed and execrable Bunter all the whole," said Hurree Jamset Ram Singh. "Not the absurd Smithy at all."

Harry Wharton eyed the fat Owl curiously. He had believed the Bounder's denial that he was the culprit. But it was a surprise to learn that the culprit was William George Bunter. It was still more surprising that Bunter, being the culprit, had owned up. His confession had extricated Smithy from a very bad scrape: but Bunter was not, as a rule, wont to bother much about other fellows' scrapes.

"You've kept it dark a pretty long time, Bunter," said Harry.

"Oh! Yes! But I say, you fellows——."

"Well, it was decent to own up, even after all this while——."

"Was it?" gasped Bunter. "I—I—I mean, yes, of course—I—I'm a pretty decent chap, you know——."

"You ought to be jolly well kicked," said Squiff.

"Oh, really, Field——."

"We've all been down on Smithy," exclaimed the Australian junior, indignantly. "He was barred from the Soccer, and we all thought it was his own fault! And it was you all the time, you fat owl."

"Blessed if I can half-believe it," said Peter Todd. "Where did Bunter dig up the nerve to buzz a bag at Quelch's nut?"

"I give that one up!" said Bob, "but he jolly well did —and now he's got to go through it with Quelch."

"I—I say, you fellows," stammered Bunter. A crowd of Remove fellows had gathered round the fat Owl at the corner of the corridor, when the form came out. Bunter blinked at them anxiously through his big spectacles. He was due to go to his form-master's study and apparently he was not anticipating that visit with anything like pleasure. "I—I say, Quelch said I was to go to his study——."

"And you'd better go," said Harry.

"Oh! Yes! But—but I—I say, think Quelch will be waxy?" asked Bunter. "Smithy said——!" He broke off, rather suddenly. "I—I—I mean——."

"Eh? What did Smithy say?" asked Toddy.

"Oh! Nothing! I haven't been speaking to Smithy," said Bunter, hastily. "What I mean is, wouldn't Quelch think it jolly decent of a fellow to own up and get another fellow out of a row? Mightn't he let me right off?"

"The mightfulness is terrific," grinned Hurree Jamset Ram Singh.

"I wouldn't bank on that," said Bob. "Beaks, as a rule, don't like bags of flour chucked at their nappers."

"But I—I—I say——."

Vernon-Smith and Tom Redwing came down the

corridor. There was a faintly sarcastic grin on Smithy's face. Redwing was looking very bright. No more than any other Remove fellow had he guessed that Bunter was the culprit. But the fat Owl's confession in the form-room had come as a tremendous relief to him. His chum was out of his scrape now, free to carry on as captain of the Remove without let or hindrance, and without resorting to any lawless or desperate expedient. So, at least, it seemed to Redwing, as to the other fellows. But Redwing frowned as he stopped to speak to Bunter.

"You fat rascal!" he said.

"Oh, really, Redwing——."

"You ought to be booted all over the school," exclaimed Tom. "You all the time, and you let everybody believe that it was Smithy——."

"Well, he's owned up now," said Bob.

"Yes, after leaving it on Smithy all this while, and nearly dishing him over the Soccer! I've a jolly good mind——."

"Here, you keep off, you beast!" exclaimed Billy Bunter, in alarm. "I say, you fellows——."

Vernon-Smith caught Redwing's arm, and walked him on. Smithy had the best of reasons for not sharing his chum's indignation.

"Chuck it, Reddy," he said. "All serene now."

"I've a jolly good mind to boot him——."

"Oh, rot! Leave him alone."

"Mean to say you don't feel like booting the fat villain yourself, Smithy?" exclaimed Redwing.

The Bounder laughed.

"Not at all! Don't you know my gentle and forgivin' nature by this time? It's all clear now, and that's all that matters."

And Smithy walked his chum out into the quad: evidently not desirous at all that that "fat villain" should be booted!

"Beast!" said Bunter, blinking after Redwing as he went. "He wouldn't call me names if he jolly well knew——."

"Well, dash it all, a fellow can't do more than own up, even if he leaves it a little late," said Ogilvy. "I don't envy Bunter seeing Quelch about it."

"Oh, crikey! I—I say, you fellows, Smithy thought——."

"Smithy thought what?"

"Oh! Nothing! But I say, it was pretty decent to own up, wasn't it—frank, and manly, and straightforward, and all that?" said Bunter, anxiously. "Don't you fellows think Quelch might go easy, taking that into account, you know? I don't want to be stuck in Extra for the term, like Smithy was. I mean to say, it wouldn't be worth that, would it?"

"What wouldn't?" asked Bob, staring.

"Oh! Nothing!" said Bunter, hastily. "I—I mean, I—I owned up because—because I did it, you know. I hadn't any other reason."

"We all know you did it, fathead, as you owned up to Quelch," said Nugent.

"Oh! Do you?" gasped Bunter. "I mean, yes, of course. I—I wasn't pulling Quelch's leg, or—or anything of that kind, you know. I—I just owned up because—because it was the right thing to do, being a decent chap, you know. I—I say, do you fellows think that Quelch will look at it like that?"

"Better go and see," grinned Bob. "His temper won't improve if you keep him waiting in his study."

"Oh, lor'!" mumbled Bunter.

He rolled away, at last, with reluctant feet, to his form-master's study.

He had carried out his compact with the Bounder—he had "done his best" for him, as agreed. Smithy was out of his scrape: and the reward was to come, in the shape of spreads in No. 4 Study: that land flowing with milk and honey. That was all right: that was, in fact, extremely attractive. But the interview with Quelch was not attractive: and as he slowly and reluctantly approached the dread apartment, Billy Bunter rather repented him that he had done his best for the Bounder. If Quelch, as Smithy had predicted, decided to "go easy" with a fellow who owned up, it was all right. But if not——! It was a very uneasy fat Owl that tapped at Quelch's study door.

"Come in!"

Slowly, very slowly, a reluctant fat Owl rolled into the study. Mr. Quelch looked at him across his table. To Bunter's immense relief, he was not looking "waxy". His face was very thoughtful, that was all. Had he, after all, decided to "go easy"?

He had!

"Bunter!" said Mr. Quelch. "I have been considering how to deal with you. With regard to the act you committed, and to which you have now confessed, I feel bound to take into consideration the circumstance that you are the stupidest and most utterly obtuse boy in the form——."

"Oh, really, sir——!" gasped Bunter.

"I should certainly punish you severely," went on Mr. Quelch, "but——."

Billy Bunter was glad to hear that there was a "but".

Mr. Quelch paused. The fat Owl hung on his words,

as certainly he had never done in the form-room, when the Remove master went on:

"But," repeated Mr. Quelch, "your confession has prevented an act of injustice to another boy in my form, Bunter."

"Oh!" gasped Bunter. "Yes, sir!"

"You are aware that Vernon-Smith was punished for your act——."

"Oh! No! I—I mean yes——."

"That is now set right," said Mr. Quelch. "That is a matter of very great importance, Bunter."

"Is it, sir?"

"Certainly it is, Bunter," snapped Mr. Quelch, "and I cannot overlook the fact that it is due to your confession, which you have made of your own accord. Having considered the whole matter very carefully, Bunter, I have decided, in view of your voluntary confession, to pardon you."

"Oh!" gasped Bunter. He could hardly trust his fat ears. "Oh! M-m-may I—I go now, sir?"

"You may go, Bunter."

Billy Bunter lost no time in going!

## CHAPTER 30

## TIT FOR TAT!

HARRY WHARTON raised his eyebrows a little.

He was mildly surprised.

Why a sudden dead silence fell in the Rag as he walked into that apartment, was quite unknown to him.

There had been a buzz of voices as he came down the passage, some of them in quite excited tones. But immediately he stepped in, every voice was stilled. The whole crowd of Removites in the room were silent.

He glanced round.

After class, it was known that Herbert Vernon-Smith, captain of the Remove, was to post up the list for Rookwood. The Bounder, as he had declared that he would by hook or crook, was going over to Rookwood with the Greyfriars team on the morrow, to captain the side there. The clouds had rolled by, so far as Smithy was concerned: "Extra" was now a thing of the past. Smithy was no longer the discontented, disgruntled fellow of the past few days: he was full of beans.

A crowd of Remove fellows gathered in the Rag to read the list when it was posted: though most of them could guess, or thought they could guess, how it would run. Smithy was keen to begin his captaincy with a Soccer victory over formidable opponents like Jimmy Silver and Co. of Rookwood: and he had a very accurate eye for a fellow's form. The list was expected to run very much as it would have run had it been posted by the former captain of the Remove: with perhaps one or two minor changes just to show, as it were, that there was a new hand on the steering-wheel.

Harry Wharton had been delayed in the form-room by some of his duties as Head Boy of the form: but as soon as he was through with Quelch, he went along to the Rag. He was interested to see Smithy's list, though he did not expect to find any surprises in it: unless perhaps the Bounder, putting friendship before football, might have selected Tom Redwing in the place of a more useful man.

His glance, as he looked round the Rag, was puzzled. Something, evidently, was "on", of which he had as yet no idea. That "something" had to do with him: every face in the Rag told him as much.

His friends were there: Bob Cherry red, as if with anger: Nugent, Johnny Bull, and the Nabob of Bhanipur looking rather grim. Lord Mauleverer was frowning. Squiff, Peter Todd, Russell, Ogilvy, Mark Linley, and other fellows looked uncomfortable. Tom Redwing looked the very picture of discomfort. Every fellow in the room looked at Harry Wharton: but not a fellow spoke. Really, it was surprising. On the Bounder's face was a smile, and he gave the former captain of the form a vaunting look as he came in. Wharton did not heed it.

"List up, Bob?" he asked.

"Oh! Yes!" stammered Bob.

"Anything else up?" asked Harry, with a smile. It was plain that something was "up".

"Well, yes, rather," muttered Bob.

"The ratherfulness is terrific," murmured Hurree Jamset Ram Singh.

"The cad!" muttered Nugent.

"Trust Smithy to throw his weight about," said Johnny Bull, with a snort. "You'd better look at the list, old man."

Harry Wharton walked across the Rag, to look at the list posted on the wall. All eyes were fixed on him. It was dawning on his mind that there was a surprise in that list: and that it was not going to be a pleasant one—for him! He read it down:

J. Bull.
S. Q. I. Field. P. Todd.
R. Cherry. M. Linley. T. Brown.
R. Penfold. R. D. Ogilvy.
T. Redwing. H. Vernon-Smith. H. J. R. Singh.

It was as good a list as the Greyfriars Remove could have put up for a big fixture: with a single exception. Vernon-Smith had made only one change in the men that his predecessor would have chosen. All the Soccer talent in the Remove was at Smithy's disposal: as it had not been at Wharton's for the Courtfield match. Smithy had given himself Wharton's accustomed place at centre-forward. But Wharton had not been given Smithy's old place at outside-right. Redwing was there: and the former captain of the Remove was not in the list at all.

Harry Wharton understood now why that sudden silence had fallen when he walked into the Rag. The new captain had deliberately left him out: and every fellow in the room was wondering how he was going to take it. Smithy, probably, was expecting an angry outburst: for which he was more than ready. Everyone watched Harry Wharton: even Billy Bunter sat upright instead of sprawling, and blinked at him through his big spectacles.

Wharton, for a long moment, stood very still.

He knew what this meant. This was tit for tat! He had turned Smithy out of the Soccer, for good cause. Smithy was turning him out, in his turn!—for no cause at all, unless personal enmity counted as a cause. Redwing was a good man at Soccer: but even the Bounder would hardly have pretended that he was so useful a man as Wharton in the front line. Evidently the Bounder not only put friendship before football: but enmity also.

Harry Wharton had admitted, to himself and to his friends, that in the affair of the Courtfield match, he had carried matters with too high a hand. In that dispute there had been faults on both sides: and pride had led to a fall. And little as he liked Smithy, he had stood for giving the new captain of the Remove a chance, when it would have been easy for him to "cash in" on Smithy's difficult position. And now——.

For that long moment, while he stood looking at the list, anger and resentment were strong within him. And the remedy was in his own hands. This move of Smithy's was unpopular: that was clear enough. Actually the Bounder had gone too far in his vaunting arrogance. The excluded player could have caused—as Smithy had done before him—a split in the Form and in the team. Perhaps, for that moment, the thought was in Wharton's mind. If so, it was gone the next moment. And whatever he was feeling like, his feelings did not appear in his looks. He turned from the list with an almost expressionless face, and strolled across to rejoin the Co.

Smithy, watching him, realised that no outburst was coming. He was a little disappointed: he would rather have liked a "row".

"Taking it like milk, what?" he muttered to Tom Redwing.

Redwing's face was dark and troubled.

"You're doing wrong, Smithy——," he said, in a low voice.

"Dear me!" said Smithy.

"Take my name out, and put Wharton's in, before there's trouble."

"Likely!" jeered Smithy. "Tit for tat, my dear man. A Roland for an Oliver. Sauce for the goose is sauce for the gander."

"Do you call that sporting?"

The Bounder shrugged his shoulders. Evidently that consideration did not appeal to him very much.

"Like the list, Wharton?" Skinner asked that question, with a wink to Snoop, who grinned.

"Quite a good team, Skinner," answered Harry, unmoved: and he turned his back on Harold Skinner.

"Look here, Harry——!" began Frank Nugent. Wharton displayed no sign of anger or indignation: but Frank was angry and indignant enough for two. "Look here, are we going to stand this?"

"Certainly," answered Harry. "Smithy's captain."

"Oh, don't be a goat!" growled Johnny Bull. "You've only got to say a word, and Smithy would have to climb down fast enough."

"We'll jolly well make him!" said Bob Cherry, savagely.

"The makefulness is the proper caper!" assented Hurree Jamset Ram Singh, with a nod of his dusky head.

"Everyone's against Smithy in this," said Bob. "Look at Squiff, and Toddy, and Linley, and Browney—all of them—you can see what they think——."

"Quite!"

"Well, then——!" said Bob, hotly. "Think we're going to let that rotter get away with this? If you're not in, I'm out, I can tell you, and Smithy can look for another half-back."

"Same here," said Johnny Bull. "I'll tell him to find another goal-keeper."

"The samefulness is terrific!" declared Hurree Jamset Ram Singh. "The esteemed and execrable Smithy can look round for another outside-left."

"And a good many other fellows will say the same!" said Nugent.

Harry Wharton smiled faintly. The indignant remarks of his chums reminded him of the "ultimatum" in No. 1 Study. But his face became grave again at once.

"That won't do," he said, quietly. "That means splitting the team, and leaving everything at sixes and sevens: with very likely a seven-to-one licking at Rookwood to match the one we had from Courtfield. That's Smithy's way—not mine. It won't do for me, or for you fellows either. Soccer comes first."

"But——?" said four fellows in unison.

"Leave it at that!" said Harry. "This Co. always plays the game—and that's the game! Leave it at that."

"Rot!" said Bob.

"Bosh!" said Nugent.

"Rubbish!" growled Johnny Bull.

"Terrific rubbish," said Hurree Jamset Ram Singh.

However, having thus expressed their feelings, the Co. acquiesced: and it was left at that!

## CHAPTER 31

# BUNTER ALL OVER

"WHARTON!"

"Yes, sir!"

"You are not playing football this afternoon?"

"No, sir."

"I trust you are feeling fit, my boy," said Mr. Quelch, benevolently.

"Quite, sir, thank you."

"Your friends, I think, have gone to Rookwood to play."

"Yes, sir."

Harry Wharton coloured faintly. He rather wished that he had not encountered his form-master in his walk in the quad. His position was discomforting enough, without Quelch taking note of it.

It was a bright afternoon, but Harry Wharton's face was not bright. That was hardly to be expected, in the circumstances. Wednesday was Rookwood day: and Harry, like most of the Remove, had taken it for granted that he would be playing Soccer, and helping to beat Jimmy Silver and Co. at the Hampshire school that afternoon. Instead of which, he had watched the footballers roll off to the station, and was left on his own. His friends were playing up, as he had counselled them to do: Smithy was getting all the backing he wanted. Smithy had departed in great spirits: all the more so, perhaps, because he had left his defeated rival so completely out of it. Nugent and several other fellows had gone with the team: Wharton, rather naturally, had not cared to do so. He had intended to fill up the afternoon with a bike ride over to Highcliffe, to see his friends Courtenay and the "Caterpillar": but he had not quite made up his mind, and he was leaning on an old buttress, with his hands in his pockets, thinking not very pleasant thoughts, when Quelch came into the offing.

Mr. Quelch was taking his walk by the path under the study windows—in no danger now of a bag of flour descending on his august head! Quelch was probably thinking of matters much weightier than junior football matches. Still, he was aware of the Rookwood fixture, and aware that his Head Boy was the best junior footballer at Greyfriars: and he was somewhat surprised to see Wharton there, doing nothing while his friends were "urging the flying ball".

He eyed the junior rather sharply.

The recent election in the Remove, and its result, had not pleased Mr. Quelch. But it was not a matter in which he could intervene. Now he could see that there was a spot of trouble somewhere.

But, to Wharton's great relief, he asked no further questions. Quelch had tact: and he could see that the subject was distasteful to the junior. So, after that keen scrutiny, he bestowed a nod on Harry Wharton, and walked on, with a very thoughtful face.

Wharton was glad to see him turn the corner of the building and disappear.

He leaned on the buttress again, after Quelch had gone, his brow moody.

He was thinking of Rookwood, and the Soccer match there. In his mind's eye he pictured the scene: the blue shirts of Greyfriars, the green stripes of Rookwood, mingled on the field of play: Johnny Bull like a rock in the Greyfriars goal, Arthur Edward Lovell of the Rookwood Fourth keeping goal at the other end, and the Bounder, very likely, beating him to it with whizzing ball.

Smithy would be playing the game of his life. He was backed by the best team the Remove could put into the field—with one exception. It would be nothing like the hapless Courtfield match. Smithy and his men were more than likely to beat Rookwood on their own ground: and the Bounder would come back trailing clouds of glory, as it were, after winning the first big fixture of his captaincy.

Everything was going the unscrupulous Bounder's way: while the fellow who "played the game" was left out in the cold, loitering idly while his successful rival gathered laurels: and chiefly because he disdained to imitate his rival's unscrupulous methods. It was a bitter reflection: and no wonder that Harry Wharton's brow clouded as he thought it over.

"Poor old chap!"

That fat squeak interrupted his glum thoughts.

Wharton started as if he had been stung, and looked up—at a fat figure, a fat face, and a pair of big spectacles that glimmered in the sun.

Billy Bunter gave him a commiserating blink.

"Poor old fellow!" he squeaked.

Wharton breathed hard.

"You fat ass——!" he said.

"Oh, really, Wharton——."

"Cut!" snapped Wharton. He was not in want of sympathy: of pity still less, and pity from the egregious fat Owl of the Remove was the limit. He was strongly tempted to detach himself from the buttress, and help Bunter on his way, with a foot on the tightest trousers at Greyfriars.

Billy Bunter did not cut. Wharton was down on his

luck, and the fat Owl was sympathetic: and apparently was going to sympathise, whether the object of his sympathy liked it or not.

"Nothing to get shirty about, old chap," he said. "Here you are, hanging about on your own, while the other chaps are playing Soccer at Rookwood. Puts your nose out of joint a bit, what?"

Wharton breathed harder.

"Brace up," said Bunter, encouragingly. "Don't get down in the mouth—that's not Greyfriars style. Brace up!"

"Will you clear off, Bunter?" asked Harry.

"Eh? Well, I like that!" said Bunter, warmly. "Here you are, looking as if you'd lost a quid and found a farthing, and you can't be civil when a fellow sympathises. Talk about an ungrateful tooth being sharper than a serpent's child! Look here, old chap, don't be stuffy! Have some of these chocs!"

Billy Bunter extended a sticky fat hand, which held a sticky paper bag. The bag was half full of chocolates. Sticky smears round the largest mouth in the Remove indicated that Bunter had already been busy on those chocolates.

"Make you feel better, old chap," said Bunter. "Nothing like stickers to brace a fellow up when he feels down in the mouth, what?"

Harry Wharton laughed involuntarily. A sticky bag of sticky chocolates, in which sticky fingers had been groping, did not appeal to him: neither were "stickers" the consolation to him that they were to Bunter. But the fat Owl's intentions at least were good, and he manfully refrained from kicking him.

"Have some, old chap," urged Bunter. "I've got lots,

and I know where to get more, too!" He chuckled, a fat chuckle. "Help yourself, old fellow! I can tell you they're good—Smithy always has the best, I'll say that for him. He's caked with oof, and chucks it about, you know."

"You fat ass! If you've been grub-raiding in Smithy's study, you can expect to be booted when he comes back from Rookwood."

"He, he, he!" chuckled Bunter. Apparently he was in no dread of the Bounder's boot: though it was clear that that bag of chocolates had come from No. 4 Study: and Smithy, as a rule, was far less tolerant of Bunter's peculiar manners and customs than Harry Wharton and Co.

The fat Owl helped himself from the bag, and munched.

"That's all right, old chap," he said, reassuringly. "Don't you worry! Look here, have some! They're topping! I say, it was a bit thick Smithy edging you out of the Soccer like that! But cheer up. Look here, I'll put in a word for you with Smithy, if you like. What about that?"

"You fat ass!"

"Well, Smithy's skipper now, and what he says, goes," said Bunter. "And there's the St. Jim's match in a week or two. Smithy doesn't mean to let you have much of a show in the Soccer. But I might put in a word for you," said Bunter, benevolently. "I do pity you, old chap!" Probably Billy Bunter rather enjoyed "pitying" the late captain of the Remove.

"Roll away, you fat chump!"

"You needn't be shirty, because a chap pities you when you're down and out," said the fat Owl, reprovingly. "Won't you have some of these chocs? I can jolly well get lots, if I want them."

"No: and you'd better look out for Smithy's boot,

when he comes back and misses them from his study."

Billy Bunter chuckled again.

"Catch Smithy booting a chap, after all a chap's done for him!" he grinned. "Not likely! He, he, he! One good turn deserves another, what? Why, Smithy wouldn't be playing Soccer at Rookwood this very minute, if I hadn't pulled Quelch's leg——."

"What?"

"I—I mean, if I—I hadn't owned up," amended Bunter, hastily. "I—I wasn't pulling Quelch's leg when I owned up, of—of course. I—I owned up because—because I did it, just as I told Quelch! I wasn't spoofing him——."

"Spoofing him!" repeated Harry, blankly.

"Nothing of the kind, and Smithy never had anything to do with it. Besides, he told me to keep it dark, and I'm jolly well going to."

"You fat villain——."

"Oh, really, Wharton——."

"Oh, scissors!" Wharton stared quite blankly at the fat Owl. Not for a moment had it occurred to him, or to any Remove fellow, or even to the wary Remove master, that Billy Bunter's "confession" in the form-room had been anything but genuine. It had caused surprise: but not suspicion. But now——! "Oh, you fat rotter! So it was all gammon, and Smithy put you up to it——."

"No!" gasped Bunter. "Nothing of the sort! I say, don't you get saying that Smithy put me up to it—Quelch might get to hear. Besides, he—he—he didn't, you know. Smithy never said a word to me about it." Bunter was aware that his compact with the Bounder had to be kept a secret. He had his own inimitable way of keeping secrets! "Not a word!" continued Bunter, blinking anxiously at Harry Wharton. "He never asked me into his study, and never stood me a spread, and never said it was a lark to pull Quelch's leg, or—or anything! He never——."

"Shut up!" exclaimed Harry Wharton, hastily, as a tall, angular figure turned the corner of the building. Quelch was coming back.

But Billy Bunter's back was to that angular figure, and he was unaware of Quelch. He did not shut up. Shutting up never was much in Bunter's line, anyway.

"I tell you he never!" howled Bunter. "Don't you get saying that Smithy put me up to pulling Quelch's leg—why, I should get into a fearful row if Quelch heard—he would be in a frightful wax if he knew that Smithy put me up to owning up about what Smithy did——."

"BUNTER!"

"Oh, crikey!"

Billy Bunter spun round like a humming-top at that unexpected voice. His eyes almost popped through his spectacles at Mr. Quelch.

He gazed at him in horror! Quelch had heard! He could see that Quelch had heard! The expression on Quelch's speaking countenance gave every indication of a "frightful wax". Bunter could only gaze at him, as no doubt Priam gazed at the dread figure that drew his curtains at dead of night.

"BUNTER!"

"Oh, lor'!"

"I heard what you said, Bunter."

"Oh, jiminy!"

"Follow me to my study, Bunter."

"Oh, crumbs!"

Quelch swept on. After him rolled a dismal, dismayed, disconsolate fat Owl. Harry Wharton was left staring after them and wondering what was going to happen now.

## CHAPTER 32

# QUELCH SEES IT ALL

"BUNTER!"

"Oh, crikey!"

Billy Bunter quaked.

He had reason to quake.

His fat knees knocked together—his little fat legs almost refused to support him, as he stood before his form-master, in Quelch's study.

The expression on Quelch's face was positively terrifying. It was unnerving. It was petrifying.

Quelch had been seen in a "bait" before. Quite often his brows were knitted in a frown. Not infrequently the gimlet-eyes glinted under those knitted brows. But never before had Billy Bunter seen his form-master looking so grim as he looked now. Rhadamanthus, in his most rhadamanthine mood, could scarcely have looked grimmer.

"Bunter!" Mr. Quelch's voice was not loud, but deep. "Bunter! It appears that you have deceived me!"

"Oh! No, sir!" gasped Bunter. "I—I wouldn't, sir! I—I—I——."

"Yesterday," said Mr. Quelch, "you confessed in the form-room that it was you, Bunter, who threw the bag of flour from the window of a Remove study."

"Oh! Yes, sir!" groaned Bunter. "I—I—I owned up, sir—I—I—I——."

"Believing your statement, Bunter, I dealt with you very leniently. And it now appears that there was not a word of truth in that statement!" said Mr. Quelch, sternly. "You had the audacity, the unscrupulousness, to make an utterly unfounded statement, for the purpose of deluding your form-master, and enabling another boy to escape a just punishment."

"I—I—I——!" babbled the fat Owl. "I—I—I didn't——."

"What?"

"I—I mean, I—I wasn't—I—I never—I—I—I—it was only a lark, sir," groaned Bunter. "Smithy said it would be a lark——. I—I mean, Smithy never said anything, sir—not a word! I—I did it voluntaciously, sir."

At any other time, Quelch certainly would have pounced upon that remarkable adverb. Now it passed unheeded.

"Bunter——!"

"Oh, dear! Yes, sir! Ca-c-c-can I go now, sir?"

"Do you venture to repeat, Bunter, your statement in the form-room yesterday, that it was you who committed the act for which Vernon-Smith was punished?" thundered Mr. Quelch.

"Oh, crikey! I—I mean, yes, sir——."

"What?"

"I—I—I mean, no, sir!" gasped Bunter, in a hurry.

Billy Bunter was not very particular about the truth. He had, indeed, hardly a nodding acquaintance with it. Fibbing was his great resource. But under that grim glare, that resource failed him.

"It was not your act, Bunter?"

"Nunno, sir!" groaned Bunter.

"And why did you confess to an act that was not your own, Bunter?"

"I—I—I——."

"Answer me, Bunter."

"I—I—I told Smithy I'd do my best for him, sir—oh, lor'! I—I wish I—I hadn't now," groaned Bunter. I—I—it was only a—a—a lark, sir!"

Mr. Quelch stood looking at him. Until ten minutes ago he had not had a suspicion of the truth. It was now, of course, quite clear to him. But the hapless stammering Owl was not the chief object of his wrath. Bunter had been nothing more than a catspaw in wily unscrupulous hands. Quelch, angry as he was, could make allowances for the unlimited obtuseness of William George Bunter. Obviously Bunter had not thought out this amazing deception himself: indeed, he could have had no motive in doing so. Bunter had been merely a puppet with a cunning hand pulling the strings. It was Herbert Vernon-Smith who had thought out this scheme, unscrupulously making use of Bunter, the only fellow in the Remove obtuse enough for such a purpose. Quelch saw it all now!

And that young rascal, Vernon-Smith, had gone off to Rookwood to play football, instead of sitting in Extra: laughing in his sleeve at the "beak" he had so easily deluded!

Quelch breathed hard, and he breathed deep.

Billy Bunter eyed him, through his big spectacles, with a terrified blink. As Quelch did not speak, the fat Owl ventured to edge towards the door. A sharp rap from his form-master stopped him.

"Bunter!"

"Oh! Yes, sir!" gasped Bunter.

"The matter is clear now," said Mr. Quelch. "You were induced to make an unfounded confession by a boy more cunning than yourself, who made unscrupulous use of your foolishness, your obtuseness, your almost unexampled stupidity. I shall take this into consideration, Bunter, in dealing with you."

"Oh! Thank you, sir!" gasped Bunter. Billy Bunter was far from recognising that description as just. He was happily unaware of the foolishness, the obtuseness, and the unexampled stupidity, to which Mr. Quelch alluded. But he was glad at least that there was something to be taken into consideration, and his fat face brightened. "M-m-may I go now, sir?"

"You may not!" answered Mr. Quelch, grimly. "I shall, as I have said, take your almost incredible foolishness into consideration, Bunter, and your punishment will be less severe than that of the unscrupulous boy who prompted you to this deception. I shall cane you——."

"Oh, lor'!"

"—severely——!"

"Ow!"

Mr. Quelch picked up a cane from his table. Billy Bunter watched that proceeding with the deepest apprehension. The Remove master pointed to a chair with the cane.

"Bunter! Bend over that chair!"

"Oh, crikey!"

"At once!" thundered Mr. Quelch.

In the lowest possible spirits, Billy Bunter bent over the chair. The cane swished and descended. Billy Bunter's tight trousers fairly rang under the swipe.

"Wow!" roared Bunter.

Swipe!

"Yow!"

Swipe!

"Yarooooh!"

Billy Bunter had been "whopped" before: often, though

not so often as he had deserved. But he had never had it like this before! Quelch was putting his beef into it. Apparently he thought it his duty to be severe in this flagrant case: and Quelch was a whale on duty. He was running no risk of spoiling Bunter by sparing the rod!

Swipe!

"Yow-ow-ow-ow-ow!"

Swipe!

"Yooo-hoooooop!"

Swipe!

It was six of the best—the very best! Billy Bunter had "done his best" for Smithy, to Smithy's satisfaction. Now Quelch had done his best for Bunter—not in the least to Bunter's satisfaction! The final swipe of the six evoked a roar that must have awakened most of the echoes in Masters' Studies.

"Now, Bunter——."

"Yow-ow-ow-ow!"

"Let that be a warning to you, Bunter——."

"Wow! wow! wow!"

"Cease those ridiculous noises at once, Bunter——."

"Ooooooooooooooooooh!" Bunter seemed to find some difficulty in ceasing the ridiculous noises.

"And leave my study."

"Ow-ow-ow-wow-wow-wow!"

A mumbling fat Owl rolled out of the study, and wriggled away down the passage like a fat eel. Sounds of woe floated back as Bunter departed.

Mr. Quelch did not heed them. He was done with Bunter, and he dismissed him from mind. He laid the cane on the table, and stood in thought—grim thought! Bunter was punished and done with: but Vernon-Smith? Grimmer and grimmer grew Quelch's brow as he thought of

Vernon-Smith: the wily, wary, unscrupulous young rascal who had engineered this deception: who had made a fool of his form-master, and gone off to play football, no doubt laughing in his sleeve. He would be dealt with later: but at the moment, he was out of reach—free to enjoy the success of his deception, free to do as he liked, regardless of authority, regardless of an angry master whom he had fooled and flouted—out of reach——.

But was he?

Mr. Quelch's eyes turned to the telephone. He stepped across to that instrument, and grasped the receiver off the hooks. A few moments, and he was asking for a trunk call to Rookwood School. Quelch had been fooled: but he was not the man to be flouted! He had something to say to the head-master of Rookwood.

Billy Bunter had "done his best" for the Bounder. Really, he might as well have done his worst!

## CHAPTER 33

# ORDERED OFF!

"GOAL!"

"Good old Smithy!"

"Bravo!"

"Goal!"

It was like wine to the Bounder.

That afternoon, Smithy was enjoying life to the very full. His luck, which had always been phenomenal, had held out: everything, after all, was going his way. He was captaining the Greyfriars junior side at Rookwood: and he was backed up by as good a team as he would have wished for. Even his mistakes seemed to be turning out well. Every man in the team disapproved of his choice of Tom Redwing, and the exclusion of Harry Wharton, even Redwing himself: less a mistake than an exercise of arrogant self-will. Yet it was turning up trumps: for it was from a pass from Redwing on the right wing, that Smithy had just scored—sending in the leather with a whizzing shot that beat Arthur Edward Lovell, in the Rookwood goal, all the way.

It was close on half-time.

Jimmy Silver and Co. of Rookwood were in great form. They were playing a hard and strenuous game. But the Greyfriars team seemed just the necessary little bit the better. The Bounder himself was at the top of his form: and at the top of his form, Smithy was very good indeed. Greyfriars were attacking most of the time, and again and again the green shirts had to fall back: though they lost no opportunity of coming on again. Johnny Bull, when called upon, saved with almost automatic precision, but he did not have a great deal to do: it was very unlike his experience in the unlucky Courtfield match. But the Rookwooders, if they could not get through, were at least strong in defence, and it was near half-time when the first goal was scored—for Greyfriars.

"Goal!"

There were six or seven Greyfriars fellows among the crowd of Rookwooders round the field, and they all yelled "Goal!" at the top of their voices. Frank Nugent's voice was as loud as the rest. His chum's exclusion from the team irked him sorely: and he felt, in point of fact, more disposed to punch Smithy than to cheer him. But when Smithy, taking the pass from Redwing, made one of his lightning dashes, winding through the defence as if by magic, leaving the backs standing, and slammed the leather into the net, in spite of all the custodian could do, Frank, like the Tuscans of old, could not forbear a cheer!

"Goal! Good old Smithy!"

The Bounder grinned breathlessly. This was what he had dreamed of. Captain of the Remove: his rival down and out, kicking his heels at Greyfriars while Smithy led the team to victory. Nothing succeeds like success! Discontented voices would be silenced, when the first big fixture of Smithy's captaincy ended in victory on the Rookwood ground. Redwing had warned him that unscrupulous trickery could never turn out well in the long run. The Bounder, if he had remembered it at that moment, would have laughed! It was turning out all right so far, at all events.

The sides lined up again for the brief remainder of the first half. The Bounder's eyes were gleaming. He was feeling on top of the world. In the seven or eight minutes before the referee blew the whistle for half-time, he hoped for, or rather felt assured of, another score. This was his "day": the game was wax in his hands!

He had no eyes for anything but the game, and did not see Mr. Richard Dalton, the master of the Rookwood Fourth, come down to the ground. Richard Dalton, a young man and a keen footballer, generally alluded to by his form as "Dicky", often gave the junior matches a look-in. But on this occasion his face was extremely grave, as if some weightier matter than Soccer was on his mind. He stood looking on for a minute or two, and then tapped Frank Nugent on the shoulder. Nugent looked round.

"There is a boy named Vernon-Smith in the team from your school, I think," said the Rookwood master.

"Yes: he is playing centre-forward to-day," answered Frank.

Mr. Dalton nodded, and fixed his eyes on the Greyfriars centre-forward. Smithy had the ball, and was coming up the field with another of his lightning dashes. But this time it did not come off: Jimmy Silver, the Rookwood centre-half, took it fairly from his toe, and sent it away into the visitors' territory, followed by the Rookwood forwards. For a second, a dark scowl flashed over the Bounder's face: noted by the Rookwood master who was looking at him. The Bounder was never a good loser.

Frank Nugent turned back to watch the game, but the corner of his eye was on Dalton. Why the Rookwood master was there, with that extremely grave expression on his face, Frank could not guess, but he had a feeling that something was amiss. Rookwood fellows were glancing at Mr. Dalton, as if wondering what was "up". Once he looked at his watch, and seemed to hesitate: then he settled down to wait for the finish of the half, which was a matter of only a few minutes now.

Greyfriars were attacking again, coming down on the Rookwood goal in great style, when the whistle went. It had looked, to the Bounder at least, like another score: and his brows knitted for a moment, as Bulkeley of the Rookwood Sixth, the referee, blew the whistle. Mr. Dalton made a movement, as play ceased, and called out to the referee.

"Bulkeley!"

The Rookwood Sixth-former looked round.

"Yes, sir. What——?"

"I must speak to one of the Greyfriars men—Vernon-Smith! Please ask him to come here to me."

Bulkeley stared for a moment, in surprise, and then called to Vernon-Smith. The Bounder stared, too. He knew Richard Dalton by sight, and knew that he was master of Jimmy Silver's form. But what a Rookwood master could possibly have to say to him, in the middle of a football match, was beyond his guessing. However, he came across to Mr. Dalton.

"You wanted to speak to me," he said, not very politely.

"You are Herbert Vernon-Smith?"

"Yes."

"Then I am sorry to say that you must come off the field now, and cannot continue to play in this match."

The Bounder stared at him, dumbfounded.

"Wha-at?" he stuttered.

There were stares and exclamations on all sides. Greyfriars and Rookwood men stared, equally amazed. Everyone within hearing of Mr. Dalton's voice stared blankly.

"What on earth's up?" muttered Bob Cherry.

"Smithy can't go off," said Squiff. "What does the man mean? Is he wandering in his mind, or what?"

"Must be crackers!" grunted Johnny Bull.

"The crackerfulness must be terrific," murmured Hurree Jamset Ram Singh.

"Smithy!" breathed Tom Redwing. "What——!"

Jimmy Silver weighed in, in amazement and dismay. "Mr. Dalton, we're in the middle of a match. What is the matter? What——?"

"I am very sorry indeed to have to take this action," said Mr. Dalton. "I am acting under the instructions of your head-master, Silver. Dr. Chisholm has requested me to come here and take Vernon-Smith away, in consequence of a message received by telephone from his school."

"Oh!" gasped Jimmy.

It was clear that Richard Dalton was performing an unpalatable task. But he had to perform it. There was wonder and dismay in all faces—in the Bounder's rage as well as amazement.

"I am sorry, Vernon-Smith," said Mr. Dalton, quite gently, "but you must change at once and come with me."

The Bounder's eyes blazed.

"I'll do nothing of the kind." He almost shouted. "Do you think you can walk a man off in the middle of a match? I'm captain of this team——."

"But what's happened, sir?" exclaimed Tom Redwing. "There must be some mistake—or what has happened——?"

"Some silly mistake——!" hissed the Bounder.

"There is no mistake, I fear," said Mr. Dalton, quietly. "You are here to play in this match without leave, Vernon-Smith——."

"It's not true! I have leave, like the rest—every fellow here knows——."

"That's so, sir," said Bob.

"We all know——!" said Peter Todd.

"The knowfulness is terrific."

"There's some mistake——," said Redwing. "There must be."

"Vernon-Smith is here without leave!" repeated Mr. Dalton. "From what we are told, from Greyfriars, he was under detention for some act of insubordination, and obtained leave by inducing another boy to make an untrue confession of that act——."

"Oh!" panted Redwing.

"Oh!" breathed the Bounder. He understood now. Something had come out, since the team had left Greyfriars: his trickery had come home to roost, as it were, at the most inopportune moment.

"Great pip!" murmured Bob Cherry. "Then Bunter——!"

All the Greyfriars fellows understood, now. What Mr. Dalton said could only refer to the "owning-up" of the fat and fatuous Owl of the Remove.

"Oh, Smithy!" muttered Tom Redwing, miserably. "Did you——?"

The Bounder did not heed him.

"I'm not going!" His voice rang out sharply and savagely. "I'll go back when the game's over—I won't stir a step before the whistle. I mean that!"

Mr. Dalton compressed his lips.

"You will come away at once," he said. "I am sorry, but Dr. Chisholm cannot permit a truant to remain here, in defiance of authority at his own school. Please go in and change at once, Vernon-Smith."

"I won't!"

The Bounder clenched his hands, wild with rage and chagrin. Not for a moment had he dreamed of anything like this. Now the utter failure of his scheming, the utter and hopeless collapse of his plans, overwhelmed him.

He knew what awaited him at Greyfriars: an incensed form-master, a stern head-master, as likely as not the "sack" for what he had done. He knew very well what view Dr. Locke would take of Bunter's bogus confession. But his stubborn spirit rose fiercely in the midst of disaster. All that he had planned was coming down about his ears like a house of cards: unscrupulous trickery did not, after all, pay in the long run. He was quite reckless now: reckless and desperate.

"I won't! Do you hear? I won't go!" He shouted out the words. "I'm here to captain my side in this match, and I'm playing it out! I won't go."

"Smithy——," muttered Redwing.

"Look here, Smithy——!" exclaimed Bob Cherry.

"Don't make a scene here, Smithy," growled Johnny Bull.

The Bounder cared little whether he made a "scene" or not. What the Rookwood men might think of all this was nothing to him.

"You must go, and at once," said Mr. Dalton, quietly. "Your return to your school is demanded, without a moment's delay, Vernon-Smith. There is no alternative."

"I'll go when the match is over, if you like——."

"You must go now!"

"I won't!"

"The match will not be allowed to proceed with you playing in it," said Mr. Dalton. "It will be stopped, by my order, unless you leave the field immediately."

"Oh!" panted the Bounder.

In his rage and excitement he did not realise, or did not care, that Mr. Dalton could, and doubtless would, have marched him off with a hand on his shoulder, if that extreme step had been needed.

But it was not needed. Savagely enraged as he was, ready for any act of defiance or mutiny, utterly reckless of consequences, Vernon-Smith had to realise that his game was up. The Rookwood match was at an end so far as he was concerned. If the match went on at all, it had to go on without him. Jimmy Silver and Co. could not carry on if Dalton stopped the match.

The hapless Bounder stood still and silent. He was beaten, and he knew it now. He cast a glance at the other Greyfriars men—only in Tom Redwing's face was there anything like sympathy. Every other face was hostile. A scene like this on the football ground of another school: a player, and he the captain of the side, ordered off in the middle of a match: it was more than enough to put all backs up. Never in the history of Soccer could any football team have been so utterly and thoroughly fed up with their captain.

"Come!" said Mr. Dalton.

There was no help for it: the Bounder had to go. For a moment or two more he hesitated. But it was useless: and with a white and furious face, he followed the Rookwood master. When the whistle went for the second half, the Greyfriars side lined up a man short.

## CHAPTER 34

## FOR IT!

HARRY WHARTON stared, in surprise.

"Smithy!" he ejaculated.

He had not expected to see the Bounder at Greyfriars so soon.

Wharton had been out of gates, filling in a rather weary afternoon with a visit to Highcliffe. He had returned in good time for lock-up, but not expecting to see anything of the footballers yet: the team were not expected back from Rookwood till a much later hour. But, coming away from the bike-shed, he noted a little crowd gathered in the quad, and in the midst of them, Herbert Vernon-Smith. The footballers, certainly, had not come back yet: but it seemed that their captain had, on his own, and Wharton wondered what had happened—having no knowledge, so far, of Quelch's performance on the telephone.

A dozen fellows were staring at Smithy. Skinner, among them, was grinning, as if amused: but Russell, Wibley, Snoop, Bolsover major, and the others, were only surprised and curious. Smithy had tramped in at the gates, with knitted brows and glinting eyes, obviously in the worst temper ever, and not making the slightest effort to conceal that fact. Everyone at Greyfriars, and everyone in the county of Kent, for that matter, was welcome to note that Smithy was in a state of smouldering rage: the Bounder did not care.

Three or four fellows were asking him questions, all at once, but Vernon-Smith did not take the trouble to answer one of them. He tramped on towards the House, with the little crowd round him, in savage silence. But as he caught sight of Harry Wharton, his eyes flamed, and he pushed roughly through the juniors, and came towards Wharton, his hands clenched. Skinner winked at Snoop, and Snoop grinned. Smithy, evidently, was in a mood for a "row", and Wharton had turned up in happy time for it!

"Wharton! You rotter——!"

Harry Wharton raised his eyebrows.

Something, evidently, had gone wrong at Rookwood. The Bounder had returned early, and returned alone. But why he was in so savage a temper, and why he specially was the object of it, Wharton did not know, and cared little.

"Did you wangle this?" breathed the Bounder. "After all your gammon, you've dished me at the finish——."

"I'm quite unaware of it," answered Harry. "If you'll explain what you mean—that is, if you mean anything——."

"You know without my telling you."

"Not in the least! Has anything happened at Rookwood?" Harry Wharton was quite perplexed. "Haven't you played the match, or what? You seem to have come back on your own——."

"As you expected!" breathed the Bounder. "You jolly well know that Quelch phoned Rookwood, when he found out that Bunter had pulled his leg——."

"Oh!" exclaimed Harry. He began to understand. "No, I never knew that Quelch had phoned Rookwood, but I'm not surprised if he did, after he found out that you had put Bunter up to bamboozle him——."

"And how did he find out?" hissed Smithy. "Bunter

never told—he wouldn't dare, if he'd wanted to. Did you get it out of Bunter and tell Quelch?"

Harry Wharton's lip curled.

The Bounder eyed him with savage suspicion. All the way home in the train he had been thinking of it, brooding over it, in helpless dismay and rage: unable to account for his plans having gone so disastrously wrong, but suspecting an enemy's hand. His triumph had turned to dust and ashes: instead of coming back from Rookwood, as he had anticipated, with a victorious team, trailing clouds of glory, he had had to leave an unfinished match, leaving his men to play a losing game out—coming back in disgrace, to face a stern head-master and answer for what he had done, with as likely as not the "sack" in prospect! He had no doubt—or rather was determined to have no doubt—that his rival had worked this somehow. He could think of nothing else: and it was like him to be able to think of nothing else.

"Did you——?" His voice was a snarl, and his hands were clenched convulsively, as if he could barely refrain from dashing them into the face before him. "You've been watching for a chance to get your own back—think I didn't know that, with all your gammon? Did you——?"

"Don't be a fool, and a cad as well," answered Harry Wharton. "I never dreamed that Bunter was put up to pull Quelch's leg, any more than any other fellow did: and if I had known, I should not have said a word to Quelch, as you know as well as I do."

"Then how——?"

"That's easy! Bunter babbled it out, and Quelch heard him—that's how he knew."

"Oh!" panted the Bounder. "That fat fool——!"

"Nobody would have said a word to Quelch," said

Harry. "He heard Bunter burbling and marched him off to his study: and I've no doubt got the whole story out of him. But I'll tell you this, Herbert Vernon-Smith, that it serves you jolly well right, and that you've asked for what's coming to you. You put up that silly fathead to tell Quelch a string of lies—the only fellow in the form who was fool enough for you to make use of him like that, and it was a rotten thing to do. I believe you never did what you were nailed for, but getting that fat ass to tell a lying tale about it—pah! You make me sick. You ought to be sacked."

"Vernon-Smith!"

It was Mr. Quelch's voice.

The Remove master had come out of the House, no doubt having observed the Bounder from his study window. Sudden silence fell on the little crowd of juniors as he came. His face was like iron. One glance at that face was enough to reveal that the scapegrace of Greyfriars had the worst to expect, now that he had come back to face the music.

The Bounder looked at him, his heart sinking. He was ready, indeed eager, to wreak his rage and disappointment upon his rival, or upon anyone else: ready to quarrel with foe or friend. But even in that savage and reckless mood, that grim face daunted him.

"So you have returned, Vernon-Smith!" said Mr. Quelch, icily.

"Yes, sir!" muttered Smithy.

"Your head-master is prepared to deal with you, Vernon-Smith. You will follow me to Dr. Locke's study."

The smouldering rage had died out of the Bounder's face, and he looked almost haggard. Perhaps he had had a hope that his form-master would keep the matter in his own hands, and deal with it himself. The severest "six" that had ever been handed out at Greyfriars would have been a light matter to the hardy Bounder, compared with going up to the Head. But if he had had that hope, it had been a faint one. The matter was too serious for that. He was going up to his head-master for judgment: and what was that judgment likely to be?

In silence, he followed Mr. Quelch.

Harry Wharton stood looking after him, as he went, his expression changing. He had told the Bounder that he ought to be sacked: but as it was borne in upon his mind that Smithy actually was going up to the Head to be expelled from Greyfriars School, it came as a shock to him. Smithy had his good qualities, as well as his bad ones, though of late he had shown little of them. He had filled a prominent place in the life of the Greyfriars Remove: even fellows who did not like him, would miss him, when he went. He had made himself Wharton's enemy, but at that moment, Harry could feel only compassion. He would willingly have helped the luckless fellow, if he could.

But there was nothing he could do. He believed that Smithy had not done the act for which he had been "nailed": but his belief availed nothing. If that could have been proved, no doubt it would have helped Smithy now: but there was no hope of that.

"By gum!" Bolsover major was speaking. "This looks like the finish for Smithy here."

"If you have tears, my beloved 'earers, prepare to shed them now!" remarked Skinner, satirically.

"Oh, shut up, Skinner," muttered Snoop, for once out of accord with his pal. "Smithy's down and out, and it's pretty thick."

Skinner stared at him, and then linked arms with him, and walked him away. Snoop was evidently troubled in mind: and perhaps Skinner was uneasy lest he might say too much, in the hearing of other fellows.

Harry Wharton did not heed them. He watched the Bounder disappear into the House with his form-master, and then walked away, with a clouded brow. Smithy was "for it": there could be no doubt of that: and yet, in a way, he had had hard measure, if he really was innocent of the act for which he had been given Extra School: and Wharton believed that he was. He had been hard, arrogant, malicious, cynically unscrupulous: and now he had to pay scot and lot, for what he had done, and for what he was believed to have done. No doubt he had himself to blame, from start to finish: but——.

If he went, it was certain that Harry Wharton would soon be back in his old place: captain of the Remove. But Wharton was not thinking of that, or of the Bounder's enmity, or his wretched suspicions and bitter words. He was thinking of the reckless scapegrace, brought to book at last, standing downcast before his head-master: and he wished from the bottom of his heart that he could have given him a helping hand.

## CHAPTER 35

## LIGHT AT LAST!

BILLY BUNTER pricked up his fat ears.

Bunter was astonished.

And he was interested.

For a considerable time, after that painful interview in his form-master's study, the Owl of the Remove had been interested in absolutely nothing. Even food had lost its appeal for him. His chief activities had been twisting and mumbling. Indeed, it might have been supposed that he was understudying the young man of Hythe, who sat down on a scythe, and did nothing but wriggle and writhe!

But Time is a great healer!

After a couple of hours the worst effects of that "six" had worn off, though the fat junior was still feeling painful twinges. But he was feeling better. He was still disinclined to sit down: his accustomed armchair in the Rag did not attract him. At the present moment, he was leaning on the trunk of a massive old elm near the school wall.

Bunter seldom stood up if it was possible to sit down. But as the lingering effects of that six made sitting down uncomfortable, he had to stand: so, as he had to stand, he leaned!

Leaning his podgy back on the tree trunk, he was even beginning to find a little solace by groping in sticky pockets for remaining chocolates, when footsteps and voices on the other side of the tree impinged on his fat ears.

Two fellows were coming along the path under the wall, on the other side of that big elm. They were speaking as they came, and Bunter recognised the voices of Skinner and Snoop: and had no doubt that the two young rascals were seeking a quiet spot to smoke cigarettes: which did not interest him at all. But he was interested all of a sudden, as Snoop's voice came, quite near at hand:

"It's too jolly thick, Skinner! There's a limit! Smithy's up for the sack—you could see that in Quelch's face, and it was you buzzed that bag at Quelch, as I know if nobody else does——."

"Quiet, you dummy."

"Oh, rot! There's nobody to hear us—that's why you walked me off here, because you were afraid I might let something out——."

"You'd better not! You've kept this dark for a week, and you're going on keeping it dark, Sidney Snoop."

"Letting a fellow get sacked for what you did——."

"Quiet, I tell you."

Billy Bunter's little round eyes opened wide behind his big round spectacles. There was a sticky chocolate in a sticky paw, half-way to a sticky mouth. But in his astonishment, he forgot that chocolate: and it remained half-way on its journey: suspended, as it were, like Mahomet's coffin, between the heavens and the earth.

"Oh, crikey!" breathed the fat Owl, inaudibly.

Up to that moment, Bunter had believed, like almost everyone else, that Smithy had "done it". True, he had himself "owned up" to having "done it": dazzling vistas of unlimited tuck had tempted him, and he had fallen! Certainly he had never thought of Skinner in connection with the affair in No. 4 Study.

And now——! He was making discoveries now!

"Keep your mouth shut, Snoopey." Skinner's low voice was going on. "I only did what Smithy had planned to do

—he had that bag all ready, and Quelch would have got it on his nut if Redwing hadn't butted in, as I've told you——."

"I know! But Smithy never did it, and you did! I know he let us down, after the election, and that he chucks his weight about now that he's captain of the form, and I don't like him any more than you do. But I tell you there's a limit—I—I can't stand for this—they're going to sack the cap——."

"That's why I've brought you here to speak to you, on the quiet," said Skinner, in the same low tone. "You're going to keep mum, Snoopey. Smithy isn't going to be sacked for buzzing that bag at Quelch—he got Extra for that, and that's all he would have got, if he hadn't put Bunter up to pulling Quelch's leg about it. Did I have anything to do with that?"

"Well, no: but——."

"He must have bribed that fat rotter, somehow, to tell lies for him," said Skinner, "and that's what he's up for now. Nothing to do with me, or with you either."

"If they knew that he hadn't done what he was put in Extra for——."

"Well, they don't, and won't! Don't go!" Snoop had made a movement to walk away. "Stick where you are, Snoopey, till we settle this. You're not going to give a pal away."

"I—I ain't going to give you away, Skinner. But—but—look here, I tell you it's too thick," muttered Snoop. "Smithy's up before the Head now——."

"He's asked for it."

"I know! But—but—it all comes out of what you did, and you can't let a man be turfed out of the school because of what you did—it's too jolly rotten. You ought to go to Quelch before it's too late——."

"And own up?" sneered Skinner. "Would you, Snoopey?"

"Yes, I jolly well would, now it's come to this," said Snoop. "You can't let it go on, Skinner, when a word from you——."

"Talk sense!"

"You're not going to say anything?"

"Not a syllable! And you're not, either! And——." Skinner was suddenly interrupted by a startling and unexpected sound from the other side of the tree under which the two were standing.

"Wow!"

Billy Bunter had not intended to ejaculate "Wow!" He was too interested in that conversation to wish to interrupt it. He did so involuntarily, as he felt a sudden twinge. That sudden twinge caused him to ejaculate "Wow!" quite unintentionally.

Skinner jumped, almost clear of the ground. The next moment, he was coming round the massive trunk of the elm, with mingled alarm and fury in his face. Snoop followed him, staring.

"You!" breathed Skinner. The look on his face made the fat Owl of the Remove palpitate with alarm. His eyes popped at Skinner.

"I—I—I say, I—I wasn't listening," gasped Bunter. "I—I never heard a word that you and Snoop were saying——."

"You heard——!" Skinner almost choked.

"Not a word!" gasped Bunter. "I—I didn't even know you were there, old chap, and I—I never heard Snoop say you buzzed that bag at Quelch, and—Yaroooh! Keep off!" yelled Bunter. "Oh, crikey! Yarooooh!"

Billy Bunter fled under the elms as if for his fat life. After him rushed Skinner. In his alarm and rage, he hardly knew what he intended to do—whether to attempt to persuade Bunter to silence, or to punch the fat eaves-dropper till his arm ached. Snoop was left staring, as Billy Bunter flew, and Skinner flew in pursuit.

Seldom did William George Bunter put on speed. But on the present occasion an arrow in its flight had little or nothing on Bunter. An enraged fellow rushing on his track with clenched fists and blazing eyes was more than enough to make the fat Owl stamp on the gas, as it were. He came out from under the elms, and careered across the quad, and crashed headlong into a fellow who was walking there, before he even saw him.

"Ooooooh!" gasped Bunter, reeling from the shock.

"Oh!" gasped Harry Wharton, staggering. "You fat ass—you mad rhinoceros—you potty grampus—Oh!"

"Keep him off!" yelled Bunter.

"What——?"

The breathless fat Owl rolled round to the safe side of Harry Wharton, and blinked back at Skinner.

"Keep him off!" he gasped. "I say, old chap, you keep him off. I say, old chap, it was Skinner all the time——."

"You fat chump——."

"It was Skinner, you know—bagged that buzz at Quelch!" gasped Bunter. "Snoop knew all the time that he bagged that buzz—I mean buzzed that bag—I say, keep him off, will you!"

Harry Wharton stared at him, and then at Skinner. Skinner came to a breathless halt. Whatever he had intended, it was useless now: Bunter had already blurted out what he knew, and punching him was not feasible, with Harry Wharton in the way. Harold Skinner stood panting, while Wharton looked from one to the other.

"Now tell me what you mean, Bunter," said Harry, quietly.

"It was Skinner all the time!" gasped Bunter. "Snoop knows—he jolly well knew all along. It wasn't Smithy at all—it was Skinner did it in Smithy's study—he bagged that buzz—I mean he buzzed that bag—chucked it out of Smithy's window at Quelch's nut——. Snoop told him he ought to own up, now that Smithy's up for the sack——."

"So it was you, Skinner, and you left it on Smithy?" said Harry Wharton. "And Snoop knew, and was keeping it dark. This will have to go to Quelch."

Skinner panted.

"You're not going to Quelch——!"

"No: you are!" said Harry. "Don't be a fool, Skinner—this will be all over the school before dorm, and it's bound to get to Quelch. Your best guess is to go to him while the going's good."

"I shall deny——."

"I don't think Snoop will, if Quelch asks him questions," said Wharton, drily. "You worm, your game's up now. Look here, Skinner, Quelch has taken Smithy to the Head—they're both in his study now——."

"No business of mine," snarled Skinner.

"Smithy may be sacked——."

"A fat lot you care," said Skinner, savagely. "Smithy's chiselled you out of the captaincy, and taken your place—you'll get it back if he goes——."

"Never mind that!" said Harry Wharton, quietly. "Will you go to Quelch now, and tell him the truth about what happened in Smithy's study last week?"

"I'll go nowhere near him."

"It might pull Smithy through," said Harry. "The Head might think it some excuse for him, if he knew that Smithy never did what he was nailed for. Will you go to Quelch?"

"No," said Skinner, between his teeth. "I won't."

"If you won't go——."

"Well, I won't."

"Then you'll be taken," said Harry. "You're going to own up, you worm, before Smithy gets it in the neck." He made a stride at Skinner.

Skinner jumped back.

"Hands off!" he panted.

Harry Wharton did not trouble to reply. But it was not a case of "hands off": it was a case of "hands on": strong hands that grasped Skinner and propelled him into the House, in spite of his frantic resistance, and marched him along inexorably to the study where the Bounder of Greyfriars stood before his head-master, his fate trembling in the balance.

## CHAPTER 36

## AT THE ELEVENTH HOUR

DR. LOCKE sat at his writing-table, looking across it at the junior who stood before him.

There was silence in the Head's study.

Vernon-Smith stood erect. If this was the finish for him at Greyfriars, the Bounder had the courage to face it.

But his manner was quiet and respectful. There was no trace in it now of the self-willed arrogance, the reckless hardihood, that had been his undoing. Even the reckless Bounder was subdued, in the presence of his head-master.

Mr. Quelch, standing beside the table, had been speaking: in a cold, hard, uncompromising voice. His face seemed to be moulded in iron. From him, at all events, it was clear that the offender could expect no compunction. The rebel of the Remove had long been a thorn in his side: and now, in Quelch's opinion, the cup of his offences was full to overflowing. The sooner the gates of Greyfriars closed behind him, for the last time, the better, was the fixed view of his form-master.

Smithy was well aware of that. Only in his head-master was there a ray of hope: and it was a very faint one.

The silence was brief: but it seemed almost endless to the junior waiting for judgment. Dr. Locke's usually kindly face was sternly set: there was little hope to be drawn from it.

He spoke at last.

"Vernon-Smith!"

"Yes, sir," almost whispered the Bounder.

"You have heard what your form-master has said. It is difficult for me to believe that any Greyfriars boy could be guilty of such duplicity: but you have been guilty of it."

The Head paused: but Vernon-Smith did not speak.

"You have made an instrument of a foolish boy to deceive and delude your form-master. You prevailed upon Bunter, of Mr. Quelch's form, to make a pretended confession in which there was not a word of truth. By this means, you eluded detention. I take your form-master's view that it is upon you that the chief blame must fall. You do not deny this?"

"No, sir," said the Bounder, in a low voice. "I don't want to put any of it on Bunter. He only did what I asked him to do." He paused a moment, his face flushing. With all his faults, with all his arrogance, with all his unscrupulousness, the Bounder of Greyfriars was at heart a sportsman, as his next words showed. "Bunter was not much to blame, sir: he's got no sense, and a fellow could talk him into anything. I did the whole thing."

Dr. Locke gave him a very keen look.

"That is your form-master's view, and mine," he said. "Bunter has already been punished for his part in this deception: adequately, in Mr. Quelch's opinion. So far as he is concerned, the matter has ended."

"I'm glad of that, sir, at least," said Vernon-Smith, in a very low voice. And he spoke sincerely. The Bounder's conscience was tough: but there would have been a weight upon it, had the fatuous Owl been sacked along with him. It was a relief to know that his dupe, at least, was in the clear.

"It remains for me to deal with you," said Dr. Locke. "After what you have done, Vernon-Smith, you cannot expect that you will be permitted to remain in this school.

But if you have anything to say, I will hear it."

The Bounder drew a deep, deep breath.

He had something to say: though with little hope that it would benefit him. What he had done was serious—more serious than he had realised at the time he had planned it, blinded by passionate temper and resentment. But there was, at least, one rag of extenuation—if the Head would believe him!

"I never did what I was given detention for, sir!" he said. "Mr. Quelch thought so, and I know it looked like it: but I never did it. I was football captain in the Remove, and barred from the matches—for something that I had never done. If I'd done it, it would have been different——."

Dr. Locke held up his hand.

"It is quite useless to make such a statement as that, Vernon-Smith!" he said, coldly.

"I—I suppose it is, sir," muttered the Bounder, "but it's true all the same. If you'll let me tell you, sir—how it was——."

"You may speak."

"Somebody—I don't know who—threw a bag of flour from my study window, at Mr. Quelch. It was not I."

Dr. Locke glanced at the Remove master.

"There was no doubt in the matter, Mr. Quelch?"

"None, sir."

"If you have nothing else to say, Vernon-Smith——."

"But I have, sir!" exclaimed the Bounder, "and you must listen to me. I own that I had the bag in my study—I own up that I thought of doing the very thing that was done—but Redwing persuaded me not to, and I never did. I went out of the House, and the bag was left in my study cupboard: and I never knew that anything had happened at all, till Redwing told me later——." Smithy's voice rose a little, in passionate excitement. It was now or never: unless his head-master believed him, he was finished. "Oh, sir, it's true—I never did it—and I know that it was my own fault that Mr. Quelch thought I did—but I never did, sir, and that was why——."

At a sign from the Head, he was silent. Dr. Locke's expression had changed a little: the Bounder's passionate earnestness had made an impression on him. But Quelch's face was as grim as ever. Again the head-master glanced at him, but Quelch's face did not relax.

"There was, and is, no doubt in my mind, sir," he said. "Certainly, if Vernon-Smith had not committed the act for which he was sentenced to Extra School for the remainder of the term, it would be an extenuating circumstance. But I repeat that I had, and have, no doubt. Vernon-Smith undoubtedly planned that malicious and disrespectful act, as he now admits, and had the means prepared in his study, waiting for an opportunity: and he answered untruthfully when I questioned him on the subject. Such evidence is to my mind conclusive."

"And to mine!" said Dr. Locke. "If an error was made, Vernon-Smith, the fault lies entirely at your own door: but I cannot doubt that your sentence was just. If you have nothing further to say——."

The Bounder opened his lips—but closed them again. It had been his only chance, and it had failed him. If the Head could have believed that his wretched trickery with Bunter had been the outcome of a sense of injustice, it would have helped him. But the Head could not believe him. And the blame lay at his own door: his own hands had dug the pit into which he had fallen. It was futile to say more.

"SKINNER HAS SOMETHING TO TELL YOU, SIR——!"

There was a brief pause. Then the Head, slowly, spoke again:

"In the circumstances, Vernon-Smith, I have no alternative but to——." At that point, the head-master of Greyfriars was interrupted.

There was a sound of scuffling feet in the corridor, and a knock, or rather a bang, on the study door. Dr. Locke broke off, staring at that door in indignant astonishment.

It flew open.

Dr. Locke, Mr. Quelch, and the Bounder all stared at what was revealed by the opening door—a Remove junior in the grasp of another Remove junior, who held him by the collar.

"Wharton!" thundered Mr. Quelch.

"Skinner has something to tell you, sir——!"

"What—what——?"

"Go in, Skinner."

"I—I——," panted Skinner. "I——."

"Do you want me to call Bunter and Snoop here?"

Skinner gave him one black and bitter look, and made no further resistance as Wharton pushed him into the study. Harry Wharton drew the door shut, and walked away, leaving him there.

## CHAPTER 37

## BEASTLY FOR BUNTER

"I SAY, you fellows!"

"Slay him!" said Bob Cherry.

"Oh, really, Cherry——."

"Scrag him!" said Johnny Bull.

"Oh, really, Bull——."

"The scragfulness is the proper caper," agreed Hurree Jamset Ram Singh. "Come in, my esteemed and idiotic Bunter, and be slayfully scragged."

Billy Bunter paused in the doorway of No. 1 Study. He wanted to roll in. The fat Owl, who had a really marvellous nose for scenting out a spread, was aware that a study supper was on in No. 1. He was anxious to make one more at the festive board. But he did not want to be "scragged". Almost filling the doorway with his ample person, William George Bunter blinked uncertainly at the Famous Five through his big spectacles.

"I say, you fellows, wharrer you got your rag out for?" he demanded. "I haven't done anything, have I?"

"You fat villain," said Frank Nugent.

"Oh, really, Nugent——."

"Better cut while you're in one piece, Bunter," said Harry Wharton, laughing.

"Oh, really, Wharton——."

"You fat, frabjous, footling, flabby, foozling barrage balloon," said Bob Cherry. "We've been licked at Rookwood, three goals to one."

"Well, that ain't my fault, is it?" asked Bunter, blinking

at him. "I offered to play Soccer at Rookwood, as you jolly well know. If I'd played——."

"Oh, burst him!" growled Johnny Bull.

"All your fault, from beginning to end!" hooted Bob. "If you hadn't spun Quelch that yarn, Smithy would have been squatting in Extra, instead of being ordered off the field in the middle of the match. Wharton would have captained the side, and we should have walked all over them——."

"Perhaps!" suggested Harry Wharton, mildly.

"Oh, we'd have beaten them all right," said Bob, "but what chance had we, after all that?—playing a man short against men like Jimmy Silver's crowd? Licked to the wide——."

"The widefulness was terrific," sighed Hurree Jamset Ram Singh.

"All Bunter's fault——."

"And Smithy's," said Nugent.

"Well, we're going to boil Smithy in oil, if he isn't sacked," said Bob, "and as for that fibbing, flabby, footling fat octopus——."

"I say, you fellows, Smithy ain't sacked," said Bunter. "He's in his study now, with Redwing. They were jawing when I looked in, and I heard Redwing say—don't you chuck that loaf at me, you beast!" Billy Bunter backed out of the doorway as Bob Cherry picked up half a loaf from the supper table.

"Ha, ha, ha!"

The fat Owl blinked uneasily round the door. He was very keen to join in the study supper. But it was borne in upon his fat mind that he was not, at the moment, *persona grata* in No. 1. Why, he did not know. So far as Bunter was aware, there was no fault to be found with him by the most captious critic: he was, in fact, a shining example to all Greyfriars.

"I say, you fellows——."

"Come a little nearer," said Bob, taking aim.

"Beast!"

The fat head disappeared again.

But a moment later it reappeared. That well-spread board drew Billy Bunter like a magnet.

"I say, you fellows, be pals," urged the fat Owl. "I say, I've been through it to-day. Quelch gave me six! And did he lay them on? Wow!" Bunter gave a reminiscent wriggle. "He made out that I'd been telling him a lot of whoppers, you know——."

"Made out!" ejaculated Harry Wharton.

"Well, you know Quelch!" said Bunter, bitterly. "That's Quelch all over. Why, he put in my last report that I was untruthful. Me, you know!"

"Oh, my hat!"

"Practically calling a fellow a liar!" said Bunter, blinking sorrowfully at the Famous Five. "That's Quelch! That's the sort of justice we get here."

"Oh, crumbs!"

The fat head came a little further round the door. Billy Bunter blinked hopefully at the supper table, and uneasily at the half-loaf poised in Bob's hand.

"And that beast Skinner kicked me," went on Bunter with his tale of woe. "He didn't like Wharton hoicking him off to the Head's study to own up. I expect he would have liked to kick Wharton——."

"Very likely," said Harry, laughing.

"Well, I wouldn't mind if he did, of course: but he kicked me!" said Bunter, "and then that beast Smithy—that awful beast Smithy—I only just looked into his study, you know, to ask him as a friend whether he'd been sacked, and he chucked a football boot at my head——."

"Good!"

"After all I've done for him!" said Bunter, sadly. "I told him I'd do my best for him, and didn't I do my best? Didn't I pull Quelch's leg about that flour bag, just as I said I would? Out of pure friendship, you know—it wasn't because he stood me a feed——."

"Ha, ha, ha!"

"Blessed if I see anything to cackle at!" said Bunter, warmly. "I call it ungrateful—sharper than a serpent's child, as Spokeshave says—I mean Shakespoke—that is, Shakespeare. Didn't he say that I would have the run of his study if I did my best for him—and then when a fellow looks in as a pal, he chucks a football boot at him——."

"Ha, ha, ha!"

"Even Toddy has been cutting up rusty," went on Bunter. "He's been calling me names, and he banged my head——."

"Hard, I hope," said Bob.

"Beast! I mean, dear old chap——."

"Ha, ha, ha!"

"Well, I think you fellows might be pally, when everybody else is letting me down all round!" said Bunter, pathetically. "Anybody would think that I was some sort of a rotter, really, instead of the most decent chap in the Remove, and chance it. I really wonder sometimes whether it's worth while being upright, and high-minded, and a cut above other fellows, when a fellow's treated like this!"

"Oh, ye gods and little fishes!"

"Well, it discourages a fellow," said Bunter, shaking his head. "Quelch making a fellow out to be a liar, and whopping him—Smithy being as ungrateful as a serpent's tooth—and you fellows too jolly mean to ask a fellow to a study supper, and I can jolly well say—Yarooooooh!"

The fat head had come a little further in, and was in good range. The half-loaf flew from Bob Cherry's hand. It landed on the precise spot where Smithy's Latin dictionary had landed. There was a roar from Billy Bunter as it landed, and he went back quite suddenly into the passage.

Half a loaf is said, proverbially, to be better than no bread. But Billy Bunter would certainly have preferred no bread, in the circumstances. There was a frantic roar as he sat down in the Remove passage.

"Yarooh! Wow! Beast!"

"Ha, ha, ha!"

"Ow! wow!"

"Come in again," called out Bob. "I've got a tin of sardines to follow."

"Beast!"

Billy Bunter did not come in again. Doubtless he would have liked the sardines: but not the tin. A sad and sorrowful fat Owl rolled away, feeling that life, even at Greyfriars, was hardly worth living for a really decent and quite admirable fellow in a form composed chiefly of beasts!

Harry Wharton and Co., with absolutely no sympathy to waste on a dolorous fat Owl, resumed dealing with the study supper. But there was another interruption, as the door was pushed open, and Herbert Vernon-Smith walked into the study.

## CHAPTER 38

## UNEXPECTED!

HARRY WHARTON and Co. eyed the Bounder curiously, and not very amicably. Bob Cherry frowned, and Johnny Bull indulged in a snort. All the footballers were feeling sore over the fiasco at Rookwood: and if they were not quite disposed, as Bob had expressed it, to boil Smithy in oil, at least they were thoroughly fed up with him. Smithy had pushed himself to the top, and his captaincy had resulted in disaster for himself and everyone else concerned. The general expectation was that he would be "sacked" for what he had done. But if he was not sacked, and fancied that he could carry on in his old arrogant way after what had happened, he had, in the opinion of the Co., quite another guess coming. But he seemed quite at ease as he strolled into No. 1 Study.

"Sacked?" asked Bob.

"Thanks for askin'," said the Bounder, with sarcastic politeness. "No!"

"Pity!" grunted Johnny Bull.

Vernon-Smith laughed.

"Thanks again," he said, "but you can blame Wharton for that. I should have been sacked like a shot if he hadn't butted in."

"More ass he!" grunted Johnny, uncompromisingly.

"I couldn't agree more!" assented the Bounder, coolly. "Not quite what I should have done in his place, I rather fear."

"Hardly," said Frank Nugent, with a curl of the lip.

"We common mortals can't quite live up to Wharton's high standard," said the Bounder, with sarcastic regret.

Harry Wharton's cheeks reddened.

"That will do, Vernon-Smith," he said, curtly. "If that's all you've come here to say, you can cut, and the sooner the better."

"But that isn't all," said Vernon-Smith. "You pulled me through, and you were an ass for your pains. That rat Skinner would have seen me sacked, and never turned a hair. You made him come to the Head and own up: and it worked the oracle. When it came out that I never had done what Quelch nailed me for, the Head simply couldn't get on with it—and even Quelch, I think, didn't want him to. So I came through with lots of stains on my character but not bunked. Why did you do it, Wharton?"

"Why?" repeated Harry.

"Yes, why! You had me just where you wanted me—or where I should have thought you wanted me, at any rate. I never gave you a show. I diddled you out of the captaincy, taking advantage of your silly temper and silly obstinacy——."

"You can pack that up!" snapped Nugent.

"Wharton knows it as well as I do, and as you fellows do," answered the Bounder, unmoved. "I never gave him a fair show, and when I had the upper hand, I pushed him out of the Soccer, tit for tat! And afterwards, when I was down and out, all he had to do was to stand clear, and leave me to it—and walk back into his old place after I was turfed out. Why didn't you, Wharton?"

Harry Wharton laughed.

"If you don't know, it's no use my telling you," he answered.

"Well, perhaps I do know," said the Bounder,

musingly. "It's what you would describe as playing the game, I suppose."

"Not your line of country, Smithy," said Bob.

"Oh, we live and learn," said Smithy. "I can play the game too, if it comes to that." His look became more serious. "Look here, Wharton, I've been rather a rotter to you—and but for you, I should be catching the morning train home. I'm sorry."

He went on again without waiting for a reply.

"There's something else—I've just posted up a notice in the Rag, which you fellows had better read when you go down. Official notice to the form, from the captain of the Remove, you know. Interested?"

"Not at all," answered Bob.

"Not in the least!" said Frank Nugent.

"Couldn't care less," said Johnny Bull.

"The couldn't-care-lessfulness is terrific."

"Well, I think it will interest Wharton, at least," said Smithy.

"Why me especially?" asked Harry.

"Only because it's my resignation of the captaincy of the form," answered the Bounder, carelessly. "Having made such a ghastly muck of it, and feeling that I owe you something for saving my bacon, I'm standing down. That's all." He turned to the door, the Famous Five staring at him blankly. He threw a last remark over his shoulder, as he went. "You wouldn't vote for me at the last Form election, Wharton, but I shall vote for you at the next. Cheerio!"

With that, the Bounder of Greyfriars walked out of No. 1 Study.

He left a blank silence behind him.

"Well!" said Nugent, at last.

"Well!" said Johnny Bull.

"Well!" said Bob Cherry. "You never quite know what to expect, from Smithy. But this——!"

"The unexpectedness is terrific," said Hurree Jamset Ram Singh, "but as the English proverb remarks, it is the unexpected that happens to a bird in the bush and makes the cracked pitcher go longest to a stitch in time."

"Good old English proverb!" chuckled Bob. "Anyhow, the jolly old unexpected has happened this time. We won't boil Smithy in oil, after all! Smithy's got his good points, though he does keep them rather dark."

Harry Wharton's face was thoughtful.

"Smithy's a sportsman, when he doesn't forget to be one," he said. "There's been faults on both sides—but it won't be my fault if we don't pull together better after this!"

"Hear, hear!" said Bob.

And it was a cheerful party that went down to the Rag, to read the last official notice put up by H. Vernon-Smith, captain of the Remove: captain no longer.

The Form election was a "walk-over" for Harry Wharton. He was back in his old place, to the general satisfaction. But there was one fellow in the Remove who had a somewhat disgruntled outlook. That one was William George Bunter. Billy Bunter had, according to his lights, done his best for Smithy. True, it hadn't worked out according to plan. But was that Bunter's fault? Yet he found nothing more hospitable than a boot in No. 4 Study. Which Bunter could not help thinking was very hard on a fellow who had done his best!